THE ICICLE
ILLUMINARIUM

A Random House book
Published by Random House Australia Pty Ltd
Level 3, 100 Pacific Highway, North Sydney NSW 2060
www.randomhouse.com.au

First published by Random House Australia in 2014

Addresses for companies within the Random House Group can be found at
www.randomhouse.com.au/offices.

National Library of Australia
Cataloguing-in-Publication Entry

Author: Gemmell, N.J.
Title: The Icicle Illuminarium
ISBN: 978 0 85798 567 5 (pbk)
Dewey Number: A823.3

Cover design and illustration by Allison Colpoys
Internal design and illustration by Allison Colpoys
Typeset by Midland Typesetters, Australia
Printed in Australia by Griffin Press, an accredited ISO AS/NZS 14001:2004
Environmental Management System printer

Random House Australia uses papers that are natural, renewable and recyclable
products and made from wood grown in sustainable forests. The logging
and manufacturing processes are expected to conform to the environmental
regulations of the country of origin.

THE ICICLE ILLUMINARIUM

N.J. GEMMELL

RANDOM HOUSE AUSTRALIA

BASTI

KICK

SCRUFF

BERT

PIN

BUCKET

and Banjo!

For Justin, India, Will, Luc and Mimosa —
gorgeous godchildren, all!

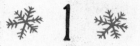

1

A FATHER MOST CHANGED

'**Caddys major, intermediate and minor, put down your snakes!**'

Well, we most certainly do. This is Charlie Boo, after all. The bravest, cleverest butler in the entire universe – trained in martial arts in Rangoon and hat-frisbeeing in Haiti, and an endless source of chocolate airplanes that appear, thrillingly, at unexpected moments. Which could be now. In fact, Scruff's got his tongue out in readiness. Four green tree snakes are unwrapped quick-smart from four necks. Not missing out on this one. Four green tree snakes are plopped on the lion skin in front of us.

But – oh no! – Pin can't resist. He leans down, sneaks his snake an extra smacker of a kiss, then decides that, actually, his two sisters and brother should be getting a kiss too because it's the day after Christmas and no one's been fighting all day – an absolute miracle when it comes to us. You'll soon find out.

'Master Phineas,' Charlie Boo tuts with a twinkle in his eye. 'Does *everything* have to be smothered in sticky, icky love in your world?'

'Oh yes, Mr Boo. Specially *you*!'

Charlie Boo leans back in mock horror as an enormous bear hug comes at him and, yep, almost knocks him over. Then he lifts the little boy high into his arms, says, 'Well, if I must, I must,' and surrenders to the ferocious onslaught of cuddles and kisses with a smile of pure bliss on his face.

'I was under the impression – until you lot came along – that butlers were strictly not for befriending, let alone loving. They were meant to be for one thing and one only. Obeying.' He attempts a stare. He attempts a glare. He raises an eyebrow but it wobbles and collapses.

The rest of us get a right old giggle going on. Nup, sorry, Charlie Boo, you're not getting any help from us at this moment. Because we're still on a giddy Christmas high and it's proving impossible to climb down from it. We've got more presents than we've had in our lives and snow for the first time ever, which means sledding with all our brand new neighbourhood friends right in front of our Uncle Basti's amazing Kensington Reptilarium, in London, our glorious new home. And most incredible of all, we've got a father just back from the jungles of Malaysia! Plus, PLUS, a dingo dog! Who we thought had been left behind forever, lost somewhere in the desert of central Australia – or worse, taken in by a cop.

Bucket most conveniently gives a sharp, joyful bark at this point, needing to be appreciated too. Pin obliges and gets a big slobbery licky kiss in return, which seems to cover his entire face, in fact, almost swallows it up.

Oh, and did I mention that horrid old World War II is over and it's never, ever coming back? So right now there's a lot to be silly with glee about.

Charlie Boo, however, has gone all serious on us. His face doesn't reflect any of our zippiness. Quite the opposite. Saggy and droopy, suddenly weary of life. 'I have something extremely important to tell you, my little friends.'

The change in his voice snaps us to attention.

'Master Phineas. Miss Thomasina. Master Ralph. Miss Albertina the Younger.' Pin, me, Scruff and Bert are each gravely stared at in turn. We hush.

'It's something even more pressing than the development of that most, er . . . singular Twelfth Night extravaganza you've got going on.'

Oh. Is *that* what he really thinks of the show we're developing for the last festive night of the Christmas season, the twelfth night of Christmas? But it's going to be fabulous! It's somewhere in early January and it's our enormous spectacle of a circus involving whip cracking and double backflips and singing and costumes from the fashion house of one 'Albertina of Kensington' as well as four dancing snakes weaving their heads back and forth, simultaneously, when a dead mouse is waved in front of them.

'Do you realise,' Charlie Boo says softly, 'that while you've been busily devising your grand and extravagant amusement, you've been neglecting here, to some extent, someone most . . . neglectfully. I don't think you do, do you? Someone who's been lost for months in a farflung outpost of terror. Who escaped evil captors then spent weeks with flesh-eating savages, swinging on vines and consuming grasshoppers and shooting poisoned darts or, or, something like that, all for —' he shakes his head, with that twinkle back in his eye '— you lot. Goodness knows why.'

We all look to the corner of the room. To our father. Awake, but with these weirdly blank staring eyes. Golly galoshes! We rush over. Yes, something is desperately wrong here and look at us, too busy and zippy and shouty to notice. This is no time for green tree snakes! What were we thinking?

'Cor blimey,' I whisper. And there it is. The first bit of swearing and it's breaking a two-day drought – a possible record in the Caddy books.

Charlie Boo whispers to me that we don't have long. What are you talking about, I ask, not liking the way he's sounding here. We're told the recovery process will be lengthy and gruelling and it won't be with us here, at the Reptilarium. That our dad's too ill. Terribly weakened. Malaria, perhaps.

We gasp. All peer closer at our beloved, cheeky Daddy. His frail body is completely swallowed by his zebra-skin armchair. His bullet-ridden bush hat – that's seen just about every country on earth – is most horribly askew and he never wears it like that, he's too proud of it. Bert straightens it with a careful tenderness and kisses him gently on the cheek. He gives her absolutely nothing back, there's just a slow closing of his eyes. His legendary red-checked handkerchief is too jolly around his neck. It doesn't match the rest of him.

'Your father's fading,' Charlie Boo continues, 'and he needs to be put to bed immediately and loved most fiercely – yet gently, Master Scruff, gentleeeeeee,' he adds as Scruff tiptoes back from the fearsome bear hug he was about to administer. 'Your father is your responsibility now, my bouncy Caddy kangaroos. While you have him.'

'Stop talking like that, Mr Boo!' I cry. 'Say what you *mean*.' Because grown-ups never do that enough and I get so sick of it.

'He needs proper help, Kick. Urgently.'

I stare at the pale ghost of the legendary desert adventurer before us. The master spy, croc wrestler, brumby wrangler, champion woodcutter and crack shot. Who now just looks . . . broken. His silk dressing gown has slipped open and his hip bones jut out too sharp, like the prow of Pin's abandoned toy ship from the desert sand at home. His rib bones are like the corrugated iron of our roof. His cheeks could hold a cricket ball in the well of each one of them and his eyes – one green, one blue, the fabulous Caddy trademark – are barely alive with life. I press my hand to my mouth in horror. Whisper, 'Daddy.' All he can muster is a weak smile back.

Charlie Boo lifts our papa's terrible frailness too easily into his arms. 'Come on, young man, let's get you to bed.'

Pin – dear little Pin – suddenly cottons on to the gravity of the situation. Attempts to drag Dad out of Charlie Boo's arms, trying, as always, to be the circuit-breaker with us crazy lot.

'Hey, ow! A mighty Pin cuddle right now will crush these brittle old bones,' Dad scolds his youngest child. A bit too far, mate, in my book.

Pin feels it. His mouth is suddenly like an upside-down Sydney Harbour Bridge. There might even be a cry.

Scruff's onto it. He grabs my cricket ball from the floor and throws it in the air, snatching it in a spectacularly neat catch. Diversionary tactics. Splendid. 'Come on, Mr Bradman,' he coaxes Dad, 'give us that googly you've always got tucked away in you.'

Googly. It's the magic word that giggles us right up – and the signal for a session of Caddy madness to begin. But both boys don't fully get it. Dad's really, really sick here, worse than Spanish flu, worse than plague.

Dad shakes his head and tells his Scruffter that there's no ball games allowed inside this place. 'Not that it stopped us at home.' We all laugh, thinking of the poor battered bread tin in the kitchen that was always our stumps. It hadn't seen a loaf for years. No mum, no fuss. 'Home,' Dad whispers, his eyes lighting up for a tick.

It'll be a long time before we can get him back from London at this rate, to our crazy playground of a homestead smack-bang in the centre of Australia. The tin slippery dip from roof to dirt, the chook house Pin'd hold his school in, the windmill we'd all jump from into the water tank (best diving board in the west), and Scruff's eggs happily frying on the bonnet of Matilda because it's so darned boiling in those parts. It'd be forty-eight degrees right now and I tell you, I need the big blaring sun strong on my back again, so much, after this endless London cold that's so darned sneaky it's like it's curled up inside us and gone straight to sleep.

Pin salutes and cries that Daddy is our hero, trying to get his father's eyes to re-ignite.

'Captain, I salute *you*.' Charlie Boo nods in appreciation.

'Oh yes, I am the captain and I am invinciple,' Pin announces to one and all, end of story, in the most grown-up of four-year-old voices.

'Indestructible, more like it,' murmurs Charlie Boo.

Dad glances at the dawning realisation in Scruff, getting the hang of this new situation here. 'Just hang in there, ol' Scruffter me boy,' he whispers, ruffling his eldest son's hair but barely touching it before his hand drops. 'We'll get our beer together yet. Just you wait.' But the worry in Charlie Boo's face is telling us that there's a lot they haven't explained about the injuries Dad got in his horrid old jungly prisoner-of-war camp. Can someone be a bit honest around here? And excuse me, but who'll be looking after us while Dad's so sick?

I sigh. Because hang on, yep, I know the answer to that one. Yours truly. Taking care of the whole pesky lot of them at the grand young age of thirteen. Great. Chief mum and dad and governess all at once; along with fun-hunter, mystery-solver, putterer-to-bedder, nose-wiper and Pin-tracker all rolled into one.

No one will bother to ask me what *I* want. And it's not what I need right now. Too much hard work. Not mummy material at all, nup, not girl material for that matter. Who'd want to be one of them? I'm far too tough and bush-blunt for that, far too boy and desert rough. Plus my little sister Bert will be recording in her notebook, with malicious delight, every time I swear. So she can tell anyone who'll listen how badly done by she is having to put up with the likes of me. But hang on, what about me having to put up with *her?*

Dad trails his finger along my cheek and chuckles as he's always done, as if to say, 'It's okay, Kicky, it's all right.' But it's so not. Because everything is suddenly just not fair and not working out and too much. Don't go disappearing on us, Daddy, just as we've found you; it's so tough at the frontline with this crazy lot.

'When are we going to see you in a dress for more than a few hours . . . a proper lady?' Dad smiles soft. 'It's about time, Miss Thomasina Flora Caddy. Did we really call you that? Beautiful name, not that you'd know it. You're growing up, Kicky, and there's a right looker under all that frown and crazy hair, all those cut-off shorts and slingshots. But where, I wonder, where?' He gazes right into me, eyes narrowed. 'Nope, can't find it yet.'

I shake my head angrily. Brusque away. No time for jokes. Because yes, okay, I'm back to wearing dungarees after that silly mistake of the posh Christmas dress – whipped up by one Albertina of Kensington as a very Berti form of torture and, oh boy, didn't she love the triumph of that. But now my slingshot's right where it should be – tucked into my belt – and Dad's hunting knife is on a chain around my neck and I feel proper again, okay? Ready for the world. Right. Not all scratchy and constrained and pink and hot. This is my uniform and I'm sticking to it.

A blunt fringe was cut last night, just for Dad, in celebration of his return. Okay, it's a bit wonky, but there's a clear line of sight now, which means I won't have to push it away in the desert heat when we're eyeing off a roo for a clean shot or hurtling Matilda, our trusty ute, straight into the bush in a plume of dust.

Bert lifts up a lock of hair behind me. 'It's only fit for one of those Germans in their work camps, isn't it, Daddy?' She giggles conspiratorially. They all laugh.

I storm off. Have had enough of them, the whole blinking lot. They have no idea how hard it is being the boss of this crazy, bouncy, yappy, mean-as-a-midday-sun mob. Bucket jumps around me in sympathy. I drop to her. She always understands. The only one. She licks me on the lips and smiles at me with her beautiful honey eyes.

'Kickasina Tsarina!' Dad calls after me, in exactly the voice that used to stop me from gunning Matilda into the desert in a right strop.

I don't turn to him. Can't. He mustn't see my eyes smarting, no one must, I'm too big and tough for this.

'You're beautiful just the way you are. Always have been.' His voice drops. 'I'm only teasing, you know, because you're so darn teasible . . .'

I face him – deep breath – but the tears are all blinky and hot in me now. Dad suddenly winks. Smiles his beautiful smile that would have got Mum right in the heart when they met, I just know it. Cracking me with kindness, as he always does.

2

A SHOCK MOST UNEXPECTED

'Ladders, Caddy monkeys, ladders,' Charlie Boo commands. 'We're off to Bert's room, which has the most comfortable bed in the house. And can fit the lot of you. Miraculously. But, Scruff, be warned, the sheets are silk. Pale pink, no less.'

'Aaaaaah.'

'And if you want a fatherly cuddle in them – well, you'll just have to cope.'

'Urgh, double urgh.' Scruff doubles over like he's going to be sick.

Charlie Boo presses the button that lowers a chair on chains from the Reptilarium's dome. He places our father gingerly next to him and Bucket leaps onto his lap. Dad smiles and holds his chin to the top of her head; he's got his girl. Then, as if on cue, our legendary Uncle Basti emerges from the kitchen in purple pyjamas with red trim and a bright orange sleeping cap. Perdita, his beloved pet cobra, is wrapped around his neck and he holds a silver tray of grasshopper delicacies flat and high in one hand.

'My brother, my captain.' Our uncle salutes, crisp, with the other hand.

'My brother, my captain,' Dad replies, softer.

'I'll be up later to read to you. Dickens? Lawson?'

'Lawson. "The Drover's Wife." Read me home, old sport.'

The brothers smile at each other then our uncle goes to cuddle us; thinks better of it. He's not good with touching. But he takes off his sleeping cap and hands it across to Pin and tells him it's for that teddy he can never let go of, that it might be cold tonight, and we know that's as close to affection as we'll get from him. Then our uncle melts away into another room of the house, as he always does; impossible to pin down and contrary and reclusive and completely in a world of his own. Charlie Boo pushes the lever and rises majestically to the second floor like a god with his Jesus looking down at the rabbly flock that's left.

We scramble up the Reptilarium's delicious ladders that whizz sideways when a destination is reached, then fly past the cages, candlelit on each level, up past golden, glass and brass receptacles filled with water dragons and salamanders and slow worms and skinks. The great glass dome, the lid of the building, has snow falling onto it, big blowsy drops dancing in London's orangey evening light, and I smile at the beautiful sight.

We burst into the room of tall silver curtains that plunge like foam on a beach. As our father's tucked into the four-poster bed with its silvery drapes, Charlie Boo murmurs, 'This poor man has just survived the giant leeches of the most ferocious jungle on earth. He's survived amnesia. Starvation. Deathly thirst. And now, God help him, he has to survive you crazy lot. Is it possible?'

'I don't think so.' Dad smiles weakly, falling back on his silk pillow.

Bert suddenly lunges at her father, most un-nurse-like, crying for him not to leave her.

'Would you stop cuddling him in that stickily ferocious way, Miss Albertina. You're worse than a boa constrictor. And if you don't unhand yourself right now I'll jolly well fetch one, just to demonstrate. It may well gobble you up.'

'Oh please,' I respond. 'I'll pay you.'

I'm hit. By my sister. Who's punched back. Harder. Who then hits and hits and – ow! – yep, she's in it for the long haul, we're off. Charlie Boo tries to break it up. It doesn't work. 'Madam? Miss. MADAM –' Charlie Boo takes out a trench whistle and blows on it; we snap into stillness. Amid a great cacophony of Reptilarium noise from a thousand creatures protesting with shrieks and hisses and thuds and squeaks. 'Madam Albertina – newly crowned fashion empress of the post-war era – come in, Albertina. Couturiers, in case you haven't realised, are not in the habit of attacking their number one, most beautiful Christmas mannequin. Do you copy?'

Bert pokes out her tongue at me. I narrow my eyes like a cat. The battle ain't over yet.

'Ah, my little tiger cubs, you haven't changed a bit, have you?' Dad shakes his head. He tells Pin to tie Basti's sleeping cap around Banjo's neck immediately, so as not to lose it, then tickles Bert because he needs her smiling again, needs her cranky face wiped off. I know why. Because when we're happy, he's happy, he's always saying that. But he can't tickle for long, he has no energy for it, he's so . . . sapped.

'Now listen here, I've got something important to tell you.' A big sigh as if he can hardly bear it.

We huddle close. A pause. He tells us he's going on another mission. Nooooo! Impossible. Too soon, he's not ready.

'Dismantle your battle face, Kicky. It's called the Sanatorium Mission. The task: to get fixed. Pronto. In a proper place that will set me right. First thing tomorrow, in fact. So this is all of me you'll get, I'm afraid, for now.'

Cue all manner of wailing and exclaiming: 'No!' 'Too short.' 'What will happen to my beer!' That one from Scruff, of course.

'You'll stay here with Uncle Basti. Until I get strong enough. And don't you worry about that beer, Master Scruff. I'll be telling Basti to keep it on tap. Just you and me. It'll only be a few weeks.' He winces, placing his precious hat on Scruff's head. 'Look after this for me, mate. And don't you grow any hairs on your chest while I'm gone.'

'Oooooooh, Scruffty Scruff, you're my hero.' Bert flutters her eyelashes.

Pin hooks his hand gravely around his father's neck and draws him in and covers his face with tiny pecks. Our youngest Caddy is pure, fat love, always has been. Dad snuggles into his dear little neck and breathes him in deep, like he's trying to singe the memory into his brain.

'I bet you'll get a chocolate ration there every day,' Scruff says. 'Can you save it for me? I mean, us?'

Dad explains in exactly Basti's posh voice that he'll be far away from us, taking the waters in Bath, no less. He ties his scarf around the neck of Banjo, Pin's teddy. 'Something to remember me by, me old Banj. You will look after them for me, won't you?' he asks the teddy most earnestly. It waggles in an enthusiastic yes. Pin is enchanted. 'Daddy, book?' he says hopefully. Because it's bedtime. Pin starts reciting *The Jungle Book* in exactly Dad's bedtime-story voice then says, 'Hang on, I do Kicky now,' and proceeds with lots of swear words thrown in and skippings-to-the-next-chapter.

I slam my hand hurriedly over his mouth. 'I've been a good mum, I promise!'

'Well, hopefully she won't have to be the mum for too much longer,' Charlie Boo chuckles as he rubs ointment into Dad's foot.

Eh? We all look at Charlie Boo. In sudden silence. Shock. *What* did he say? He just implied – did he? Did we hear right?

'But Mum's dead,' I whisper.

Goosebumps scooting up my back.

3

NO, IT CANNOT BE

'What's going on here?' Bert shakes her head with her hands scrunched at her temples.

'Mum's not dead?' Scruff asks.

'Not as far as I know,' Charlie answers cheerily, grabbing some spare blankets and quite oblivious to the shockwaves his casual remarks have caused.

Thumping heart. Dry lips. Bert grabbing my fingers, almost breaking them. Pin holding his hands to his chest in wide-eyed hope. A mummy? But he's never had one. Since he was a baby she's been gone. He could be getting a mummy back now, as well as a dad? What's going on? Grown-ups. Why are they always so mysterious?

Charlie Boo talks on, measuring out a bandage for Dad's foot. 'Darius Davenport should be able to help out in that department, shouldn't he, Mr Caddy? That'll be your next big mission, no doubt.'

We all turn to Dad.

He's deathly pale. He looks at us. At Charlie Boo.

'Out,' he thunders. Suddenly changed. Completely. Scarily. 'Remove yourself, Mr Boo. From my children, from my room, from my life. Find a job to do. The lot of you. Stop talking nonsense. Just GET OUT.'

We look from one man to the other, not knowing what's going on. Mum's dead. Isn't she? There's a memorial, in our garden at home, under the desert rose. She's gone for good. I clutch my head, trying to think. But hang on, what were we actually told? What did we always believe? It was four years ago, so long, just after Pin was born.

'What . . . Dad . . . where's Mu–?' I begin.

'OUT!' he roars. Like he can't bear to talk about it. Can't bear to deal with any of us all of a sudden.

We shrink back. Gosh. A father completely changed. Snapped. Just like his brother, Basti, sometimes is. Like he's . . . damaged. For good.

Shell-shocked. We know that word now. Like us kids are too loud in his head and it hurts, really hurts, deep inside him. Something is very wrong.

'Confused by malaria, no doubt, along with everything else,' Charlie Boo hurries us out fast, 'and then look at me, no idea what I'm rambling on about. Sorry,' he tuts. 'All the excitement, yes. Forget everything, you heard nothing in there. Too much going on. Bed, now, the lot of you. Off, off.'

'But Bucket?' Scruff asks. 'She's still in there.'

'Oh, she can stay,' Charlie Boo murmurs. 'She's more relaxing than the lot of you put together. She's a good nurse.'

We look back as he shuts the door. At Dad's eyes, closed already. At one hand over his forehead like he has an enormous headache going right through his eyebrow. At the other hand holding his beloved Bucket, our darling girl, the Cleverest Dingo In The West.

I look at Charlie Boo. He's completely rattled, muttering 'sorry, sorry' to himself, to us. What did he say about a mother? Why is he so flustered? What did we *want* him to say? Did we deliberately mishear whatever it was?

Because we know now that sometimes people who we think are gone can return. War does that sometimes, it jumbles families up. Then suddenly someone comes back. From a camp, another country, a memory loss, another life. It's happened once with Dad. Lost but not. Could it possibly happen again? I never know what grown-ups mean. It's like they speak this weird double language, it's all layers and pretending and covering up. Was all that really about Mum? Why is Dad so upset?

Maybe she did similar work-things to him, secret, government stuff. Spying. Who knows. They were so alike, two peas in a pod. Maybe her job was as top secret as his. Does Basti know anything more? The War Office, the government?

I know one thing. We'll get to the bottom of this. Have to.

I hold my fist to my mouth with the amazingly deliciously fabulous thrill of it. Could we possibly be a family, a real, proper, together-family in our desert homestead all over again? A dad. AND a mum. Plus a Bucket and, oh all right, everyone else. There's the familiar tingling. Of the call to arms, of action and adventure and the needing to know. I *will* work this out.

We will.

I look at the rest of them. They've all got their skills. We can do this.

'Troops,' I announce, as soon as Charlie Boo's departed, 'we've got a mystery to solve. While Dad's away at his fixing-up place. Imagine if we get Mum back and she opens the door to him the day he comes home!' Bert gasps with the sheer glorious loveliness of it – she's the romantic. 'We need to get on to it fast.'

'Aye aye, captain!' 'Yes!' 'Let's go!' Three hands shoot into a crisp salute. Excellent. The Caddy kids are well and truly back. Now we just need a plan and we'll be off.

Tomorrow! As soon as Dad's left. He is going to get the biggest welcome-home present of his life!

INGENIOUS PLAN
NUMBER 452

'The Lumen Room,' I command, 'quick.'

Because my room – the library – is just too risky. We can't have anyone eavesdropping and Bert's room is right next door. We can't worry Dad. He mustn't know we're doing this. His bizarre explosion of fury tells us this – it's not in any way good for his health. He needs rest. Serenity. Calm. He's not going to get that around us. We run to our favourite place, the room of a thousand glow worms, the most beautiful space in the house.

Thick, velvety darkness. Stopping us into a hush. 'We've got to wake them up,' Scruff whispers. 'Can I?'

'We can't alert anyone, mate,' Bert warns.

'Me! Me!' Pin jumps in.

Scruff shoos him off with a weary 'okay'. And so with his teddy held high Pin runs gleefully around the room, as fast as his pudgy little legs will carry him, close to the walls but not touching. Bert can't resist, she joins in too, silently giggling, and then Scruff comes on board and what the heck, so do I. So there you have it, four Caddys running around a room in absolute silence but giggling until our mouths hurt, faster and faster, creating a huge wind, chasing each other's tails, and then Pin suddenly stops abrupt and bang! We all jam into him. Collapse in a heap. 'Ow,' we whisper, cradling elbows and knees and then, 'Look!' Pin softly exclaims and points.

At the roof. A single glow of light, in a corner. Then another glow worm, and another, until their light is oozing like an upside-down lake flooding right across the room, one wall then another, and another, until we're surrounded by a buttery golden loveliness.

I whisper my thanks. Berti tells us she's going to find a cloth the exact colour one day and make the most beautiful dress that's ever existed from it. I say it'd be impossible, the colour's too magical, it couldn't exist. Pin insists that Mummy will find it, she's the best, she can do it.

Mum. Yes. Our beautiful mother. Why we're here. Who Pin lost as a baby and only knows from the rest of us. What have we told him? Not much – too hard – and then over the years it's faded into just a few pinpoints of fact. She was far too glamorous for the desert life, I always thought that. She had red hair. Freckles that always sprung out in summer. She loved reading like me, the only thing we had in common, I used to think. I can do her hoot of a laugh. Her voice soft, 'Kicky, oh Kick.' But what do I really know about her?

She had a secret life, she told me that once. 'Before kids' she'd been in a very different world, but I never properly asked. Wasn't interested. There'd be hints. It was in England. It was full of silver shoes with sparkly buckles that look madly uncomfortable, Paris holidays, balls. Champagne, which she'd never had since because Alice Springs didn't have it. 'What have I done with my life?' I remember her crying when Bert lost all the diamonds from her debutante tiara in the red dirt. She had matching red-leather travelling trunks stacked high by her bed, a man's watch and a face that crumpled into a frown as the desert dust blew in from the south; I remember that so clearly, towards the end, the face that seemed permanently creased by worry.

What does everyone else remember? I wonder. We need any clue here, even the tiniest, that could wing us off in the right direction. 'Troops, we need a debrief.'

Bert pulls out her notepad in readiness from the pocket of a French maid's apron she's wearing over a black velvet evening dress held up in great folds by a succession of brooches that go up to her waist. All thanks to the treasure trove of the Reptilarium's attic, which holds centuries of wonder and is a bottomless source of delight. And wouldn't Mum just adore the spectacle of my sister right now. She'd clasp her hands, cry in raptures, 'Pet! You've *done* it! What a champ.' She never got me. Berti was the daughter she'd been waiting for.

I ask them if there's anything we're missing here about Mum. Blank looks. Scruff volunteers that she was really pretty.

'Nothing like Kick,' Bert adds.

'Thanks,' I snap. She'll keep for now.

'She was a crack shot,' Scruff adds. 'Remember the snake? When I was little and I was in the chook house and there was this King Brown and I yelled "Mama!" She was cleaning Dad's pistol in the shed. The snake slithered in front of the door. I was stuck. And with a single shot she blew its head off. Bang!

Just like that. It was mi-racca-lus.' He mimes holding the pistol. 'She was the best shot in the desert.'

Pin's eyes are wide. Bert sighs that she had the most beautiful clothes. We always knew that, I snap. 'No, Kick. They were from somewhere else. That's the key. She must have travelled a lot, before us, because they were really exotic. The materials. You wouldn't get them even from Sydney, I bet. It was more like Istanbul, Delhi, Cairo, cities like that. She never talked about those places but I reckon she'd been there. And remember she had all that lovely red luggage in her bedroom, stacked up and locked. What was in it? I was always trying to get it open but couldn't. It's still there. Maybe we should be opening it.'

Bert's right. We need to get home. To solve this. Crack open those chests. First up, get out of the Reptilarium. Which is extremely locked. And without anyone knowing. So, this is Plan Number 452 in my endless array of plans to set things right. I take Bert's notepad and write it bold.

'So what have we got here? Maybe she was an adventurer, a spy, just like Dad.'

Blank looks. Maybe she was just a mum. A frazzled one at that. There's not much to go on here and our father never talks about her going – we never ask – don't want him hurt so his broken face comes back. But what have we gleaned from Dad over the years?

She was the love of his life. She made him laugh. She was his best mate. They were a team. She always threatened to leave the homestead because it was becoming too much: kids, mess, dust, runaway chooks, sleeplessness, rabbits, spiders, feral camels, the huge swamp of it, but then she had Pin, our medieval kissing post who giggled us all up. She'd never, ever leave him if she could help it. Surely? No one could.

Dad once told us once that our mum needed to go away to instruct God how to look after us, because we were such hard work. But what exactly did he mean by it? Did she go to a convent? We always assumed it was heaven but maybe not . . .

Bert says she used to always call her Pet. And she'd had long, black hair with beautiful pins holding it up. 'Ivory, red coral, jet . . .'

'Topaz, jade,' I add. We catch each other's eyes. No one's told us how to do our hair for years, no one cares. She did. We've had no one to teach us how to be ladies, thank goodness, apart from some traumatic interventions from shrivelled old aunts or governesses who'd sucked on too many prunes and always seemed to leave quick smart. They'd just give up. Goodness knows why. Bert seems to have cottoned onto the lady thing, in some instinctive kind of way, but I'm still completely hopeless at it. Who'd want to be one of them anyway? All obedient and sighing and squealing and quiet, shoes that hurt, fiddly stockings, lace hats in the dust. Mum loved her ivory umbrellas and silk pyjamas, yes, yet she could tame not only a brumby but a bull whip. Where did she get it all from?

Scruff volunteers that she was a crack shot. Well, with beef stew. And chocolate cake. But yes, poor Scruff's now getting mighty sick of my feeble attempts in comparison to her. Endless fried eggs, and bread and dripping, and roasted roo tails with witchety grub desserts (baked in coals with sugar sprinkled on top, thank you very much).

'The car came and took her away,' Bert says suddenly. 'I'd forgotten that.'

'What?' She's never told us this before.

'In the dead of night. I thought it was because she couldn't cope.'

'With what?'

A pause. 'Us. Our naughtiness.' Oh. 'She was in her nightgown. Some man was holding her arm tight. I don't know who. I couldn't sleep. I was looking out my window, at the car. She glanced back, mouthed at me, "Pet." Really upset. She went away to die, didn't she, Kick? That's what I thought. Because she never came back. And she'd found Pin's birth really hard. I just thought she went to a hospital. Or maybe, maybe, I imagined it? What happened, Kicky? Please tell us.' Bert scrunches up the hair on her head like it hurts. 'It was so long ago. You out of anyone should remember.'

But I don't. And it's driving me crazy here. I can't bear to tell them all I'm failing with this. That we've reached a brick wall before we've begun.

Pin punches the air, exclaims. 'Darius!' We look at him – his suggestion is genius.

'Charlie mentioned him,' Bert says, 'but I can't remember who he is.'

'When we first arrived at the Reptilarium Basti threatened to get rid of us,' I say. 'Remember? He said he'd send us off to his friend Darius, who works at Brompton Cemetery. Preparing dead people or putting them in coffins or something horrible like that . . .'

Bert's eyes shine. 'Coffins! Ghosts! What are we waiting for?'

I look at my brother, the one with the ghost phobia that stops him in his tracks. 'I'm so sorry,

Scruffty-mate. But he might be our key to all this. Dad's certainly not going to talk, and I'd hate to see him cranky all over again. Charlie Boo certainly won't be saying anything else. And we can't count on Basti.' Because he lives in a world of his own making, is deeply unreliable, always off with his own projects, in cahoots with Charlie Boo as well as Dad and no doubt alerted already about this. Scruff starts biting his nails. Always a bad sign: it means super nervous. He asks when we'll be doing this.

'Tomorrow. Right after Dad's gone.' He nibbles his nail again – it'll be bitten to the quick before long. 'We have to work fast, mate. Sorry. The four of us have to get out of here . . . somehow.' I look around dubiously. 'Dad just needs to be thinking we're safe and sound, helping Basti in the Reptilarium. Just waiting quietly to go home.'

'Since when have we ever been quiet?' Bert giggles. We all burst out laughing. Because the answer's never. And who on earth would think we're safe and sound with a mad uncle and a house full of the most dangerous reptiles on earth?

'The library, troops!' I rub my hands. 'We need a good night's sleep. We've got an attic raid tomorrow. Then a daring and miraculous escape. Plan 452. Our most ambitious of the lot. We need to stock up on compasses, warm clothes, flying goggles, the whole kit and caboodle. We might have to cross continents, could end up in Iceland, Egypt, Siam – who knows! But first, we've got to find Brompton Cemetery. Plus – crucially – we've got to do it before Dad gets back.'

'Yippeeeeeeee!'

We scurry off to the library with its warning sign:

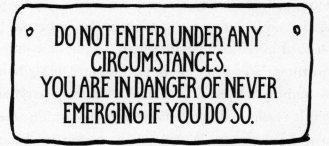

DO NOT ENTER UNDER ANY CIRCUMSTANCES. YOU ARE IN DANGER OF NEVER EMERGING IF YOU DO SO.

Because of all its delicious books, I choose to believe, but you never know in this crazy house. The excitement's bubbling over. The magical Kensington Reptilarium is full of hissing and squeaking and chattering and rustling, as if all the animals have cottoned on to our excitement and are whispering our plans, in shock, amongst themselves. Outside, snow gently falls over the square. And there are new friends out there, across the garden, impatient for all the bush skills we've promised to teach them. But it'll be a huge day tomorrow – the Grand Caddy Bush Demonstration will just have to wait.

As will home. Its tall blue skies. Its ghost gums like shinbones on the red hills to the east that glow golden in the evening light. 'It's like they've trapped the sky in them, Kicky,' Mum said once, 'like they can't bear to let all the beauty leak out.' She loved gazing at it from her wicker chair on the verandah, her feet up on the long wooden extension arms, most unladylike. 'A girl's got to do what a girl's got to do,' she'd hoot at my shock. I can't wait to go back to it. All the laughter, that's what I remember the most. Hold Pin tight in the envelope of my arms. A mummy. The first ever time for him. Imagine that.

He stirs and draws my arm over his tummy, deep into his warmth. We've got an adventure to get cracking on with here. Tomorrow. As soon as Dad's gone. We'll sort his life out, and Mum's, and ours — oh, don't you worry about that.

Plan 452: our most spectacular yet!

5

A SQUARE
FULL OF FUN

'Arise, Caddys one, Caddys all. It is eight – o –
ni-iiiine precisely. And a certain beloved father is
soon to depart.'

'Er, what did you say, Mr Boo?' I tease, desperate
to hear his stern Scottish vowels mangle the word
'nine' so exuberantly once again – he says it with
about four syllables added into it.

But he's having none of it today. 'You heard,
Miss Thomasina, you heard.'

'Kick.'

'Thomasina. Such a beautiful name. Now, as
I said –' The Boo glare, at me, then at Bucket, who's
curled up with me overnight. The Boo eyebrow
raised, the Boo eyes at the Boo watch.

'But where's our mum?' Onya, Scruff, launching straight in to it. The nub of the problem here.

'Yes! Yes!' we all tumble in chorus because maybe Charlie Boo has had a softening overnight and is ready to tell us everything. Yes? 'Can we rescue her? Is she stuck?'

'Deary me, wasn't I the rambler. We will forget that unfortunate conversation from last night immediately.' Oh no we won't. 'I repeat, immediately.' The Boo eyebrow once again. 'I know nothing. In fact, I never know anything in this place, including, for instance, where you've hidden the entire secret stash of Christmas chocolate rations. Master Ralph?'

Scruff gives his magnificent 'I didn't do it' face in response, which fools everyone but his family and Charlie Boo.

'The head of the house would like to know immediately. As would I.'

'Excuse me,' Scruff responds indignantly, 'but do you have any idea of the enormous pressure I live under here? Two stinky sisters *and* a brother who are all desperate every second of the day to get their hands on my secret supplies. One needs certain things to get by in life. Man to man. You know.' Charlie Boo's face says he does not. 'There's, like, crucial information for survival that must be kept to one's self, Mr Boo.'

'Well said, old boy!' booms a voice from the doorway. 'Chocolate stashes are sacrosanct in my book.'

Uncle Basti, of course, resplendent in his morning attire of yellow velvet as blaring as a sunflower. The suit, the matching shoes. Only broken by a jumpy red shirt far too big for him, a green tie, one pink and one blue sock, round mirrored sunglasses and a chameleon perched on his head. Who is red, er, no. Green, er, blue.

'*What* is this cacophonous cacophony in here? We have an invalid in the house. And you're meant to be in a library, my dear family-types, in case you haven't noticed. A library.' His voice drops to a whisper. 'Which means deathly quiet. And, er, dog-free. But I'm never going to win that one, am I?'

'Nope!' Bert giggles.

Scruff sidles up to him, rolling up his sleeves. 'Basti, me old mate, what's all this about our mum? Come on, you can tell me, man to man.'

Our uncle sighs exhaustedly. Looks at his nephew, then Charlie Boo, then Bucket, who puts her head quizzically to one side, then his nephew once again. 'I am so very sorry. But there's absolutely nothing you can do, my boy. You must accept it. Your mother is gone and that is a fact. Full stop. End of story. You must forget Charlie Boo ever said whatever he said, in his most unprofessional lapse. He's getting old, you know.'

Charlie Boo raises a startled eyebrow at his boss.

'You *are*,' Basti says. 'And my bouncy little tiger cubs, as you bid farewell to your father please don't – under any circumstances – mention any of this ridiculousness. His poor heart has been weakened most terribly by his ordeals, and we don't want to give him any more stress. Do we? Because the consequences –' he sighs '– could be fatal.'

He's right. Keep Dad out of this. As much as we don't want to. But the thought of him opening the door to Mum when he comes back! It will keep us going. We will never be persuaded from Plan 452's course.

The doorbell suddenly rings, most insistently. Basti sighs. 'Far too vigorous, too young and too early for any of my acquaintances. Off you go. Why on earth did I let you into my world? Why? Why?' He hits his head in frustration then suddenly smiles. 'Because it's good for me, of course. Dinda keeps telling me this. You lot, apparently, stop melancholy and madness and indulgent thoughts. All thoughts, in fact, except despair at never again having a peaceful moment in my life.'

'Love you, Uncle Basti!' 'See you soon!' We race downstairs to the front door, followed by a wildly excited Bucket. Friends! Snowballs! Sleds!

Oh yes indeed. A cacophonous cacophony of brand new mates. Hannah, Violet, Lauren and Anton, Dave, Hen, Georgie, Noah and Becky, Max and Charlotte, Otto and Chasper, Eva and Luke, who've all raced from their neighbourhood houses and crowded around the Reptilarium, calling us out, snug as bugs in their winter hats and coats. 'We want to see a whip cracked!' 'Where's your slingshot?' 'Do your freckles go all over?' 'Even your belly button?' (Scruff being Scruff answers yes to that one and volunteers to show it, which has Bert and me in fits of, 'Stop, stop!') 'Can you ride a kangaroo?' 'An emu?' 'Is your dog really one of those dingo things?' 'I'll swap you a sled for a hunting knife.'

'Not on your life,' I smile, 'it's special,' clutching the knife on its strap of leather around my neck.

We pour out of the Reptilarium, Bucket yapping wildly then throwing in a desert howl for good measure. We all race into the snow-bowered garden square, rolling and squealing down its vast expanse of sloping white. Perfect for sleds! And brand new skis!

And bits of crates! And a snowman called Lily C, which Bert decides is not stylish enough and must be instantly re-dressed – Albertina of Kensington style – or, in the tactful words of the Grand Dame herself, 'enhanced'.

Scruff's up a tree quick as a flash, lassoing a rope around a branch and calling me over to tie a short log to the bottom of it. He smiles, winks – we've done this before, on a river gum at home: instant swing.

'Me first!' Pin is off, promptly crashing into the tree trunk and tumbling off – oops! – up he pops. (Yep, indestructible as well as invincible.) Max has found an old whip in his father's study, souvenired from a cattle muster in Argentina, and hands it across with a dare – 'Show us what you're made of, Aussie girl!' Oh, just you wait.

With a sharp quick flick I promptly remove the beanie from his head. 'Anything else?' I spin around. 'Any heads that need removing? Toes?'

'Max's nose!' cries his brother, Luke. I curl the whip under a crisp leap from Bucket then wrap it magically and harmlessly around Max's wrist. Everyone gasps. Claps. I could grow to enjoy this.

'Nice one, Kick. You must take after your father with that!'

I spin to the Reptilarium. It's Dad. On the footpath, leaning between Charlie Boo on one side and his brother on the other. Ready to set off.

'Daddy!' The four of us race across the road.

He looks no better than last night. Is helped into Basti's waiting limousine ever so gently by the two men. Dinda from next door clatters outside in heels far too tall, wielding an enormous bouquet of orange and black flowers that match most fabulously her tiger skin-coat. But she's had no time to do her hair – it's still in huge golden rollers. Rather divinely, I can tell from Bert's look.

Basti is now standing all nervous and awkward beside her – at being out, in the open, at being next to the undeclared love of his life. Love. Urgh. It's such weird stuff. Look what it turns perfectly sensible people into? Quivering wrecks. It's like he suddenly can't talk. Why do people bother with it? It takes up so much time and fret.

'She'd look incredible in anything. A potato sack,' Berti sighs.

'When's their wedding thing?' Scruff butts in. 'Who wants to take bets?'

Bert rolls her eyes. 'You know nothing about love. I, on the other hand, most certainly do. There'll be many obstacles to overcome before Basti and Dinda get to their church. Which will be a small but beautiful one in the countryside with white roses around the door. But get to it they will. In a December, to commemorate their spectacular finding of each other all over again. They will be in matching creations. From myself. I've already begun designing them, in fact, plus the interior of the reception hall, which will be medieval with shields and dead zebra heads and a roaring fireplace.'

'Zebra heads?' Pin is aghast.

'Since when have you been an expert on . . . kissing stuff.' Scruff wrinkles his nose at that horrid and deeply forbidden word that has to pass from his lips.

'Kissing! Kissing! Did someone say kissing!' I plant big giggly smackaroonies all over his squirmy head; Bert joins in, Pin tackles his legs and proceeds to smother his knees with wet licks.

'Caddys major, intermediate and minor,' Charlie Boo roars. 'Could you please direct your energies to someone in actual need of them.' He indicates our father, now snug in the long, low panther of a car with a tartan rug over his knees. We crowd around the door, jostling and shrieking for kissing space, Bucket leaping and snuffling around us trying to get in close.

'Steady on,' Dad laughs.

'I fear someone's kisses may well be directed towards my grandson Linus soon enough,' Charlie Boo murmurs to him.

'What?' I snap, blushing.

'Not saying,' he teases.

'Is she growing up, Mr Boo?' Dad asks. 'Is she reaching that stage already?'

'No,' I squeal furiously.

'We'll have to find a dress for her first,' Dad says.

'I'll do it!' Albertina of Kensington jumps in.

Dad grabs my hand, laughing. 'You're our chief tigress, aren't you, Miss Kicky? Spitting and yowling and fighting the world. Always have been. As fierce as your mother, you know. And don't you go changing on me.' I look at him, clotted, want to ask him so much. Not now, Kicky, please, says his face.

He turns to his commando of a son, who's at the ready here with whip in one hand and slingshot in the other. 'Scruff, you're my wild one, my chief defender, yarn spinner, bar mate and crack shot, so you, I do believe, have to be in charge of the hat.' Dad winks at his eldest son, whose face is shining right up. 'Until I can get my googlies perfected, and then we'll be off with that cricket game all over again. But we need that bread tin, right?'

'And what about Peter Pan airplanes?' Bert asks. 'You know, where you'd hold us flat like an ironing board and fly us round and round? They were my favourite, Daddy.'

'Oh yes, I'll put that on the list, my love, my little pet.'

'And camping trips? Where we track goannas and cook 'em up in the coals?' Scruff jumps in.

'And duddles?' adds Pin.

'Yes, yes, all of it,' Dad smiles. 'Now look after our Bucket girl, won't you?' He plays with her ears affectionately. 'And, Pinny, you have to mind my scarf. It's your big grown-up task while I'm away. I think you'll manage. You're extremely capable. In fact, my children seem to turn out more sane and sensible the further down the line they go. How did that happen?'

'Oy!' I exclaim.

'Oh, you are so teasible, Kicketty Kick. It's rather delightful, you know.'

Charlie Boo starts the car. Pin gives his father a grave salute.

'Don't do anything I wouldn't,' Dad winks to all of us.

I smile, taking that as a signal to proceed immediately with Ingenious Plan Number 452. And won't he get a shock – the best shock of his life – at its grand and spectacular climax. But as the car pulls away it's like he sees something in my face, like he reads my mind and all the grand scheming in it. 'Stay safe!' he yells in sudden anguish. Like he'll never see us again. 'You're not going anywhere, are you?' His hand trails out the window.

We all grab on to it. 'We love you, Daddy!' 'Get better soon!' 'We'll have you home in no time!'

Then the four of us plus one dog tear all the way down Campden Hill Square, waving and yelling and barking and whistling our desert whistles that make brumbies' ears prick as well as roos, until the car turns into Holland Park Avenue and is swallowed by traffic, by London, by the vast crazy busy-ness of it.

Dad's last gesture is a V for Victory sign tall out the window.

I hold out one, high, back. Oh yes, we'll bring him victory all right.

6

PREPARATION

We're going to find her for him. Oh yes.

The love of Dad's life. We're going to get us a family here that's all fixed up. It will be the most amazing adventure of our lives. I just know it. So let's get cracking! I turn to the others. 'Right. Mr Darius Davenport, here we come. Brompton Cemetery. However we find it.'

'Dinda could help,' Bert suggests. Anything to get close to the glamorous fashion photographer next door who she's got a ridiculous girl crush on. Wants to be, in fact.

'Nope, too aligned to Basti,' I say. 'In love.' Scruff covers his ears in horror at that squirmy L word again. 'We're alone with this one, troops. Have to be.

Because any grown-up who finds out about us will put a stop to it, quick.' I look at Pin. His face reflects the enormity of this knowledge. That he's now like a baby camel raised in captivity who's suddenly let loose with a whole world ahead of him, an entire desert and there's a lot of excitement out there, but scariness, too.

'Pin? Get it?' I warn. 'No telling *anyone*. Or Mum might be lost forever.' He nods gravely, puffed up with the hugeness of the task. 'Now, what are we going to call this operation? Mission . . . what?'

'Mission Chocolate!' Scruff volunteers. We roll our eyes.

'Mission Desert Rose,' Bert says quietly. 'The first phase of Plan 452.'

The name's perfect. Exactly right for Mum. 'Good one, sis.' She smiles at me.

'Boy heroes, you ready?'

Two crisp salutes.

'Girl hero?'

'Aye aye, captain!' I look at her, incredulous. Could it possibly be that we're on the same wavelength? Nup. Impossible. Has never happened before in our lives.

'I'm going to get Mum opening that door to him if it's the last thing I ever do,' she vows. 'It's the most romantic thing in the world. Ever. Imagine their kiss.'

'Uuuuuuuurgh.' Scruff's arms are now in revulsion over his entire face. I'm with you, mate, I'm with you. Don't want to think about it.

'Bucket?'

A bark of readiness. She's our master tracker and hot water bottle and body guard all rolled into one. Essential to Mission Desert Rose.

'Right. The attic. About turn. We need some kitting out.'

And so there we are, climbing the Reptilarium's ladders with a great clatter of glee then zipping across floors on their ingenious rails, whizzing and giggling as we get closer and closer to the great glass dome. The clouds are so low they almost seem to brush us like cow bellies grazing grass and we put out our hands to them in wonder – the big blue is all so far away at home.

'We'll be out there soon enough,' I say.

Bucket waits patiently down the bottom while we crawl through the small golden door tucked under the dome, which opens into our wonderland of wonders – a vast accumulation of junk, from centuries ago. Stuffed camels, army tents, billycarts and cannons, hot-air balloon baskets and a battalion of mannequins. We arm ourselves with ropes and old whips and strings of bullets just for effect and feather boas along with a bellboy's hat from Claridges (Bert) and a pirate hat (Pin, of course) and a toy silk jacket (Banjo) with Basti's sleeping cap double-knotted around its neck along with Dad's scarf, and long riding boots (me) and a child's chest plate from Roman times, or Norman, goodness knows what but it's all rather fabulous (Scruff) and he's topped it off with Dad's old bush hat for good luck.

'Come on,' I urge them after half an hour, 'we've got to get out of here before anyone cottons on to us.'

Charlie Boo's with Dad so he's out for the day, thank goodness; Basti's busy with all his Reptilarium tasks, lost in the bowels of the building but it won't be for long.

Bert lingers, perfecting her outfit. A billowy black feather from a funeral horse's corsage, a tiny Victorian velvet blazer with gold trim. 'I might be spotted, all right? By potential clients.'

I roll my eyes.

'Who knows where we'll end up, Kick.'

Well, she has a point. She even grabs an old dog's jacket made out of a mangy mink. 'Will you stop accessorising even the dog?' I urge. 'Just come *on*.'

'Bucky might get cold. She's from one of the hottest deserts on earth.'

We head downstairs. Fan across the Reptilarium. Each with the mission to find a way out of here. Report back to the Glow Room. It's not looking good. All doors: firmly locked. Ditto ground floor windows. Especially the broken scullery one that we used to sneak into Dinda's once. Repaired. Sternly. Nup, no way out.

What to do? I spin, thinking. They always expect me to make things right and by golly I'll deliver on this one like nothing else, if it means a proper family again plus that icky kiss at the end of it. 'I do know a window that's open, actually, but it's really, scarily, high up.' I bite my lip. 'It's tiny. Plus –' I look at Bucky and sigh '– we've got a dog in the mix.'

'She *has* to come with us.' Bert holds her collar fierce.

'I know. I know. Okay, troops, let's do this.' Deep breath. 'We're from the bush. We can solve this.'

I flash a V for Victory sign. Just like Dad's.

'All for one and one for all, or whatever it was,' Scruff says.

We're off.

7

A ROPE OF SILVER

We gaze up at the sky. A tiny window right at the edge of the dome. Gulp. Silence as we contemplate the sheer scariness of it.

'I notice it every time we're up there. It's got this flimsy little catch –'

'Because no one would be stupid enough to escape through it, perhaps . . .' Bert trails off.

'Precisely.'

'Except us!' Scruff exclaims.

'Yep, it's our only way out,' I say. 'But the problem is, troops, that it leads us onto a really tall roof. With a sheer drop. Captain Scruff, how would you be tackling the next bit?'

No further prompt is needed. 'Well, at home, General Kickasina, we'd be removing all our shoes because, as you know, we're better in bare feet. Years of practice. Then we'd be climbing up one by one through that hole I sawed so amazingly in the roof, to the washing-basket crow's nest – thanks for donating that, Mum. Not that you knew.'

'And one day, I promise, we'll get all the washing done for you,' I murmur, thinking of the great piles of it languishing at home.

'Then someone would have to haul Pin onto their back, for the really tough bits.' Scruff looks at yours truly. They all do. 'Then there's the dog, of course.' Yep, me again. Thanks. Anyone else care to join the party up there on my back? 'Then we'd just launch ourselves off the side of the house, whooshing down and down like we're jumping off the moon –'

'Screaming blue murder,' Bert joins in.

'On that slidey thing we constructed out of those flat pieces of tin we found in the shed. Gee, we were good, weren't we?'

Bert rolls her eyes. 'Yeah, really subtle, that. No one will notice a washing basket and tin slide in London, will they?'

'Would you *stop* being thirty-two?' Scruff snaps at her. 'You're being a bit too parent for my liking.'

'Rope,' Pin declares serenely over the two of them.

We stare at him. He's right. As he so often is. But we don't have enough for the entire building's height. 'What else have we got that's rope-like?' I ask. 'Bert, come on, we need something really long here.'

'Easy peasy.' She smiles like a cat with the richest cream. 'Thank you for asking, Kick. As the most intelligent one here I'd suggest curtains.' I let it pass, she's got a point. 'My room's got – two – four – *eight* of them. Plus sheets. There's a closet full of them in the dressing room. Pink satin, Scruff. Brace yourself.'

We rush to her bedroom. The curtain rods are awfully high. How to reach?

'Climb them, like a fireman's pole, but going up,' Scruff exclaims. And before we can say stop, wait, he shimmies up a silvery streak as tall as the ceiling and pushes a strip of fabric off its rod. But how to come down once the second curtain's gone? 'Pile up all the cushions you can find,' he commands, hanging off the curtain rod like a monkey, 'and just watch this superboy leap! I've been practising for this moment for days, troops.'

'But every single cushion here is pink,' I warn.

He shuts his eyes, braces himself. 'Well, we'll just have to cope, Scruffter boy.' Then he flashes an enormous grin. 'It's all a matter of holding your nose!' Which he does as he takes a wild flying leap. Again, and again, until we have eight enormous fabric strips and a pile of sheets swallowing the floor.

'But will this be long enough?' Bert mutters to herself as she ropes it all together with a canny knot Dad taught her, just for those moments when you're tying down a camel pack or, alternatively, escaping from a London house.

'It'll have to be,' I snap.

Because there's no other way to do this. And we need to have double the length so we can loop it over something and then bring it all down after us, so no one knows we're gone. 'More sheets, we're not done yet!' I command, and Bucket barks at the sea of silver and pink before her, in excitement as well as terror.

'I think we need to muzzle you, girl,' I murmur, looking around for something, anything. 'But with what? You're not allowed to scupper our plans. Yet we can't leave you here because we might need you for your nose – you could sniff Mum out anywhere, couldn't you?' She whines in agreement. Does a little jiggle of excitement. I swear she understands everything. 'Plus that grumpy Perdita the cobra might eat you up if you stay here.'

Banjo the teddy is languishing on Bert's bed with Dad's checked scarf around his neck. Perfect. I pick him up.

'Kicky . . .' Pin growls.

'I promise I'll give it back. As soon as we're free.' Reluctantly Pin allows me Dad's precious scarf but stuffs Banjo firmly into his belt; they'll be going on this operation together whether any of us like it or not. Then we all cram onto the flying chair that will whizz us to the ceiling, our escape hatch, Bucket across our laps and a mountain of material spilling down below us like a great dragon's tail. We have lift off, slowly – too slowly – there's too much of us – excruciatingly slowly, creaky, come *on* – then just as we near the dome the kitchen door opens.

No, no, no.

Breaths held.

Out steps Basti. In his white lab coat, wheeling his trolley loaded high with Insectarium delicacies. Feeding time.

Nooooooo!

I crash down the lever and the chair lurches to a wild swaying stop; Bert gasps and Scruff slams her hand across her mouth; Pin wobbles and almost tumbles out; I grab him back as well as Bucket, who's not liking this one bit. We all gaze down. Nope, our uncle's utterly oblivious, phew, singing away as he measures out a mixture of mashed cockroach and earthworm. Then, just as I lift the lever to proceed on our course, Pin's pirate hat tumbles down, down – thud – to the ground.

'My hat!' he yells.

'I say ... what?' Basti gazes up, squinting to work out what's going on. '*Childus Desertus Australis* times – good grief – *four*? Plus one canine.' He can scarcely believe what he's seeing crammed into the seat. 'Explain yourselves,' he snaps.

'Oh, you've caught us!' I laugh down at him, trying to smooth the panic from my voice. 'We're just rehearsing here. It's a big surprise, Uncle Basti. Our grand show of celebration. For Twelfth Night. To say thank you to everyone. For everything. It's a big secret. Mr Boo's in on it. He approves. He says it will cheer you up no end.'

'And Dinda too,' Pin throws in.

'It's a *dress* rehearsal,' Bert adds. 'And I've got this idea to make the stage curtains using silver cloth, and to turn the entire Reptilarium into this huge theatrical set. It'll be amazing. Just you wait.'

'But you can't look!' Scruff cries. 'Not yet. It'll spoil it.'

'Especially the finale involving one Rasti the lovable red rat and Minda the Mighty Mouse, black-haired, of course,' I laugh.

Basti clasps his hand to his chest. 'Oh, I *do* love the thought of a jolly good show! Just make sure you return those curtains tonight.'

'Of course!'

'Oh, and Basti,' Scruff adds, 'you know that grasshopper mash you've got there? Um, you might like to think about making a new batch. I got a bit peckish last night. Started experimenting. Added what I thought was sugar to what I thought was cake mix . . . but it was baking powder and . . . well, I know that makes ants explode. So I can't imagine what it might do to a skink?'

'Oh, you vexatious creature!' Basti roars, all changed. 'I *knew* there was a reason why I shouldn't have let your species into my world.' He flurries back to the kitchen to make up an entirely new batch. 'No chocolate ration for a week! Make that two. A year,' he grumps.

'Okay.' Scruff grins meekly, and raises a cheeky V for Victory sign at our departing Uncle's back.

'Exploding ants. Nice one, mate,' I wink.

'We just lied to him, Kicky,' Pin says gravely.

'I know, Pinny Pin. And it's not good, not good at all. But sometimes you have to. To save your skin. And our mum's skin. And buy about fifteen minutes of escape time. So come on. Trust me, little captain. Please.'

'I always do!' His beautiful big eyes shine with anticipation and chuff. 'This is the best adventure of our lives and then there's that great big kiss at the end of it. I don't forget, Kicky.'

We reach the top of the Reptilarium. Slip off shoes for extra grip. Look dubiously at the tiny window that's our key to outside, to the world, and to Mum. This has to be done.

I'm out in a flash, into a blast of cold air. Brrrrrr. It's brisk out here. Plus there's accumulated snow. Not pleasant. Pin's hauled up behind me with Scruff pushing his little bottom through the tiny opening. Bert then lifts Bucket through, all wriggly protesting limbs, then helps Scruff up and last but not least hauls herself out with all the champion gymnast's easiness that she's famous for. We crawl along the terrifying edge of the roof next to slippery slate tiles; everything is so cold and grey and precarious and too far-up. 'Don't look down!' I warn.

'I'm scared, Kick.'

'Do we have to do this?'

'I want to go back.'

Even Bucket's whining through her muzzle. Am I mad here? Yes. Why have I dragged them all into this? I shut my eyes for a moment, push on. 'Mum's out there somewhere,' I urge, 'she might be needing us right now.' I flurry briskly across to a gargoyle.

Then there's an unearthly scream, from Bert.

Like nothing I've ever heard in my life.

WHY, KICK, WHY?

Pinny has stumbled, is almost over the edge – one leg, one arm – tipping and scrabbling at an ancient lead gutter that looks like it'll come loose any moment.

Scruff grabs his brother's waistcoat, he's slipping through it, I race over and flop onto my belly and grab his trousers, Bert's got his shoulders and all three of us haul our darling bundle of preciousness up. That wasn't good. We hold him tight and kiss him through his shakiness.

'I'm okay, Kicky, I'm okay,' he trembles over and over.

'*What* are we doing here?' Bert screams at me, furious. 'This is madness. Is there a plan? Really? Actually? You can admit it, you know.'

I shut my eyes on a prickle of tears, nod. What *am* I doing? Am I crazy? There's no plan beyond this roof. I'm always doing things like this — cottoning on to mad crazy schemes that then have to be carried out, ferociously, no matter what the consequences. Because I can't lose face. Because I go too far and then can't turn back. Because I can't bear the thought of Bert's sneering at my failure. Any acknowledgement of pathetic hope-lessness. So I drag them all into it, whatever it is. Stealing Matilda and gunning her into the desert, jumping off the water tower onto far away mat-tresses, attacking police with rotten eggs. So now we've got this far with Plan 452, the most ingenious plan of the lot, and now we can't go back. Because Basti will be doing his rounds now. Oblivious. I'm stuck with this. We all are.

'If any of us die it's your fault,' Bert spits at me. 'Plus my feet are freezing off. This wasn't my idea. I just want you all to know that.'

Oh yes, we know. And you'll be taking all the credit when Mum's back with us, won't you? Presenting your grand red robe to her, explaining about opening the door to Dad. Yep, you'll be owning it, sis. And right now I just want to push you off the roof myself but need to carry on here, biting my tongue, to get you all on the ground safe and sound. It's so easy to criticise, isn't it?

'Come on,' I say cheerily, even though it feels like the hardest thing I've ever said in my life, 'we're almost there.'

Pin, of course, is the first behind me. 'Aye aye, captain!'

'No, *you* are, mister.'

'No, *you*, Kicky.' I want to turn and give him the biggest hug of his life in that moment, but can't.

A dragon gargoyle guards the house. The curtain is tied in a loop around the scales of its belly. We snap the cloth tight, testing it.

'Will it hold?' Scruff asks dubiously.

'They're *my* knots,' Bert responds.

'That's what I'm worried about.' Ever the trusty lieutenant.

'Me first,' I smile grimly. 'Pinny, jump on my back. Hold tight.' He almost throttles my neck in the process. 'Just ease up a tiny bit,' I choke out.

Deep breath. Bert, we just have to trust you on this one – we've climbed down ropes from the water tower at home but have never done something like this.

Okay, we're off. Wheeeeeeee! We slide down the cloths, feet springing from the walls, down, down, and land with a thud at the bottom. Closely followed by Bert, who makes it look easy, of course; then Scruff, with his victory sign strong for the last bit coupled with a poked-out tongue. Easy peasy, troops!

'I say, what are you doing?'

We jump with fright. Dave and Hannah. Right behind us. Gazing up at the billowing silver rope of cloth.

'Esca—' Pin begins.

'Practising!' I jump in. 'For when we get home. We're going to climb Ayers Rock.'

'What's that?'

'This great big boulder right in the middle of Australia. It's about as tall as St Paul's Cathedral.'

'Wow. You desert kids do such fun things. Can we come home with you? And what about your dog?'

Bucky! Good grief, of course. We all gaze up at Bucket's anxious dingo nose; our girl's peering over the roof, whining and pacing and coming back. 'Who's going to do the honours?' I look around.

No takers, just six pairs of eyes looking at yours truly.

'Right.' Big sigh. This is not going to be easy – Bucky's an awfully long way away – it'll be like climbing the water tower at home but with no footholds so worse. Yet without another word, back up

I go, increasingly puffed, then slide down the make-shift rope as fast as I can, mainly one-handed with an utterly still, terrified dog cradled in my free arm and clinging on around my neck for dear life; my hand that's supporting her clutching at the rope whenever I think we're both going to plunge to our deaths. Which is quite a bit. I flop on my back at the bottom from the sheer exhausting effort of it all. Am rewarded with a big doggy lick of gratitude but no thanks, of course, from any of the humans here. Never any thanks from them.

Bert unknots a knot and we drag the rope from the roof and stuff it along the side of the house. No time to lose. We don't need Basti coming outside and investigating.

'See ya!' We wave to our mates.

'But where are you going?'

Would they stop with the questions here? 'To get some supplies,' I say. 'For our big performance. On Twelfth Night. There's this shop called the Seven Sisters Circusarium – and it's waiting for us. We have an appointment. See you on the night. Front row. We'll save you a seat.'

And before our friends can respond we're off, just like that, walking tall down Campden Hill Square with Bucket yappy with excitement around us now her mouth has been mercifully released. Pin's in front, walking backwards, one big ball of chuff as he stares at the whole ragtag crazy lot of us, our deeply eccentric mishmash of feather boas and medieval armour and bellboy hats.

'I can't believe you said that word, Kicky,' he giggles. 'Circus-airy – what?' And we all have turns in trying to get it out proper – with dismal results. Too gleeful right now to concentrate. We're out! *Out.* It actually worked.

'Now, Brompton Cemetery. Fact Man?' I turn to Scruff. 'Navigator extraordinaire?'

'Why thank you, ma'am. And actually, I looked up a map in the library last night. There's Holland Park tube station, most conveniently, right at the bottom of this hill. And I must say, London's train system is a ripper, troops.'

'Yippeeeeeeee, Scruffy the best!' Pin laughs.

But we have no money. For tickets. Er, forgot about that.

The ticket seller looks at us dubiously. OKAY, yes, we're a sight. A barefoot sight, in deepest winter no less. We smile hopefully. Hold out our hands. He's not convinced. How to charm him into help? He looks hugely sleepy, like he can't wait for his shift to end and get home to a lie down and a nice hot soup.

'We're almost-orphans. From Australia,' Pin announces hopefully.

'I gathered.'

'We need to get to our mama,' Pin says.

'At Brompton Cemetery,' I jump in. The ticket seller looks suspicious, sorry and alarmed all at once. 'But we can't pay.' Pin's eyes fill with tears. The man raises an eyebrow. 'We do have a dingo,' I say. He backs away. 'Yep. An authentically wild dog straight out of the central Australian desert. How about . . . um . . . a ticket for a trick?'

'That's four tricks I'd be after.'

'Just four?' I grin. 'You're on.' Click fingers. Bucket jumps up on two paws and dances. She's handed over to Scruff with a flourish. He snaps his fingers and Bucket leaps up and grabs Dad's hat from his head. Bert whistles, indicates. Bucket jumps high and places the hat back on Scruff's head and is rewarded with a double backflip from the champion gymnast who manages to keep her feather boa intact.

'One more trick, or the little fella comes home with me for lunch.' The ticket seller winks at Pin.

'Oh yes, please!'

'Pinny,' I say stern, 'the circus audience is waiting,' and with a gleeful laugh he opens out his arms like an aeroplane and zooms around the ticket hall with a dingo dancing on her back legs right behind him, then making little leaps, just like a kangaroo. We've spent years in the desert perfecting this.

'Well, I never!' The ticket seller waves us through with a bow.

'Hang on, how exactly do we get to Brompton Cemetery?' Bert asks.

'Take the Central line heading East. Change at Notting Hill gate to the Circle line. Change at High Street Ken to the District line. Get off at West Brompton. Got that?'

We laugh and nod, sort of, then set off, four kids from a tall blue sky who've never been underground in our lives, let alone on a train, and with a dingo to boot.

'Hold your breath!' Bert instructs, as the lift cranks us down, down, into the bowels of the London earth, to its blast of stinky warm air.

'It's a dingo,' Scruff's exclaiming to anyone and everyone who's looking at her. 'Isn't she beautiful?' Bucket is smiling and prancing at her most adorable best. 'She's the first real-live dingo London's ever seen outside a zoo. You're very lucky. Would you like a pat? We're from the bush, the Australian bush. Any chocolate?' He's babbling on at ladies and gentlemen left and right and centre like he's been living in a very confined space for far too long – actually, he has – but all the people are mostly too busy or too polite or too shocked to talk back. Well, we are a sight. And I don't think we're going about this right.

'Scruff,' I nudge, 'I don't think London people are used to all your chitchat.'

Because we have to concentrate here, we need all hands on deck with so many train changes on this journey, so many screeching brakes and platform gaps and stairs and tunnels and endless readings of the maps in the carriages, debating 'next stop', 'no, next' and then suddenly, finally, we're at West Brompton, thank goodness.

Pin leads the charge off the train. 'Mama's getting close, Kicky,' he whispers wondrously, coming back to take my hand. 'I can just feel it.'

My heart swells. I squeeze his little fist. Something huge, I just know it, is around the corner for all of us. We'll get to Mum, we'll get to the bottom of this. And then go home. As a family. All six of us at last. We've actually never had that.

'I'm so over you being mum.' Bert pricks my bubble as soon as we're away from the platform.

'So am I, sis, so am I. I can't wait to hand the reins back.'

'It was that roof episode that finally did it. You could have lost little Pinny. Killed him. Just like that.'

I shove her, she pinches me. 'You be careful with us, all right?' she cries.

I stop abrupt. Right. So. It's going to be a long road ahead for the two of us.

The boys are oblivious. Scruff's run ahead with Pin. He turns back and whistles his most piercing desert whistle, one long, one short. It's the signal to regather, fast.

'Hurry up, slow coaches. Look, look! Ahead!'

9

WHERE THE GHOSTS GO

A poky-up city of the dead.

That's what this is. We're all shivery and silent as we gaze at it. We've never seen anything like it. Row upon obedient row. Headless statues, armless ones, winged angels staring at the ground. What are they so ashamed about? Crosses and marble needles into the sky and feeble grass trying its darndest to poke up and get a grip in this place. But the snow and the cold won't let it. It's all so different to home, where hard little plots are scraped into a furiously unwilling earth, roped by rusted railings and then pillowed by a stern iron cross. It's always just one or two people in the middle of a great nothing. Like a warning. But here it's thousands of dead people, crammed

70

too close. I shiver again, a great big brrrr of a thing. Gosh, all these ghosts. And we're stepping into it.

Is Mum among them? Is this some trick of that sneaky adult-talk that always means something else and we're the mugs here and we'll just have to slink back? I gulp. Shut my eyes. Snap them open. Nope, we have to press on.

We walk through an arched entranceway of cold-looking stone. Knock at a tiny door in it.

A man opens the door, suspiciously. He's looks all stooped by a life of too many low ceilings and walls too close and there's a wet look about him, like his palms would be permanently damp. In any other circumstances Scruff and I would be off with our giggles by now, but not this time. Too much at stake.

The man can't quite look us in the eyes, his head is angled to the side. Splodges of – what? – stain his skinny black suit. I don't want to think too much about that. I know Scruff is. I reach for his hand and it gratefully slips into mine and squeezes tight. The man's hair is grey and hangs limp to his shoulders. It might've been dashing once but now just looks dirty and his skin is yellow-grey as if it's never seen the light. I want to drag him out into a desert blast of it but it looks like he'd turn into dust if I did. Plus there's an old smell about him. Sharp. Unnatural.

Preserving potions, perhaps. Mixed with cobwebs and dust.

'Hello. We're looking for Mr Davenport,' I start. 'Can you help?'

'Mmm, really?' He looks at us sideways.

'We need to see him on an extremely urgent matter.'

A pause. 'I am he.' Reluctantly. As if children are quite the most unpleasantest things in the entire world. He stares down at our bare feet. Flinches. No invitation to step inside, of course, no warmth.

'And who be you?'

'We're from Australia. We're staying with Sebastian Caddy.' A tic in his right eye jumps. 'We're his nieces and nephews.' The air between us is suddenly crackly with silence and shock.

'Mmm, he's made contact?' Disbelief in his face. 'But I thought he never wanted anything to do with you. None of your branch was family to him. That's what he told his lawyer. Mmm.' That murmur is a habit that's starting to drive me bananas. It's like every time he does it he's thinking, considering, and his eyes slide away; he can never look at us quite straight. 'Oh yes, I know these things. He'd lost touch with his brother years ago. Mmm. Are you impostors, by any chance?' He glances down again at our bare feet like he's never seen anything like them before. 'His estate is extremely valuable. And he's quite vulnerable. One must always be careful. Especially now, at Christmas. Awful time. Mmm.' He starts shutting the door on us.

'Look into our eyes,' I calmly instruct.

Mr Davenport peers close, head to the side. One green, one blue, just like our uncle. He steps back, pale. It's the look of someone . . . what? Threatened, perhaps? Shocked out of his skin, I know that. 'Well, well.'

'We're a family now!' Pin jumps in gleefully.

'Plus we're starving,' Scruff throws in. 'Any chocolate in the house? Just a man hunch you've got some, Mr Davenpit.'

'Daven*port*,' he hisses. 'And certainly not for the likes of you, boy. Mmm.'

'Will we get to see some coffins?' Bert, of course, being very Bert. In fact, she's almost beside herself with excitement at such an exotically fabulous place. She spent several years, from age six to eight, with a cupboard obsession. Loved getting inside them, making them her hidey-holes, goodness knows what she did in them; begged to sleep in her mother's cupboard most of all, loved any space that was dark and enclosed.

'Coffins?' It's the first smile of the day that we get. 'Why yes, little girl, excellent, mmm. The Tower of London has nothing on the attractions here. Did you know that that esteemed place used to hold a menagerie of exotic beasts?' We shake our heads, wide-eyed. 'Well, it's got nothing on the catacombs of Brompton. Oh yes. I can't offer you African beasts but I can offer you something else. Mmm.' He chuckles. It makes me hold Scruff's hand tighter. 'Come come, this way. Let me think . . .'

What about? I'm about to catapult a thousand questions into his head but he puts a long finger stained a mysterious yellow to his lips and whispers, 'Ssssh, don't want to wake anyone, do we? Mmm.'

Hang on. He's Basti's best friend, isn't he, so he must be all right. Surely? And we don't want to be rude. So follow we must. Yes? What would Basti do in this circumstance? Get cross at our reluctance, no doubt.

Mr Davenport grabs a clanking bunch of keys from a hook on the door. Crisply locks up the gate-house – three locks, checked, tight – then leads us past rows of tombstones. Our bare feet are red and raw as we crunch through snow as resistant as frozen grapes.

'Singular, aren't you?' he murmurs, staring down at our feet once again and shaking his head. 'You're sure you're not here for the money? Mmm?'

We're struck dumb. Extremely un-Caddy-like. We don't know what he's talking about.

We follow his curved back down steep open steps to an enormous double door. Two serpents face each other on the black iron grilles, mouths open and hissing their fury. Forever. Yep, they're cranky at each other, endlessly. It's me and Bert. She traces the delicate detail in their scales, in raptures over everything in this place. 'No wonder Basti likes you, Mr Davenport,' she murmurs.

'Oh yes, he christened those two snakes Wallis and Eddie. Such a wag. We're old school friends, you know. Mmmm.' A pause. 'The best.' Another pause. 'And now you're here.' He savagely unlocks a rusty old padlock holding together a rope of iron as thick as my arm. 'So that's that. Yes. Here.'

We step inside. Fear blows its warning onto the back of our necks. A rash of goosebumps races across our skin, all of us, I just know it. Well, except maybe Bert. But it feels like we're entering the bowels of the earth here, that we're walking through the gates of some terrifying underworld – and we may never, ever get out. As we creep along the stone floor, a bank of cold hits us like the breath of a thousand ghosts – wily vents from somewhere are keeping the corridors well aired.

Bucket has to be dragged into the subterranean gloom. Her paws are resisting at every step, she's whining. What are you telling us, girl?

Bert claps her hands silently in glee. Scruff looks terrified. Pin holds my hand in an iron grip. Because the air's alive with death and we've never been in a place like it. All that is vibrant and living and light-filled has been sucked out of it as we walk further and further on. And I now completely regret not telling anyone where we were going. Stupid, stupid Kick. Not even a note was left. A sign. What was I thinking? Or not thinking, more like it. So. No one knows where we are. We are here, and we are completely lost to the world. Completely, utterly vanished. And never meant to talk to strangers, of course.

What if we never come back? It will kill Basti. He'll blame himself. Then Dad. What have I done? How can we get out . . . was it a right we just took, a left?

'Amazing,' Bert is whispering, oblivious, as we walk further and further into the earth along narrow brick tunnels. We can smell the soil's dank secrets pressing close. Coffins are stacked on shelves.

'My dear friends are swaddled in the silks and velvets of their Sunday best, then sealed in lead to hold the frights of the world at bay, oh yes,' Darius explains helpfully, running a loving hand over a particularly mangy-looking casket that's so rotted it looks like cardboard. 'This is Mr Rattly in here, a most splendid chap. Mmm. Good evening, my friend.'

'H-how do you know all that?' Scruff asks, but his question's unanswered.

So many dead people, so close, tucked into the walls' pockmarks. Coffins with elaborate hinges but whitish mould on them. Coffins with great rust streaks down them, or it's something else, I hope Scruff's not looking too close. Coffins green with rot. Old bits of cloth burst through the edges of some, others have burst open and we catch glimpses inside of swathes of brown-stained fabric, encasing . . . what? *What?* 'Don't think about it,' I tell myself, 'eyes straight ahead, don't look.' I can almost feel Scruff's wildly thumping heart bursting through his chest. Lean back, waggle fingers and my hand is gratefully grasped.

'Did you tell anyone of your visit, my friends?' Darius enquires without looking back. 'Mmm?'

Before I can jump in with, 'Yes, Basti's waiting for us, must be off!' Pin says obediently, 'No, it's Kick's big secret.'

'Splendid. I do love secrets.' And he glides ahead, a hand lingering at one passing coffin then another, tucking a piece of wayward cloth inside with a tut.

I shut my eyes. So, now he knows that we're here all by ourselves. That no one else knows. It's the worst information of the lot. We need to get back into the light. Get home. Find another way to track down Mum. This isn't worth it. Bucket's right by my heels, ever faithful, watching out for all of us. Scruff's pulse is leaping like a flea. I squeeze his hand.

'Are these really all your friends?' Bert asks.

'Mmm.' Mr Davenport smiles the chilliest of smiles. 'I lead quite a singular life.'

We're losing our sense of direction here as we twist and turn through the narrow corridors. Remember it, girl, remember. A sharp left here, then a right, then another, or was that left? Hang on, can't think straight. Breathing heavy, fast.

'Would you like to live down here?' Darius enquires mildly.

It stops Scruff, Bert and me in our tracks. Too stricken, can't answer.

In a gloomy corner is a mess of bones. The skulls a rich amber, the teeth loose. 'The servants,' Darius whispers fondly. 'Still here to look after their masters. Faithful to the last. As am I. Mmm.'

That's it, Scruff's off. But Darius hooks a hand around his arm, fast, and yanks him back tight.

'Oooow!'

'Now now, little boy, we can't have you separated from your family, can we? You might get lost. There are pits to fall into here, oh yes. Coffins to come crashing down.' His voice drops. 'Little squeaky friends in dark places to bite you and haunt you and terrorise your sleep. Mmmm.' I step back – gasp – a cobweb brushes across my face and I scrabble its stickiness off.

'Now, who would like to see a dead body?' Darius turns to Bert. 'A rare treat.'

'Oh yes, please!'

'I thought as much.'

Darius pushes at a heavy iron door engraved with a lady's face and the hair of a hundred writhing snakes. The lady looks shocked. Like she's been snap frozen in this place and can never escape. Inside: a circular room. Musty corners. Low light. Four marble slabs in the centre.

'Scared now, Kicky,' Pin whispers.

'I know,' and he's scooped into my arms. Bert's having none of it. She lies on a slab with her hands folded across her chest. 'How do I look, Mr Davenport?'

'Get off,' I snap.

She pops up, does a handstand against a coffin propped on the wall and falls neatly into it. Too neatly for my liking. I back away. Near the door. Ready to dash. Try to signal the others that we need some escape action here.

'I need to get outside,' Scruff stumbles, 'I've got crosstro-phobia, I think.'

'I'll take him,' I blurt, 'but just one last thing before we go – do you know where our mother is, Mr Davenport?'

His back freezes at a cupboard he's been scrabbling at. 'Your *mother*?'

'Oh, don't worry. We'll be going now. It's Scruff, his condition. Places like this do it to him. And we thought you could help us but actually, you know, I think we made a mistake.'

'We'll do anything to find her and we thought we'd start with you,' Bert jumps in. 'We're trying to track her down.'

Darius spins. Looks at us quizzically, head on one side. Then he smiles that smile of glittery coldness. As if he's got the measure of us now. 'Flora Caddy. Mmmm. A fascinating person. Indeed. You're extremely lucky to have a mother like that. Oh yes.'

My heart beats fast. Flora Caddy. He said her name. He knows our mum's name. And most wondrous of all: *he talked in present tense.* Like she's alive. This is all worth it. She's close. He's a link. I drop Pin and rush forward. 'What do you know?'

'She looks just like you, mmm, of course.' Darius traces a long, cold finger down my cheek.

I gulp. 'Really?'

Scruff jumps in. 'We need to get her. Fast. For Dad. It'll make him better. It'll be his cure. Can you help us?'

'Oh, he's sick is he? How unfortunate.' Then Darius holds up a finger to silence us. Cocks his head as if listening to something far, far away. 'Ah, that's the telephone. Who would have thought.'

We've heard nothing. But before we can say anything more he slips through the iron door and slams it shut. Is gone. Just like that. We rush to it. It's bolted on the other side. 'I won't be long,' comes a muffled sing-song voice. He sounds almost happy all of a sudden, lighter.

Noooooooooooooooooooo.

We bang against the thick iron. It's no use. Rattle the lever. Can't get out. Stuck. Deep under the earth, and no one knows except one Darius Davenport, the creepiest man on the planet. I slide to the ground. Press my ear into the chilly iron.

No sound from outside now. No sound in here except our ragged, panicky breathing and Bucket whimpering in a corner.

Then a squeak. From a pipe above us. I gasp. A rat. Great. I have a rat phobia. Cobras? Pah. Water dragons? Please. But rats. They're the only things that get to me. Can't bear them. Another squeak. I press my hands over my ears. Please no.

'Do you think Mr Davenport likes us, Kick?' Pin asks.

'I'm not so sure,' Scruff answers, wobbly.

'Of course he does,' I snap. Not believing it one bit but need to keep us buoyant here, can't let panic leak out.

'So what do we do now?' Pin curls in my lap.

'Yes, Miss Bossy Boots,' Bert enquires, 'what exactly do we do now?' She raises an eyebrow just like Charlie Boo does at his most stern.

'We wait, troops, we wait.' I shut my eyes. 'He'll be back.'

'I'm not so sure about that,' Scruff says soft, gazing with terror at the thick, damp walls around us. Breathing in deep the smell of the earth.

10

MYSTERIOUS POTIONS AND COMMOTIONS

We wait. And wait. And wait.

Not much to do in a room with four slabs but get mighty worked up. Bert finds a bundle of bandages in a cupboard and fashions turbans for all of us. Even Bucket, poor thing, who flatly refuses to have anything to do with it or, indeed, this place. She won't move from the sanctuary of her corner and keeps pawing the turban off.

'You know, I think *I* should be taking over Mission Desert Rose,' Bert declares at one point, getting way above herself.

I let it ride. We don't need a fight on top of everything else – Scruff's about to climb the walls here and I'm not far behind him. Our sister, on the other hand, is in her element. She's far too jolly and big for this space, doing back bends and handstands on a marble slab and getting Pin laughing by singing 'Bound for Botany Bay' while marching on top of the slab with hands outstretched like a Frankenstein who of course has had a makeover and is now extremely stylishly dressed.

A sudden clang of the bolt on the door. We're still. Breaths held. What's next?

The door swings open. Darius.

Completely changed.

Flushed, energised, a bit fevery, brimming with scheming and plans. We rush over.

'Now, where were we? Mmm?' Darius rubs his hands. 'Your mother. Yes. The delectable Flora Caddy. Mmm.' Every time he mentions her he practically purrs. 'You'd like to see her, wouldn't you? The idea is consuming you, mmm, I can see it.'

I nod, my heart feeling like it's up somewhere in my mouth. Because just like that our world turns upside down. We *were* right to get here, to climb down a silver rope and abandon a new house. Because Mum *is* alive. This is our first bit of concrete proof.

'Mum is alive . . .' Bert whispers, hoarse, like that phrase is all rusted up inside her. She's tearing up.

It's catching. Because I need a mother fast. It's too hard being chief wrangler to this lot and I'm growing up in odd ways without any of them even knowing; things are happening that I can't stop and there's so much I want to ask. It's the endlessness of the worry about them that's really doing my head in. I could do with some help. And now that Mum feels close I'm ready to cut loose from the lot of them, fast, just shake them all off.

'Tomorrow, mmm.' Mr Davenport nods to us, chuffed. 'It's all been arranged.'

Jumping and cheering. But here's a lot to be done here. 'Right, troops. Action stations,' I command. 'We need to get home fast. Tell Basti. Organise ourselves.'

'Put back his curtains,' Pin jumps in.

'Bake a welcome-home cake!' Bert adds.

'Is there travelling involved?' I ask Darius.

'Oh yes. A vast distance.'

'Sooooo, if we run back right away, Basti mightn't even know we've been gone?' Scruff exclaims and Pin claps with the sheer perfectness of it all. We might even miss getting into trouble! He hates getting into trouble, from Basti most of all.

'Let's get going!' I smile. Darius raises an eyebrow. 'Come on,' I urge. 'What are you waiting for?'

'Mmm, you're very bossy, aren't you?' he replies. 'Quite terrifying, in a little girl, in fact.'

'I am not a little girl,' I bristle. 'And my father, for that matter, says he wouldn't have me any other way.'

Scruff steps in, saving me from myself, as he always does. 'Ignore her, Mr Davenport. She's always rubbing people up the wrong way. And believe me, I'm used to saying this.' He sighs. 'To just about everyone we meet.'

'I think your father will expire of an instant heart attack if he ever finds out that you escaped from the Reptilarium and wandered the streets of London all by yourselves. Mmm? No, we can't have that. I'll break it to him gently. Via Basti. Leave it with me. I know your uncle better than anyone. And I'll take you on your way first thing in the morning. It's quite a journey. Mmm. We'll need an early start.'

'Where are we going?' Bert asks.

'It's a surprise.' Darius smiles and for the first time there's the tiniest chink of warmth. For the first time we can glean something boyish and handsome in his face, something from before life and weariness crusted over it. Well, well, things might just be looking up here. 'Sleep here tonight, yes. Excellent. Mmm.' He's now rubbing his hands and pacing, deeply thinking. 'I'll phone Basti. Alert him.' He spins. 'Now, who would like to see me in action? A singular experience, mmm.' He looks directly at Bert.

'Yes, yes!' She squeals. 'Mr Davenport, you are the best.' Glances at me in triumph. Life sorted, thank you very much. Owning Mission Desert Rose and everyone who comes in contact with it.

But open coffins? A corpse? Ah, don't think so, nup – and Scruff and Pin are with me on this one. Yet before we can say, 'We'll pass, Mr Davenport, thank you very much,' he wheels in a trolley from outside the door that rattles and clinks with all manner of glass bottles and potions and rolls of white cloth. He rubs his hands. Beckons.

'What are they?' Bert crowds in close.

'Just you wait.' Darius lifts a glass stopper from an enormous blue bottle. Pours its purple liquid into a square of clean cloth. Holds it under our noses. 'This is the beautiful secret of my profession,' he purrs. 'The most exquisite smell imaginable. Myrrh, amber, top notes of wood smoke. Mmmmmm. Magical in the depths of winter. Come . . .' And one by one we breathe deep, the cloth close. It's just as he said, like a campfire in the cold, and we breathe in deeper, deeper, then he slams the stopper back with a crisp clink. Looks sideways.

Oooh, hang on, feeling a bit strange here.

The others, too. They're holding their heads, which I can tell feel so heavy all of a sudden; I can't keep the weight of mine up. Pin reaches out and slides down my legs and slumps to the ground, followed by Bert then . . .

Oooooooh, a rash of sweat, it's mightily hot and I can't get myself upright here . . .

I'm all bendy . . .

Have to sleep, sleep, it's like an enormous rake is pushing through me, pulling me down into the lovely stone ground. Lovely, lovely, yes. Must sink into it. Rest. A vast weakness takes over, so insistent. I'm down. Gone. Beautifully gone, like I'm floating on this friendly stone. The last sight: Bucket, in the corner behind a marble slab, looking at me quizzically with her head cocked. Silent. Like she can't believe what's happened to us . . .

And then a deep, velvety dark is wrapping me up snug and tight. All of us. A jumble of bare feet.

11

SO NEAR YET SO FAR

Wake.

Ow.

After what feels like a sleep of the dead, for hours and hours, days, nights. Groggy, horribly thirsty, trying to shake away awful fustiness in my head. Limbs feel like lead. Hard to move them, can't, hang on, they're tied. I'm STUCK!

What happened? Where are we?

Looking around in panic. In a van. The back of it. Not moving. The others in a line next to me, still asleep, bound tight. Where . . . what? No, not just any van – a hearse. I breathe shallow, fast; this is not good. We're in a transport for coffins and who knows what was in it before us. Or why we're in here.

The windows are blacked out, it's grubby, it must be a working van not a ceremonial one. Can't move. Shout. A gag – too big – is hurting across my mouth. Wriggling furiously. Am tied so hard. Can barely move.

And the oddest thing of all: we've got shoes on now. I stare in wonder at my brand new feet. But someone has found some very odd, old boots, in each of our sizes, and slipped them on while we were out cold. Bert will be appalled – not her style at all. And how did they survive Scruff's stinkiness in the foot department? I shudder to think where the shoes have come from. Who did it? What's ahead?

Crane my head and can just see outside through a long, thick scratch in the window's paintwork. Pale light like it's sick. Right, early morning. The cemetery still – I know those blond brick walls. But a delivery yard so it must be out the back. A private parking place.

No one to see us. No one to help. Of course.

A car. Long and low, panther black. It looks familiar. Could it be? I crane, it hurts. Can just make out three people walking from a garage.

Basti. Charlie Boo. Darius.

Oh, oh, oh! The *AGONY* of it. Wriggling madly here but can't move, shout out, can't even thump the van floor.

Basti and Charlie Boo are agitated. Beside themselves. Our uncle's dressed sloppily, it's so unlike him; jacket buttons are done up wrong and trousers are hanging a bit too loose, like there's no belt, and his shoes are mismatched and, most odd of all – he's wearing no hat. He must have left in a hugely distracted rush. He's holding his hand to his forehead. Worried. Feeling sick. We must still be lost to them. He's panicking, glancing around.

'They must have run away.' I can just make out the talk; we're not parked too far out; this is unbearable. 'We're trying everything we can think of, Dari. Charlie thought they may have made their way to you. Something he mentioned once . . .'

'Basti, old boy,' Dari puts an arm around his shoulder, 'they were here, you know. Charming children, mmm. They told me of their astonishing arrival into your world. I had no idea. You didn't tell me. Mmm?'

'It happened so quickly. They've completely taken over my life. Like a whirlwind. Terrifying, yes, but exhilarating, old chap.'

'Marvellous.'

'Where are they now?' Basti looks around in despair.

Darius shakes his head gravely. 'If only I knew. They asked me about their mother. Came to find her, in fact. Mmm. It felt like they were on a mission. What could I say? I mean, honestly. So they headed off, just like that. Wouldn't take an extra coat. Even some biscuits to see them on their way. Just left. With great exuberance. Mmm.'

Noooooooooo. I can't BEAR this.

'They said they were going to find the archives office and the War Office, Australia House, everything, get right to the bottom of it. For their father's sake. They didn't want you disturbed and wanted to do it all by themselves. Extremely self-sufficient. Honestly, I wouldn't worry, old chap.'

'Oh I do, I do.'

'Why don't you call the police, mmm? Dear boy?'

Basti recoils. Police. A fate worse than death. We all know that. The authorities want to shut his precious Reptilarium down, his whole life. They're still looking for it, no doubt. No, that's the one option not open to him.

'I suspect they'll be fine and won't be returning until they've got to the very bottom of the mystery,'

Darius continues. 'Mmm. They are one determined lot. Said they'd get back to the Reptilarium when their father's better, with their mother, and it'll be a wonderful surprise for him. That it'll cure him completely. A bit terrifying, actually, the focus. Between you and me. The colonial . . . energy. Especially that scowly, prickly one – who did most of the talking. I'd hate to come across it on a battlefield. Mmm. Imagine!'

'Kick,' Basti and Charlie say in unison.

'Yes,' Darius says, 'I wasn't quite sure *what* was under all that bite. Boy? Girl? Beast?' He laughs a yellow-toothed laugh. Uuuuurgh! I punch out in fury but it goes nowhere: I can barely move.

'I'll mobilise the grandkids, Sebastian,' Charlie says. 'Search the length of London. You stay put, in the house, in case they come back. We *will* get to the bottom of this, and before Hector gets home. They're just like their parents. You know that. Adventurers to their bones, explorers, can't contain them . . . and silver curtains! Who'd have thought.' He almost chuckles his admiration.

'They seemed so desperately keen to just head off,' Darius murmurs. 'Gulp the world, forthwith.'

'It's not the first time I've lost them,' Basti sighs. 'It's becoming a habit. Why did I *ever* let them into my life?'

'Because you're a good person,' Charlie smiles.

'Mmm, are you really that fond of them?' Darius asks.

'Oh yes,' Basti murmurs, 'extraordinary, I know.' As if he can't quite believe it himself.

Darius just nods. 'And their father? Mmm? It's been so long since you were communicating.'

'War does strange things to people,' Basti says. 'Great hardship can bring people together most astoundingly. Because you can realise that family is all you've got in the end.'

'Mmmm,' Darius murmurs.

'My brother's heart is weak. He's been sent to Bath to recuperate. It's touch and go. I left it too long, Dari...' Silence. What does it all mean? 'And now, how can I tell him that I've lost his most precious things in the world – his children? It'll do him in. I can't tell him,' Basti murmurs, rubbing his little finger like it's suddenly itchy with a stress rash. 'Nothing feels right. They've been here ... you've met them ... they ran off. Children – such vexatious, bewildering creatures. Yes? No? Just trying to think this through, old chap. To make sense of it all.'

A dog barks from somewhere far away, Basti turns his head to it, my heart leaps. Bucket? Bucket! Yes, possibly.

'Mmm, a pack of wild dogs.' Darius dismisses the sound with a wave of his hand. 'They've been roaming the cemetery for a while now. Their houses must have been bombed. Their owners . . . who knows . . . kaput.'

'Nothing, as a butler, has defeated me yet, Sebastian Caddy. Come on, we've got some children to find!' Charlie Boo announces determinedly. He runs to Basti's car and roars up the engine in readiness for the great London search ahead, no doubt. In entirely the wrong direction. And further and further away from us.

As soon as they're out of sight Darius slams down his garage door and climbs into the van. I maintain my lookout at the paint scratch as best I can as the car lurches forward, as it wobbles and swerves through a grey London morning. I can see best when the car slows or stops at intersections. We pass everyone on their way to work, head down, oblivious. Where are we going? And without our beautiful Bucket girl. Where is she? Does she have food? Is she all right? She hates those catacombs and I shut my eyes and pray that she's out of them. But if she'd escaped, then she would have found Basti and Charlie Boo, so she must be still stuck. I can't bear to think about it. Her whine, her fear, her alone.

Pull myself together. Have to make this right. Have to stay awake, have to maintain maximum alertness. We need to get out of this situation, yes, but we need to find Mum. Darius is the key. So he's got us well and good. 'Tomorrow,' he said, about getting to her, 'tomorrow.' Which is now.

The van makes its way slowly past bomb craters and rubble piles, past entire empty blocks. London feels as scrambled and as cold as I do. Scruff and Pin on either side are nudged with my foot but won't wake. Bert can't be reached and I think we'll just leave her quiet for now, anything for some peace. They all look so serene, with their long eyelashes and ruddy cheeks, as if they really needed this vast expanse of rest. It's so weird, but as they lie unnaturally silent around me I'm craving their loud giggly jumbly warmth like I never have in my life.

What have I done? *Why* didn't I go on Mission Desert Rose by myself and leave them safe? I stare at the shoes on us, mine a size too big but good enough. How did they get on us?

Someone is being thoughtful here, someone wants to impress. Even if they have a very strange way of showing it.

But *who?*

12

THE ICICLE ILLUMINARIUM

One by one, three little tiger cubs wake.

Headachy. Gritchy. Roaringly thirsty and fighting like cats in sacks to be free. But not getting far with that. One by one I have to explain through my very tight gag, in a strangulated whisper, that no, I don't know where we are. Or how long we've been here. Or who put the weird shoes on (Bert's squirmy horror at the sight of them is a thing to behold). And that everything will be all right, when I don't believe it one bit.

How to explain that their Kicky's let them down – mightily – here? I don't tell them what's even worse – that no one knows where we are. And anyone who *can* help has been sent on a wild goose chase. We're alone and stuck.

'I've let you down,' I finally whisper, in defeat, through my gag. At last it's been said. 'I'm so sorry.'

'You never do that!' Scruff retorts. Hmmm. His gag has been tied looser than mine; I think everyone's has. Interesting. Deliberate? One hundred per cent. 'You'll find a way out of this, Kick,' he adds.

I smile at my brother's crazy blind faith. Deluded. And I don't share it. Stare out when I can at endless roads because they can't, because I'm the one closest to the paint's scratch. We drive for hours. All through the day. There's purpose to all this. To what he's doing to us. But what?

I whisper a running commentary as the land empties and flattens out. London's chimneys and identical houses that give way to fields, hills, cows now, sheep, fences made of stone. Dinky churches. Bridges. Forests. Dark green, dense, so different to home. Villages tumbling upon villages, too soon, and in Australia of course we can drive for eight hours straight and never see another building let alone a cow. A roo. A soul. Now I see military things abandoned in fields, a lot. The van bullets along roads of narrow, high-hedged green then gradually it all gets emptier, wilder, stonier. Colder. Brrrrr. We must be heading north. The land rises. 'We're going up, troops, brace yourselves!' Great hillsides plunge down to the road. Mountains rush at us with streaks of high snow like frozen tears. Wherever we're going feels spectacularly lonely. Removed.

'I'm hungry,' says Scruff.

I shake my head, shrug. It's the least of our worries.

'Freezing,' Bert adds.

Shake my head. Again, nothing I can do.

'Duddle?' Pin asks.

That I can do. Waggle a foot onto his leg and he giggles and it's the loveliest sound, the giggle we're all addicted to.

'Again, Kicky!'

I most humbly oblige. Scruff joins in, then Bert sings 'Botany Bay', all muffly, till we're getting him laughing and squealing through his gag, which loosens miraculously and he whoops his delight at the sudden freedom. 'Woohooo!'

Darius slams the brakes on the car. Gets out. Bursts open the back door. '*What* is going on back here? Mmm?'

'Fun!' Pin laughs.

'You got a problem with that?' Scruff says defensively, all muffly in his gag. 'And where are you taking us?'

He raises an eyebrow. *Gotcha,* says his stare. 'Mmm, you'll find out soon enough,' he says through a cold smile, then tightens Pin's gag around his mouth again. 'Patience is a virtue,' he adds as he slams the door shut. Then 'Children should be seen but not heard' comes from outside. For good measure. We giggle despite ourselves.

Drive on and on. No villages or towns anymore. A deep frost shrouding everything; trees, fences, an occasional farm building. Everything feels brittle and still and waiting – for what? Suddenly the car slows. I crane. We're outside an enormously grand, sandstone gatehouse. A sign that's seen better days is attached to rusty iron gates.

TRESPASSING/POACHING/
RAMBLING FORBIDDEN.
BY ORDER OF THE LOCAL
CONSTABULARY.

Golly. And yep, we're heading in. We drive cautiously up a hill of trees arching over us, laden with snow and frost. Everything feels like it's pressing too close, swallowing us up. The light drops. Then suddenly the road flattens into the relief of a wide brightness and a white, waiting sky.

The van stops.

We ask Darius where we are as soon as he opens the door. 'So glad you asked. You've travelled a very long distance today. Into another world. Mmm. Let's just say,' he smiles, 'that you have gone from the Kensington Reptilarium to something even more . . . splendid . . .'

Four faces stare at him with great expectancy.

'It's the Icicle Illuminarium. Well, that's my little name for it. Mine and . . . a friend's.' He smiles a secret smile. 'A most extraordinary place. Mmm. And if you stick with it, it might just answer some of your questions, perhaps, in your quest to find your mother. Mmm. So don't go running away on me.'

'Is Mum there?' 'What's a luminar-um?' A rabble of voices are all jumbly through the gags.

'Why did you drug us?' I ask loudly.

'Ah yes. A technicality. To get you here quietly. Under orders, if you like.'

'Whose?' I snap.

He ignores me. 'I had to make sure you wouldn't escape while you had the chance, mmm.' He smiles. 'But you won't dare run from me now, will you? You're too far from anything out here. You'd never find your way back.' We'll see about that. 'And if you do escape, you'll never find the path to your mother, will you?' Yep, he's got us. Well and truly caught. 'Always remember that.'

He unties us all. We climb creakily out of the van, stretching and rubbing each other's backs, getting the circulation back. Then Darius strides off.

So, Mum could be ahead, close. Which stops us from doing anything but follow this mysterious man in his black suit. We climb the crest of a hill and gasp. Ahead of us is a house. No, a castle. And it's enormous. The length of a runway, a city block. Wow. And it's fabulously glamorous. We blink tears in the wind's snap.

Darius announces that it's our new home. For the time being.

Really? This might not be so bad after all. I look back at Scruff; he does a cautious V for Victory. Luxury, tennis courts, servants waiting on us hand and foot – here we come. 'But Basti needs to know where we are,' I say cautiously.

Darius nods vaguely. 'Indeed, mmm.'

We crunch along a gravel driveway but as we get closer another picture entirely emerges. Bert frowns that it looks sick. I murmur in agreement, with a sinking heart.

Because the house's front feels like the open mouth of the newly dead. Vines spill from the window sills like a corpse's frail lace collar. Grass laps at the window gaps and door blanks. Lichen and mould is triumphant on the walls and the bare bones of the roof. Huge blocks of stone lie on the wide front steps as if the chunks have been tossed down by giants who've plundered the grand house long ago. And a lot of it – most of it – is covered in this enormous white frost. It's gorgeously beautiful. Bizarre. Tragic.

I can feel Bert's heart lift at the spectacle of ruined beauty before her that she just about wants to lick; she's jaunted herself right up as she walks straight at it. *Mummy's here now, everything will be all right.* Can see her already planning the new winter collection to match the redecoration of this place, a collection in tasteful shades of frozen blue and white that uses the iciness of satin, the feathers of a snowy owl and the fur of polar bears to maximum effect.

The garden's also crying out for rescue. An enormous oak tree has been split by lightning and heaved from the ground and all that's left is the wave of its roots. Enthusiastic branches poke from the roof of a smashed greenhouse like giraffes from a too-small truck.

Oval windows on their side stare from a central triangle of the roof: eyes permanently awake but drained of life. There's an avalanche of beams and bricks on one side of the building where an added-on wing has given up.

Why are we here?

13

THE MOST SINGULAR HOUSE ON EARTH

'No one could possibly live in this place,' I say to Darius. 'Why are we here?'

'Mmm, delighted you asked.' As if he's a tour guide. 'You see, as Basti Caddy's newly found family, your future is intimately tied to this place.' The way he says 'intimately' makes me shiver. 'Patience. It's a surprise.'

There's only one surprise we want here, mate. I ask when we can see our mum. He ignores me. Hate being ignored. Want to kick him; resist. Want to turn around and run off; resist. Stomp closer to the blank shock of the house's stare, following them all, the promise of a mum luring me on. Leaves and hessian bags are banked up by the building's entrance like a litter of puppies at their mother's warmth. I think of Bucket. Wonder where she is. Want her with us.

'Darius, where's our –' Stop. Think better of it. He doesn't need to know. We need to keep her safe, don't want him hunting her down in the catacombs or wherever she is. Did he drug her too? Shoo her away? If he's completely forgotten about her I don't want him now tracking her down back at the cemetery, and doing goodness knows what. I don't trust him one bit, but we need to go along with him for now if it's going to lead us to Mum.

Darius pushes open the front door, which is already ajar, as if in readiness. No knock. We step into a long entrance hall of dirty black and white checks. A whirly shell of an oval staircase climbs to a blank sky. We crunch over glass from a dome high above us that has few of its panes left. The walls hold in the rain and the damp; we can smell it clamouring to get out.

There's a clattering from a far wing. Scruff turns abrupt. Who? What? 'A bird,' I mouth. Can't have him spooked. Need our wits here.

His face is unsure, about everything. He's wondering how long we'll survive in this place. It's a building to catch pneumonia in, or worse, death.

Mum is in here? Really? Yet she might be. Onward. Must.

Darius leads us through rooms of extravagant tallness. Corridors and halls. We push through a revolving mirrored door into a ballroom as empty and lost as a shut stadium. Floor-to-ceiling windows gaze out to a lawn of limbless statues. They're covered in curtains of ivy that snuff out the light.

Bert spins. 'What I could do with this!' she exclaims, pointing. 'Candles. Polished chandeliers. Our silver curtains. Imagine, Kicky! The party we could have in it.' Because we're good at that, instant parties, but not here, now. It's too hard, too tragic.

Hundreds of sacks of potatoes bobble the floor of one room. Mouldy grain is heaped – dune high – in another. Empty petrol drums are carefully stacked in a third. So. I see. This enormous house is nothing more than a succession of silos now. Storage rooms. It feels like a dirty secret. Like we've just seen someone very grand, undressed. And stinky and crazy with it.

A parlour of birds. They rise up with great startled flappings in a room open to the sky. Their droppings are thick on a parqueted floor and our feet slip through the muck like wet paint. On and on we go. To who? What? Darius is walking with brisk purpose, on a mission. There are strange clankings and wind sighs from far corners. Scruff is bunching close. I run my finger down his arm: I'm here, mate, I'm with you.

Signs in foreign languages, rows of iron bedsteads, broken metal tables, upturned helmets. Mysterious, rust-coloured stains that look like old blood seeping from under high doors, Was this a hospital once? Grime bruises clot walls. Ceilings gently bulge like swollen bellies. Tapestries fall into nothingness at their ragged ends. Frescoes have 'COLLECTION POINT' or 'MESS' painted roughly in red across them. In one wood-panelled games room there's a billiard table with its legs sawn off, now just a turf of rectangular green. In another, mahogany table legs in a grate. What's left of firewood. A welcome gift from someone who didn't own this, or didn't care for any of it.

The Cottesloe Library announces a plaque. 'A library!' Bert exclaims. Darius sighs in impatience, as if he really can't be bothered with our wonder, there's something else that needs to be done here.

'Kicky, your favourite thing!' Pin says, pushing open the doors before Darius can stop him. I shut my eyes. Oh, there is hope.

But no, chaos. Sinking hearts as we think back to Basti's beautifully cherished library – where we could be now – brimming with its books to the ceiling and leather armchairs. But this. The few volumes that are left have been thrown across the floor and they're only in foreign languages, mainly Latin or Greek, and the only order is in the shelves of one bay where twenty gas masks are obediently lined up with tin hats propped on each. Too ordered, neat. As if waiting for one last battle. Ours?

A dusty gramophone sits forlorn in a corner with a smear of records around it. Music, sound – they're the enemy of any library I know. We tread across a strange white flaking on the slippery floor and bend to pick pieces of it up – what on earth is it? Low flying planes, Darius tuts, and tells us that every time the R.A.F. passed over during the war the ceiling would flake like snow. Eventually the pilots were redirected but it was too late, there was hardly any paintwork left. Bert asks if this building was a hospital once.

'Mmm, indeed. For wounded soldiers. From the allied countries. But eventually even they were defeated by the vast challenges of a stately home. The damp, the rot, the decay. Ghosts, mmm.' He smiles wryly. Scruff presses closer.

Pin tugs his coat, asks who lives here. 'You?'

'Goodness, no. Just you wait. It'll be worth it.'

We finally reach the far corner of the house. Right at the back. White and gold double doors.

Behind them, a high-pitched wailing.

We gasp. Someone's here! Could it be . . . Mum? Has she taken up singing?

Darius turns and smiles. Flings the doors wide with a flourish. 'Your Ladyship. They have arrived.'

Our eyes take a moment to adjust to the dark after the frosty white of the rest of the house. We step forward. What is this place? The wailing is opera music that plumes through this secret wing, which is crammed with a series of rooms off a long corridor. Rooms that seem to be clutching fiercely to whatever is of value in this place – it looks like all the lost treasures have been rammed into them. In secretive haste. It's a great jumble of portraits and statues, gilt-edged chairs, harpsichords, stuffed deer heads and stacks of rolled-up rugs. All waiting for release. Which feels like it will never come.

A woman. Ahead.

Her back to us, at a window. A gloved hand resting on a cocked hip. The other hand languishing high on the frame. We can't make her out except that her hair is snowy white in a cloud about her head. She's silhouetted, dark. Framed by the glary

white of outside. We squint. She looks slim, glamorous, from the curve of her back. It just looks posh.
Like Mum.

Breaths held, all of us. Transfixed.

'They're here,' Darius says, louder.

The lady doesn't turn. As if she can't. Isn't able to
bear it.

Pin can't help it. He runs straight at her, his little
arms outstretched . . .

14

A NEW MUMMY

Pin stops, in shock. As the woman turns.

Why on earth did we think it was our mum? Because we're desperate, of course. Hallucinating. Exhausted and hungry and starting to see her in everything. I rub my eyes. They're cranky and scratchy and tired, not working properly anymore. Nothing is.

Because the woman before us is wrong. Cracked into oldness. Scariness. She's wearing a ballgown of emerald green and matching tulle that's in a wispy cloud around her shoulders. But it's cold in here. And daytime. And there's no ball. Excuse me, madam, but you're dressed like a movie star and you're far too old for it. You've seen better days, as has everything in this place. You're like a mangy old bit of mink that we don't want to wear.

I back out fast, pulling several Caddy hands with me. Now's the time to escape.

But Darius is right behind us once again, ready to stop any running for it. As if he senses it.

The woman cranes, steps forward, stares at me hesitant. A tiara's tilted on her head and there are some bits of it missing and she flurries it straight like we've caught her out. A black velvet necklace hangs around her neck; a key on the end of it that she keeps fingering. She wobbles closer on spindly silver heels. Why do ladies do that to themselves? They need sensible boots to navigate this world, don't they get that?

Bert's wasting no time re-dressing her in her head, I can tell; holding up her hands like Dinda does and framing an imaginary shot. But Pin is stepping back, unsure, and he's never unsure about anyone. It's a sign. Not a good one.

Because everything to do with this new person is blaring, 'Beware, Back Out!' Her hair is piled high in a crazy bird's nest. The bright red lips crooked and too big. The face frozen in a mask of jolliness – party time! – except it's not.

She surveys us in wonder, but no, doesn't dare. She's like a bird, fluttery, nervy, trapped in a room with us. Then her face slips and something much realler and older and tireder comes out.

'So . . .' The word hovers in the air. 'Here you are.'

She does not come forward. There's no eagerness. In fact, there's a staleness in her face, deep, worn, droopy lines, about a lifetime of disappointments and chances never coming off. Note to self: *Never, ever, become this. Never be so defeated by life.* Chipped red nailpolish hovers at her cheeks. Then she snaps to attention, as if remembering what she's actually meant to be doing here. 'Come come, my sweeties,' she purrs suddenly, motherly soft. 'Closer. Let me see what we've got. I've always wanted more little mousies. And my, you're quite the menagerie, aren't you.'

What's the real her? She's turned from bird to cat.

Darius pokes us forward. The wooden blocks of the loose parquetry lift with the suck of our soles then settle back, resigned, with a plop. Everything, it feels, is falling apart here – this entire world has given up. Her especially, but in a loose cannon kind of way. The room's ringed with dim paintings climbing to the ceiling. Only the whites of the eyes glare out. So many eyes, watching, waiting, as if wondering what on earth's next. In fact it feels like this entire place is holding its breath. For what?

The lady hovers a touch, not quite. 'My, how . . . *robust* you are. You boys look like you could crack me with a squeeze!' A too-high laugh. 'Three big bonny lads . . . who would have thought.'

'I'm a girl,' I say blunt.

She shakes her head in bewilderment. Her fingers trace our noses, shoulders, but an inch from our skin as if she can't bear to actually connect. 'Little mousies,' she murmurs, 'lost. Lost.'

Pin – who's been known to cuddle a lamp post if he can – shrinks into my skin as if he wants to be enfolded in it and disappear. Nup. The Pin-detector is on high alert here and it's telling us to get out, fast – anywhere but this place. But Mum . . . we have to find out. Imagine getting this far and then abandoning her. Nope, just can't. With my arm strong around Pin I ask the woman what her name is.

'Ugh ugh ugh!' she remonstrates. 'Little mice should be seen but not heard.' Would grown-ups in this country *stop* saying that. 'You have much to learn in life.' Then she smiles coquettishly. 'But you know, I'll allow it. Just this once.' She draws her tulle protectively around her shoulders. 'My name is Adora Ellicott. Lady Adora. And you're most fortunate to have been invited. Few people are.'

'Few would want to,' I snap, most Kick-like. 'Where are we? What's going on?' I continue the pounding. Lady Adora shrinks back, startled – and what kind of name is that? I sigh in a right grump.

'This is my family seat,' she says sulkily.

'Your what?' Scruff looks dubiously at her bottom.

'Oh, you colonials! So uncouth.' Then she leans her cheek into wallpaper that's falling away like great strips of sunburn. A single fingertip tenderly traces the faded pattern of a flower. 'Where are we, young . . . lady? Why, The Swallows, that's where. One of England's great stately homes. It's been held by the Ellicott family for four hundred and fourteen years. Swallows – such a beautiful name. So appropriate.

'This land was given to the original duke by Henry VIII to guarantee his loyalty to the Tudor succession . . .' Lady Adora's eyes are closing like a cat's as she rests her cheek on the wallpaper. 'Mmm, the king, yes. Do you know, in the Duke's journeys to London, outriders would go ahead to clear peasants from his path so he wouldn't be defiled by their sticky gaze –' She peers at us. 'Yes. Sticky. Exactly.' Strokes the wall like it's a person. 'You really need a roof over your head, don't you? A mummy, someone to clean you up. Wash out your mouths with soap. How odd you sound. That funny accent. My poor, bereft little mousies . . . new to all this. Fresh blood . . .'

But before we can jump in with a thousand indignations she gallops on. Asks if we like our shoes – that she told 'Dari' to find some for us, couldn't bear the thought of our dear little desert feet so ill-prepared. 'He has quite a selection, you know. From, er . . . clients.' She laughs a secret laugh, then purrs directly to Scruff, 'We weren't expecting you at all, young man. Quite the shock. Here, in England. And so . . . robustly. Spoiling our plans. And there's Dari, panicking, as he does. Didn't know what to do. "Bring 'em here!" I laughed. And so he did.' Her face crumples into a frown. Darius is pale, as if he's suddenly realised he's made a terrible mistake.

'And here you are. Glowingly healthy. Tall. Tanned, in that crude Aussie way.' She laughs a laugh with no joy in it, asks us if we think we'll live to a hundred. 'Good strong bones, mousies. No wartime rations for you. Yah.'

'Where's our mother?' I cut in. If there's no purpose in being here I'm pulling my troops out.

A glittery silence. Adora comes up close, worrying the key around her neck. 'No one likes other people's children,' she whispers. 'It's a hard lesson to learn but don't worry, I'm an exception to the rule. I'll be prepared to like you. Just.'

'Darius says our lives are now tied up with this house,' Bert tries a new tack, rubbing her arms with the cold. 'So, are there any old clothes in here? Curtains, sewing boxes?'

'Oh, is that what he said? Ever the trickster.' She cups Darius's chin. He says nothing, shakes his head, goes to explain but she talks over him. 'Well, he's right of course. In a sense. I have plans . . . *we* have plans.'

Bert blurts that she can help because she's a fashion designer and loves interior decorating too; blurts that she could do both.

Lady Adora snaps that she and she alone will decide what happens around here. 'For a start, those frightfully vulgar accents bother me. They make you all sound a bit stupid. They . . . grate. Have you even been educated? Can you write?' I want to hit her, my fist is clenched. 'Something must be done.'

Darius murmurs his mmm, almost bending towards her as he speaks, like a vine angling for the light. Lady Adora sulks all of a sudden; she's tired and has had enough. Rings a bell. 'We're going to tuck you little mousies up snug and tight – before we decide how to proceed. We're digesting the vast shock.'

'Proceed?' I ask, tight. 'What's The Swallows got to do with us?'

'Why, everything, my dear. Daddy was so naughty, frittering away all the money; one too many leopards in the kitchen, I suspect,' she trills. Then she comes up close, her voice cold, quite someone else. 'I will not be the one to lose this. Four hundred and fourteen years and counting. It will not be ending with me.' Then she puts a hand over her mouth like some mortifying thought has bubbled up and she has to swallow it, quick. Gathers herself.

'Where's our mother?' I demand again.

She bats me away. 'I'm tired, I said. Your questions, tans, energy. Off you go. Squeedly? Squeedly!' She's calling out to goodness knows who but I'm not letting this pass; the dragon is well and truly uncurling here, roaring up.

'Is our mother here?' I demand. 'Otherwise we're off.' She just rolls her eyes like I'm mad. That's it. No point being here. 'Let's go, troops,' I bark and as one we turn and run out the room, up the corridor, out the double doors that Darius had flung open with such a flourish.

'Flora Caddy?' The scream behind us. We stop, stunned. She's said our mother's name. 'The *Honourable* Flora Caddy?' She's making it sound like an insult. We turn. Come back, in defeat, she's got us. 'We were in the same class at school.' She knows her. 'She used to win all the prizes, of course. Hockey captain, Head Girl, all of that. Came out, what, 1928? Belle of the debutante ball, with her rosebud lips that every man was so desperate to kiss. Oh, they all loved her, didn't they? Flocked, flocked. All . . . hovery. Sticky. And that vulgar hoot of a laugh. Who could forget it. Blood not quite blue enough, you knew that, didn't you? I bet you've got the Flora bray, too. Always at the centre of her little web of . . . giggly . . . what? Giggles. Well, she never invited me to her little soirees in Eaton Square.' Lady Adora's face screws up in revulsion. 'Dari, they're asking me about Flora Caddy. Can you believe it?'

He nods, murmuring his murmur, bending a little more.

'Then she just disappeared on us. Off to Or-stray-ya or wherever it was. Married her cowboy, rode her kangaroos, had a thousand children.' She looks us up and down. 'As she would. And couldn't she yell, oh my. Voice like a foghorn. But when dis-tressed –' Lady Adora laughs '– then she'd whisper her little whine . . . "Addy, Addy, stop, you're being beastly."'

'*Stop stop stop!*' I slam my eyes shut, hands pressing on my ears. Because Lady Adora is doing exactly Mum's voice here. That used to drive me bananas. It's like this woman has snapped something in my brain; the memory of how frustrated I'd get with my mother, how terribly I'd attack her; the dragon inside me would just roar out at her, so horribly, when I just wanted to hurt her, stop her, get her quiet. Lady Adora has made me remember exactly how Mum sounded on that last night I saw her – 'Kicky, Kicky, stop . . .' – as she tried to get me to clam up with the shouting and the swearing about life being so unfair because I always had to look after everyone and fetch the baby and feed the chooks and she was always going on about the horror of my overalls and how I had to pretty myself up, be a proper girl, a young lady, like I was never good enough and she was always so critical and then, and then, I just snapped, I don't know what happened but I roared back that Mum didn't love me like the others, she was always so mean to me, singling me out, making it harder than the rest and I hated her for it, I said I hated her, *I actually said it*. 'Go away, I want any mother but you. I want someone else.'

The last words.

Hovering in the shocked quiet.

Then she was gone. So she did go away, oh yes, exactly as I'd asked. And I have to live with it. Which is why I'm determined to find her now.

Where *is* she? I plead now, broken, cracked. Because I need to make it up to Mum, say I didn't mean it, tell her how I love her so much it hurts. The guilt is like a great weight pressing down on my chest. Did *I* make her walk out?

'Aha!' Lady Adora pokes like a magpie into my distress. 'So *you* care about something as much as I do. Oh, I can see it. We'll make a fine pair, you and me. You know why?' Her voice drops to a whisper. 'Because we *care too much*. Oh yes, I recognise it in you. Because I was that once.' I shrink back. Want out, away. She leans closer, so close I can see the cracks in the makeup, the swervy lips, the eyes rimmed with too-wobbly black. *Never be this.*

'Your precious mother is where you'll be going very soon, my little mousie tomboy. Patience, patience . . .'

Heart thudding. She mentioned Mum. She knows where she is. We have to stick with this. I look around wildly. So. Can't run away. Can't go to the police. Because it'll all unravel too soon and Basti's Reptilarium will be found and he'll be kicked out and be sent to a home for damaged war veterans and his entire world will be lost. Again, my fault.

Her Ladyship calls out for Squeedly once more, clanging the bell with furious violence now. A woman in a housekeeper's uniform appears, running, pulling up abrupt. As pale and dusty and beige as her boss is vivid and loose; and puffed. She looks like she's sucked on a lemon for days, months, years. Nope, *she* won't be of use to us. It's in her face.

'Take them, Squeedly. Off, off, away. It's been sorted, no doubt.' She turns her back on us and walks to the window where we first found her, hands high in the air in a fluttery dismissal. Then she spins back to me and lifts up my chin with a finger and tells me we'll be going on a grand adventure and we're going to have so much fun with it, just be patient. She winks right at me. I back away. What does she mean? Pin grabs my hand like he's protecting me. I put my arms around all of my family. No one is splitting us up here. What's going on?

'Is there any food?' Scruff sees his chance. 'What's for tea?'

'He's asking for tea! My dear mousie boy, why not use your legendary bush skills to survive? All those things your perfect mother with her perfect talents taught you. Oh, you'll get something to eat in good time. But off now, off, off, to your room.'

I glance back as we leave.

Lady Adora is twittering and muttering, stroking the wall and murmuring, 'Soon, my precious, soon.' Quite mad with it.

And I'm not sure if she's talking to Darius – or the house.

15

MOST PECULIAR
SLEEPING
ARRANGEMENTS

**Mrs Squeedly's back is stern ahead of us.
Extremely stern. Nope, she definitely won't be of
any help. It's in her walk.**

We climb stairs bowed like saddles from centuries of use. Behind us walks a man who seems
to have appeared from nowhere. He's magnificently silent. Monstrously tall. A granite mountain
of unknowability. Or should I say obstruction –
because there's no way we could duck behind
that bulk and get out. In fact, his express purpose
looks like it's to stop us from going anywhere in
this place. Pin keeps turning and staring up at him
in wonder. There's a twinkle in his eyes. This is
not good. It means: this obstruction is a challenge

and Pin will surmount it, oh yes, there'll be Caddy cuddles yet.

How long will we be here? And what's at the top of these endless stairs?

An enormously long room, that's what. As wide as a church. Scruff winks, mouths, 'Playground,' chuffed; and throws in a sneaky V for Victory sign. Because this room has got a waiting wooden floor as large as a paddock, a gallery of spectator benches high on both sides and a peaked, glass roof running its lofty length. There are oval windows like eyes at one end and a woefully sagging net across the middle. A tennis court? But hang on, it's not the usual size. It's longer and narrower. We turn to the silent mountain man. What is this? He doesn't respond. Stares straight ahead. Right. We look at Mrs Squeedly, our next best bet.

She sighs like surely we know. Er, no. Tells us it's called a *real* tennis court, built for Henry VIII. That he was extremely fond of the game. That it demands a high roof and light, which is why it's here, close to the sky, 'Off you go.' We promptly run into the middle of the enormous space, can't help ourselves, and jump over the net, back and forth, back and forth, Pin on the back of me like a jockey with his racehorse. 'Yippeeeee!' 'We need racquets!' 'Balls!'

The room quickly echoes with our shrieks bouncing off the high walls and ringing up to the sky. Yep, the Caddys can certainly make a go of this.

Mrs Squeedly yells across the room that there's a changing shed in the far corner and we might find something useful in it but she has no idea, she hasn't looked in it for donkeys.

'Donkey, Kicky! Be a donkey,' Pin cries. Which I most certainly do.

Abandoned hospital beds are crammed up one end of the room and piled high with a jumble of pillows and blankets. 'For us?' Mrs Squeedly nods, all the while staying close to the door with Silent Mountain Man just behind her. She then glances around, as if trying to find something. We do too – can't see anything. Scruff asks her what she's looking for. 'The resident . . . ghost.' Mrs Squeedly hesitates.

Scruff turns pale. 'Y-you're joking. Aren't you?'

'Of course I am. Ghosts do not exist, young man. Do not, full stop. But Lady Adora is convinced of its presence. Is driven quite mad from it, actually.' She smiles the oddest smile, can't quite squash it down. 'Her Ladyship thinks there's a little child in this house who mocks her night and day. She can't be freed from the torment.' She looks around at the roof beams, as if talking to someone else. What's going on here? 'Maybe you can all help. Distract her. She needs distraction.'

'Please, take Bert, she's terribly distracting,' I plead. 'She'll make any ghost disappear quick-smart.'

I am kicked.

Mrs Squeedly rolls her eyes. Tells us the estate has a chequered past and she should know: she was born on it and so was her husband. That in the seventeenth century a reckless son of the fourth duke almost gambled the property away; and in the eighteenth, a female skeleton was found locked in a cupboard. Bert has a squealy shiver. 'I said, ghosts do not exist.' Mrs Squeedly glares. 'But family traumas most certainly do. One duke tried to burn the house down so a hated son wouldn't inherit. There are priceless portraits downstairs colandered by darts.' And dripping with pigeon droppings, I want to add but don't. 'Lances, swords, armour – all used within the family, no doubt.'

'Wow,' Scruff says. 'Armour . . .'

'It's what's known as a calendar house. Three hundred and sixty-five rooms. One for each day of the year. Most beyond repair.'

'It'd take an awful lot of money.' I spin around.

'Quite, young lady.' She smiles at me, sadly, as if bingo, I know something here that I shouldn't.

Well, I don't, thank you very much. Please enlighten me.

'When's dinner?' Scruff asks, only ever focused on one thing.

'You eat when you eat, young man.'

Bert wants to know why everything's so rundown. She's told crisply that Lady Adora's father, the fifteenth duke, passed away a decade ago. A hunting accident, apparently. And just beforehand he'd lost all the family money through gambling, dubious investments, lions and leopards wandering the lawns and then, God forbid, the house. Leaping onto the kitchen table, clawing at tapestries, wearing diamond collars no less. We're informed in no uncertain terms that Mrs Squeedly was once head of a household of one hundred staff and now she is – 'we are' – all that's left. She quickly glances at the man behind her. Tells us that one day, perhaps, the house will be returned to its former glory. That there'll be staff again. Their former positions. Scruff's not interested, he just wants to know what all the war stuff is.

Mrs Squeedly sighs. 'The War Office took over in 1940. Gave us a fortnight's notice. Items of value were stored in the northwest wing. The army requisitioned the building for a hospital then abandoned it. Too big a job. Her Ladyship is driven quite mad with worry over it.' Mrs Squeedly goes towards the door, the unknown man still behind her.

'Wait,' I cry, 'who is he?' To Silent Mountain Man. 'Are you locking us in?' I jam my foot in the door. 'Who are you?'

'It's me you'll be dealing with,' Mrs Squeedly snaps. 'He does not partake of idle chitchat. Does not do children. So do not provoke him – for you will not enjoy the consequences.' The warning is dire. We look at him. He is indeed silent. Mountainous. Kind of terrifying. Pin makes a dash for it, as if to test him. In a flash a huge arm shoots out and grabs his squirmy body and my brother is deposited, sternly, right back next to me. The man's face is unmoved through the entire episode.

'Who is he?' Bert whispers in awe.

'He was employed as a cobweb sweeper at The Swallows, aged nine. Eventually became Chief Winder of the Clocks. Dreamed of Head Butler. And now –' Mrs Squeedly pauses '– he upholds all the traditions of the house that I cannot. Except for marrying the housemaid. Strictly disallowed by the lady of the house. Lady Adora's grandmother, that is.' She smiles at the man. 'Quite the scandal in its day.'

'Cor, she must have been a looker.' Scruff sounds just like his cheeky dad.

'That would be me.'

'Oh. But . . . you . . .'

Scruff is trying to stuff his giggles back down. Yep, failing. With a huff the door slams shut and it's only then that we burst into a right proper, up-to-the-ceiling hoot. 'Would you stop insulting the staff?' I chastise Scruff in exactly Lady Adora's voice. 'Nothing but maggots and gruel for you, little mousie!'

We're finally alone in this room. Try opening the door: firmly bolted. The ceiling's too high and there's a horribly tall, slippery roof of slate tiles outside. Nope, we're not getting out of this place anytime soon. We'll have to make the most of it. Look around. The day is leaking its light. Night will soon crowd greedily in. And the ghosts. It doesn't feel like Mum could possibly be in this building – but Adora and Darius know of her. Know of her fate, where she is, it seems; and I need to wheedle that out of them. But how? The four of us gaze from a window to a wild, bleak moor that stretches ahead to water freezing and black. We can hear the great restless boom of it. Its swell is meekened by the snow, its surface just a gentle rise and fall like a giant's slumbering breath.

This is one very big estate, and a very isolated one. Worse luck. Far, far away from help; from shouting or screaming or army flares (sorry, Scruff). No village in sight, no public roads. On the cusp of the sea cliff is a lonely old chapel, a skeleton of stone with its flesh, light. Fat use that is to us now.

The last of the sunlight peeks through the clouds like a rip in a curtain. I push open a windowpane as far as it'll go and wily winter rushes in and curls around us, right under our clothes. I slam the window shut. Rub a violently shivering Pin. Can't let this defeat us. We need to prepare – cosy ourselves right up here – make this tennis court a bedroom not a space. I gaze at the messy jumble of hospital beds behind us. Scruff'll be in with me tonight. And Pin. And quite possibly Bert.

We arrange the beds in a row, crammed close. Pile on the blankets for a cold, cold night because we're used to evenings so sticky and stinky that not even a sheet can be endured under the mozzie net. We lie on our backs, in a row. Oh, it won't last. It's soon dark and Bert scrambles for a switch on a forlorn table lamp abandoned nearby on the floor. It works, thank goodness, weakly, but it's enough. 'For Scruff,' she says quickly. He doesn't respond but we know it's for every single one of us. A vast canopy of stars is high above the glass roof. We can actually see them here – in

London we can't. We must be hugely away from any other light.

The wind picks up. Glass rattles in the panes but they hold firm and protesting on their latches. One window whooshes open – we all jump. Giggle, shiver. The house is alive with sound from too many secret places. No wonder Lady Adora feels haunted. There are wind sighs and creaks, rattles and scurries and Pin huddles close, then Scruff, then even, even, your ghost-hunter ladyship. Well, hello there. Bert mumbles that Scruff needs her close.

'No I don't.' He scrunches his face in revulsion at imminent girl germs but we let it ride; we're all together in one piece here, that's the point.

Silence. Thinking of what's ahead. Of how on earth we got into this.

'It isn't your fault, Kick,' Bert says suddenly. Astoundingly.

'Don't blame yourself,' Scruff adds quick.

I look at them. Roll my lips in tight. Smile a glittery thanks because the guilt is almost sinking me here. Because I do blame myself, oh I do. How could I be so stupid? Too insistent and bossy and cranky for my own good. If I hadn't stormed us all out of the Reptilarium the three of them would be snug as bugs right now, feeding Perdita the cobra and playing sleds in the square.

And I'd be the only one having to deal with this.

I roll over and cuddle Pin's warm little body, breathe it in deep. He thuds against me with his whole weight. I shut my eyes . . . the bliss of it. He's clutching his Banjo teddy like he'll never give him up and I bury my nose in the softness at the back of his neck, the little dip of a curve; 'the double cream,' Mum calls it. Then Dad took it up. Was always trying to snuffle it out, with all of us, to kiss. An arm winds around my back and tickles my stomach. Scruff.

'Come on, little mousie,' he chuckles, 'there'll be cheese in them thar parts.' In exactly Lady Adora's voice. 'Albertina, now that's a name I can approve of.' Bert pretends to vomit and before I know it, the little monkeys have got me laughing.

'But what about that big mountain man?' Pin asks. 'He'll rescue us.'

'Mr Silent Mountain?' I ask.

We crack up. 'Silent Mountain!' *Yes.* 'Silent Mountain!' Forthwith he shall be known as that. Scruff stares at me intently, cocking his head and crossing his eyes and that's it, we're all gone as we attempt our most mountainous, most silent, most cross-eyed silent mountain man impressions, trying to beat everyone else.

Ah, we'll be right. We've got each other here and it's enough. Dad never wanted us split up. No matter what, I'll never be alone. Even with Bert. So at least I have this, that we're together, just how Dad wanted it. I think back to Lady Adora, two floors below us with her tiara and tea-sets, and no matter who's with her in this house she seems so utterly, utterly by herself. Stranded.

And howling inside with it.

16

THE SONG IN THE WIND OF THE NIGHT

The bolt is screeched open. We scramble to the door.

A tray is handed to us by – excuse me for a giggle here – Silent Mountain, and before we can grab him and crack him into life, into talk, he's gone, just like that, as if he can't possibly commune with the likes of us. There's just a quick catching of his eyes, which gives us nothing, and then it's shut off. The door is bolted. Of course. Mustn't forget that one, eh?

We stare at what's before us. Four feeble half glasses of milk in a miserly row. One loaf of hard bread with lots of seeds in it. Scruff's looking doubtful, but hunger will get the better of him, we all know it. A chunk of old cheese. Is that mould? Those green spots? Urgh! Silent Mountain, you're not delivering in this department.

It'll have to do. I slice off the icky bits with Dad's old hunting knife on its chain around my neck. Hand everyone a piece. Four equal portions or we'll never hear the end of it.

The food perks us right up. It's too early for sleep. What to do? Work out an escape plan from this room for a start. I instruct everyone to fan out on a Desert Rose reconnaissance mission: for what we can find, and what we can use in this space. We go over every inch of this tennis court and its spectator benches and change rooms and bathrooms, trying to find a way out. A clue to Mum. Lady Adora. Darius. Anything that can help us.

Within twenty minutes we're all back with warped wooden racquets and grubby white tennis balls, old nurse's and tennis uniforms, cricket jumpers, a box of war medals, one crutch, a pile of tennis magazines and three towels of varying rattiness. Great.

'No sign of Mum?' I ask.

Heads shaking. We look around in despair. Was she actually even in this house?

'But I'm still –'

'– starving. I *know*, Scruff,' I snap. We're all hungry here, mate. Plus the temperature's dropping as night rolls in. I tell them to jump into bed before we all freeze to death, snuggle up. Not for fun, for survival, but I don't tell them that you can actually freeze to death. Bert holds up old bits of curtain and sheets, scraps of old tennis dresses and uniforms and declares that she can do something with them, she'd just need a needle. She's on my wavelength – we need to prepare here, bunker down, get warm.

'I don't think you'll be getting anything in the way of sewing stuff from Lady Love-ora or whatever she is,' I say. 'She doesn't strike me as the practical type.'

Bert giggles. We settle, propped in a line against the hospital-issue pillows. Listen to the wind whistling. Bert flips off the light switch. A scrabbling, in a corner. Scruff whimpers. 'Someone's here,' he whispers. 'Can you feel it, troops? Right in the back of your neck.'

We look around. Another rustle.

Yes, yes, we can feel . . . something. But no one says anything, no one wants to set everyone off. The ghost? A person watching? Someone else stuck in this place? It's like a spider, a daddy long legs, is picking its way slowly up our backs. Shallow, quick breathing. Pummelling hearts. Hands clutched. Is it one of those poor, abandoned people

Mrs Squeedly spoke about? Brrrrrrr. Scruff shivers. It's contagious, it spreads to all of us. 'Hello?' Bert declares, too loud.

Just the wind, sighing in far corners, answers back.

I wish there were books here. To stop the thinking, to crowd the worry out. It's going to be a long night. Scruff declares again that he's starving and it wouldn't be Scruff if he didn't say that.

'Silent Mountain will help,' Pin says confidently, 'some time,' and that's it, we're off, giggling all over again.

Then one by one they fall asleep around me. Fast. I envy their lovely oblivion. So tired, so tired, too much in my head. Because what on earth does Lady Adora mean when she says she has 'plans' for us? Can't shut down my brain, can't turn the worry off. Bucket's out there alone somewhere, maybe still in the catacombs, and Basti's going mad with our vanishing and Charlie Boo's rallying all his grandkids to look for us in entirely the wrong place. I gaze up at the strange heavens, the stars we can't make out. It's so different here. A softer sky, and where's our mighty Southern Cross? Dad was always taking his bush bearings from it – but we have nothing to guide us here.

The waiting house creaks and groans. There's some weird kind of expectancy in it; the aching, sad breath of an abandoned building in the dark. Somewhere a startled bird flaps away. I shiver. The ghosts are active tonight. Pin wakes. Goes to cry just as he used to as a baby, wanting milk. I sssssh him quiet and he crawls instinctively into the cave of my arms, cuddling his Banjo. Finally, finally, my own sleep comes as I squeeze him tight. Like I'm never letting his deliciousness go.

But our mother did. Walked away from us. Just walked off. Why?

'You're the worst mum ever,' I said to her more than once. Wanted to hurt, see her flinch. She used to make me so furious. That she wouldn't let me go bush in the high heat of summer, or drive Matilda, or swim in the water tank, or cut my hair short. It was always no, no, no, endlessly no. And then she was gone.

Muddled dreams of somewhere far away, a strange lullaby; its soothing voice telling us to rest, sssssh, go to sleep. Like a sound inside a shell inside the deepest ocean. 'Mum?' I snap awake. 'Is it you?'

No, the voice is stranger than that, higher. I'm chilled to the bone but too tired to jump up and fetch another blanket. Just can't make my limbs move here, everything's too blinkin' hard in the dead of night. I glance outside to a world snap frozen. Frosted tree branches are like bleached coral against the sky. I slip into a cocoon of five scratchy army blankets and ram close to my hot water bottle of a little man. Somehow, restlessly, fall back into sleep.

Wake again. Bolt upright. Almost jump out of my skin.

Above us, a boy.

A *boy?*

Lying like a panther on his belly along a thick crossbeam. Exactly above us, staring down.

Is he alive? Real? Am I dreaming this?

I flick on the lamp. Yes, a real-live staring boy. But he's so pale. Unearthly. Lit by moonlight, glowing in a ghostly way, like he's never known outside. A thin, quizzical face is tilted sideways as he stares at us in wonder. A pointy chin. Huge eyes with big black circles around them. It's the early hours of the morning yet he's completely awake. There's a shock of sticky-up hair as luminously pale as his skin. He suddenly widens his eyes and pokes out his tongue in a very Scruff-like way. I splutter a laugh; nup, definitely not a ghost. Then he cups his face in his fists and sings a song like an ocean call, like I heard in the depths of last night; it's the voice of a choirboy.

It's the saddest lullaby I've ever heard – and the most beautiful.

'Lost, lost, forever they were lost.
No one ever ca-ame.

Gone, gone, forever they were gone,
And Swallows' glory, back-the-same.

Crying, crying, forever they were crying,
Hungry and alo-one,

Quick, quick, we have to save them now,
Before they turn to Bo-one.
Oh-ooooh!
Before they turn to Bo-one.

Oh-oh!
Before they turn to Bo-one.'

'Who are you?' I whisper.

Pin wakes in my arms. Gazes up. Smiles. Reaches out. 'Friend, Kicky, friend! Hello.'

I hold my brother back. Ghost boy winks and does a V for Victory sign, straight at him, as if he's known us our entire lives – or he's been watching us the whole time, here, in this place.

Pin and I gasp.

17

PIN'S NEW FRIEND

'Bone.'

'Pardon?'

'The name's Bone, chaps. Bone Boy. That's the call sign if you need me. And you are now officially part of Company T, if you choose to accept your mission. T for tennis court, that is.'

What? Wait. The others need to experience this. They're shaken awake. Scruff scrabbles me off then exclaims *'What?'* at seeing the shock of another child above him. Bert's just got a speechless, oh-my-goodness-he's-cute thing going on in her face.

Where did he come from? Is he a prisoner with us?

Bone Boy swings like a chimpanzee from his beam, skinny limbs dangling. Stare to stare. Then this new face cracks open into the most enormous grin of chuff. As if we're some just-discovered, long-lost brothers and sisters and he can't quite believe it. That we're here, with him, in this place.

He wears: calico shirt, tweed waistcoat, khaki military singlet poking out, green silk scarf jolly around his neck, a jumble of dogtags, army shorts far too big and tied with a piece of rope and an airman's cap perky on his head. His long bare feet are curling like a monkey's as if they're made expressly for the purpose of climbing and swinging all over this place. In fact, he's hugely comfortable with this room. As if he owns it, as if he's become a part of this building, is absorbed into its very bones. And over a very long time. I draw back. Not so sure about this all of a sudden.

'Bone Boy. My call sign,' he repeats to the rest of the Caddys now awake. 'If ever we're under attack. Remember that, Company T. But you can also call me Commander Bone, if you like. Of the Icicle Illuminarium. That's what Mr Davenport and Lady Adora call it all giggly among themselves, and I do too now, because it's rather good. Don't you think?' We nod, uncharacteristically speechless at this barrage of talk. 'Jolly good, chaps! We're going to have a spiffing time! Eh? And in the greatest building that ever existed, no less. You'll never want to leave it, oh no. Now, this room is HQ. Repeat, HQ. Headquarters. If only the Squeedlys knew.' He claps his hands in delight. 'T Company, you are about to have the adventure of your lives.' A flash of the most beautiful smile once again, a smile that makes me think he's been very loved because all the sun of the world is in it and it just makes you want to smile right back. Which Bert does, of course, wider than I've ever seen in my life. I roll my eyes at her. Oh please.

Bone Boy laughs and swings wide, back and forth, then jumps off his beam with a double somersault that lands him neatly on his feet, right in front of us.

'You've got to teach me that flip,' Bert whispers in awe at the new trick the gymnastics champion can't actually master yet.

'Roger. But plenty of time, old girl. Yes? What?'

We Caddys are all looking at each other, then back at the boy who's tumbling out his talk as if he hasn't spoken to new people for years here and it's been all bottled up and is bursting out. Oh yes indeed, Pinny, a brand new friend. I hold out a hand strong to shake. It's grasped, nope, let's say pumped.

Ow. Any lingering doubts that he could actually be a ghost are well and truly squashed at this point.

'Proper introductions. Pronto. Eh? Now you are the legendary Kick Caddy, I presume?' Hang on, how does he know my name? 'Jolly good to meet you, K.' He stares straight where the knife is hidden around my neck. 'Well, terrified actually, but delighted. And I come in peace, my friend. All right? No Jerrys here. Ha! Just so you know.' It's like he's never been taught how to put a stop on talk; like he can't wait to jump into everything and there's so little time and we have to begin, right now, in the early hours, in the pitch dark. And he's making me feel like he's been waiting his whole life to meet me. I can't help laughing. Is he all bluff?

He bows low, scraping the floor with an imaginary feathered hat. 'What an honour. Yes? And this is your merry band of troublemakers, I'm guessing. I mean, troubadours? I mean, crack troops, Special Ops. Escape and Evasion Unit, possibly?' He winks. 'Just thought I'd throw that in. Learnt a lot from the troops stationed here. All good fun, eh.'

'Scruff. Man of the family.' My brother steps forward and booms his voice an octave deeper than usual. We girls giggle. 'I do slingshots. Bows and arrows. Whips and ropes.' I think he should be saying grenades and tanks here, perhaps.

'And chocolate, too,' Bert mutters under her breath, which sets me off again as Scruff continues on, oblivious.

'I'm working on the driving but it'll come any time soon. And is there any chocolate here, mate?' We splutter a laugh. 'Ack ack guns? Ration packs? What do you call it again, grub? I need to get the lie of the land. Need some action.'

'Ah, the mighty Scruff. S, from now on. Copy? Who'll be the saviour of the entire allied world along with this ailing house, no doubt. Jolly good to meet you, old chap. I have great faith in you.' Bone's voice drops conspiratorially. 'And yes, there's an abandoned wibble wobble – a tank – in the stables. An army jeep by the greenhouse and Yankee chocolate in Silent Mountain's cookie jar, at the back of the larder. Well, it might be a bit old, it's from the American flyboys who were sent here to be patched up. By golly, the swear words I learnt from them.' Scruff is gobsmacked. 'Oh yes,' Bone nods, 'nothing escapes C.O. Bone in this house. Commanding Officer, that is. Unless you . . .?'

We shake our heads; nope, we'll leave the C.O. to him for now.

'Silent Mountain,' Bert says. 'You call him that too?'

'Captain B, I do now. Remember, nothing escapes me here.' We Caddys look at each other again; who *is* he? He points up and down at my sister's beautifully mad clothes. 'I say, rather dazzling, aren't you? Scary, too. Just like your sister. Quite the old lags, you two, I think – that means fighters, Company T, who are jolly well experienced. Just the type for Special Ops, eh?'

Bert's blushing madly, smiling, 'Really?' Quite someone else. The rest of us are rolling our eyes. She's beyond too much.

'B, you can tell me everything. All your plans, gripes, because I am the secret master of this house as well as C.O., and I am everywhere –' he grins that gorgeous smile again '– and nowhere. It's my big secret in this place.'

'What about Lady Adora?' Pin asks.

'No idea I exist!' He laughs. 'Spiffing, eh? I haunt her nights and days, whisper in her air vents, cry in her cupboards, knock on doors then disappear through walls and window gaps – until she's driven quite mad with it.' Bone rubs his hands, cackling, then leaps back on the beam, dips his toes along it and finishes in a handstand and neat straddle with his chin propped right above Bert's face. That would take a *lot* of practice. 'I have the run of this house, and the Honourable Adora Ellicott has no idea. It's how I know all your secrets. Oh yes, Commander Bone is lord and master of all the obscure corridors here. The gaps between walls. The disused lifts, the cellars. And he also has very big ears. He's been trained in espionage, from the very best. The men who were posted here. Our nation's finest. Somewhat wounded, but still our finest.' He stares at Pin. 'So don't you ever surrender to them, old boy. Don't go handing me in. Not a word about your Commander Bone to the lady of the house, all right?'

Pin is in shock, utterly silent, at the glorious vision of his brand new mate.

'There was a great debate about whether I should actually make myself known to you,' Bone continues. 'The Squeedlys weren't keen at all, but in the end I couldn't resist. What, my very own Company T? Brand new mates? Why of course, thank you very much. I'll risk it. Stop me? They couldn't.' He reaches up to a fork in the crossbeam and plucks a soccer ball from it. 'Now silly me. I forgot the most important introduction of all here. A lapse, Bone Boy, a lapse. *This* is my faithful sidekick, one Captain Dook. And he's very pleased to meet you all. Gets bored of my company. Because I talk too much. Well, there's been no one else. So he gets me all day, every day.'

It's a soccer ball. I stare at it. Don't get it.

'Pass!' Scruff yells. *He* obviously does.

'I'm in goal!' Pin adds. And they're off racing across the room, just like that. Leaving Bert and me to stare in hopelessness. Shrug. Boys. Balls. Instant best friends. It's too simple, isn't it.

'Wait.' I run after them, looking at my watch. 'It's four a.m.'

'So?' Three shrugs from three boys.

'Were you in this room all along, Bone? While we were here?'

'Bang on, K.' The grin again that could charm a brick wall.

'But we looked *everywhere* last night.'

'Not well enough. You obviously need some of my surveillance skills in your life. I observed those Tommys and Diggers and Yankees all the time they were being patched up in here, and learnt a lot. Oh, I could give you a tip or two. Special Ops, how about it? Gunners together? A crack team, us two. Yes?'

I scrunch up my face. I'm a lone wolf, mate.

'I'll do it!' Bert butts in.

But Bone's off, with a ballet of moves with his feet. He flicks Dook behind him, then spins and catches it on his knee and volleys it onto his head and lobs it back to Scruff.

'You've been here a long, long time, haven't you?' I say quiet.

'Oh yes. Lots of opportunities to practise. Over many months. Years. I've lost track, K. And now, finally, I've got someone to show off to.' He cuts in on Scruff's attempt at keeping Dook in the air with his knees and kicks the ball across to me in a beautiful sideways arc. 'It's been a long wait, my friends. For company. The right sort.'

Pin asks why he didn't say hello to us yesterday, to which Bone answers something that sends a chill up my spine: we needed to be checked out, because we might be together for a very long time.

'What?' I snap.

'I needed to know that your presence in such close quarters was acceptable.'

I throw the ball savagely back at him. 'Hang on. Spool back. A long time?'

'Aye aye, captain,' he nods, bouncing Dook on his head now, eyes on the ball.

'Damn.' I clench my fists.

'Dam!' Pin runs around in circles in triumph, urging Bert to write the thrillingly forbidden word in the notebook he keeps in his pocket for moments like this. 'Kick swore! Um aaahh.'

'Oh, I can give you plenty more where they came from, P.' Bone bends down – and proceeds to. Every single swear word we've ever heard plus some spectacular new ones from all the wounded service men; every single forbidden spit of a cuss said with a gleeful cackle followed by careful instructions on how to spell them.

'Stop! Stop!' I command, laughing.

Pin hugs him tight. This is his best new friend *on the planet*. 'I love you, Commander Boney Bone.'

'As you should, old boy, as you must.'

'So what did you deduce last night? On that reconnaissance mission, when you were checking us out.' Bert flirts. 'Will we do?'

'Jolly splendid and spiffing, the entire lot of you!' Bone grins. 'Now –' he rubs his hands '– as the master of the hidden world in this grand and glorious HQ, is there anything you need while you're stuck with me?'

'Books!' I jump in.

'Roger, K. I know exactly where they're stacked.' He bows low. Wow. Just like that.

'Proper food.' Scruff.

'Bang on, S. All the secret stashes are my specialty.'

'A sewing machine.' Bert.

'Stand by, B. Consider it an order. Or would you prefer Albertina?' My sister smiles the most ridiculous smile I've ever seen in my life. 'And will you make me a Scottish kilt while you're at it? I've always fancied one.' Bert blushes again. Oh pathetic.

'A mum!' Pin says soft.

We all stop. A prickly silence. Yes, that more than anything. Of course.

'That, old boy,' Bone says, 'is Lady Adora's department, I'm afraid.' A pause. 'I'm sorry.' Another pause. 'I don't have a mama either, if it's any help. We are all alone in this place.' He looks around. 'Family together, eh?'

'Where's yours gone?' Pin asks.

Bone shrugs. 'Mrs Squeedly is the closest I've got, P. And she'll do just fine. I don't have a dad, either.' Then 'Catch!' he yells too loud and kicks the football over to Scruff, who promptly misses it. 'The army chaps mucked about with their footies endlessly on the front lawn and I learnt a lot from watching them. Found my Dooky boy one day in a far corner, all alone, just waiting for a friend. He's been my soulmate ever since. Hangs about something awful.'

Scruff takes a running kick back to him. 'Now, we just need a pitch.' Bone indicates the window, the vast outside. 'Plenty down there, of course.'

'What are we waiting for!' Scruff shouts. 'You could get us to them.'

''Fraid not, S. Her Ladyship would have a fit if she saw me out and about, anywhere in this house. You see, I'm everywhere but nowhere – and we have to keep it that way. Or . . .' He runs his finger under his throat. We nod. Got it. Worst luck. 'And you lot, of course, are meant to remain in the tennis court. If you're caught anywhere else you'll blow my cover. I'd attract all the enemy fire for letting you out, and we can't have that.'

'How long have you been here?' I ask.

'Can't remember. Too long. Since the year dot. This is my home. And now, yours.'

'Ours?' A thudding heart.

He smiles. 'It's not too bad. Just remember to consider me lord and master of these barracks – not Her Ladyship – and you'll be fine. So. My world. Not hers. Got it? My Illuminarium, not hers. Not that she knows it. You see, I can teach you a lot, Company T, but she can't teach you anything except whimpering into walls and sighing and hopelessness.'

Bert says with great authority that Darius is in love with Lady Adora. Bone snorts his disgust at the word, Scruff too.

'I know these things,' my sister continues. 'But she'll never love him back. You can see it. She's stringing him along. She's far too picky and emotional for her own good. She wants something from him, I'm just not sure what.'

'Ooooh yes,' Bone murmurs. 'So just remember, Commander Bone is the one who'll be finding you chocolate and sewing machines and jolly good fun. Roger? Oh, and books! Most crucially, K, books.' He stares straight at me, straight into me, and good grief I'm blushing here myself. He likes me, I can tell, it's in his eyes.

'Really?' I'm saying wobbly, stepping back, this is going too fast and I can't quite read him, he's too bossy and assuming too much and Bert's staring at me funny but hang on, I need to get this straight, *this,* our new home? For as long as him? So we'll end up with skin as pale as his? Big saucer eyes? Black circles from endless nights of haunting sleeplessness?

No way out?

He nods, as if reading all my thoughts. Smiles his gorgeous smile all over again.

Yep, yep, and yep, says his face.

18

THE EVILEST OF EVIL PLANS INVOLVING THE ONE AND ONLY BASTI

'We have to get out of here, Bone. All together. As soon as we can!'

'Oh no, no,' he steps back, horrified. 'This is my home, K. My field of operation. I'll shrivel and turn into a puff of smoke if I'm taken from it. And besides –' he grins '– I've got friends in it now. It's perfect. Why would I want to leave?'

This is getting stranger by the minute. 'You *want* to stay here?'

'How on earth do you survive?' Bert asks.

'Magic!' He wiggles his fingers and flurries them up her arms. I swear she shivers in, what, girlishness – there's even, good grief, a squeal.

At that moment, clomping. Loud, angry, up the stairs. We freeze. Caught! With Bone, who's not meant to be here or know us. He scuppers up a beam.

'Commander?' Scruff exclaims. 'Where are you going?'

'Situation Scale A. Which means huge,' Bone hisses. 'I don't know who that is on the stairs.'

Bert leaps up beside him without a second's thought. 'Evacuate the frontline!' She whispers, 'Come on!' Bone promptly reaches down, and between him and me we heave Pin up with him quick-smart, then he helps Scruff and me and we all balance wobbly on the beam, in a panicked line, racing to the far side of the room, then we jump over a wooden barrier into the spectator stands.

Peer over.

The door's unbolted. Silent Mountain steps inside. Stands there, in the moonlight, still and quiet, as if waiting for someone, something, to crack in here.

'His eyes are bad. He won't see us from over there,' Bone whispers.

Waiting and waiting, for minutes on end, like he knows we're in here and he's not going to move until someone blows it.

'Who is he?' I whisper to Bone. 'Does he know you?'

'Now there's a tale,' he says soft. 'I was left as a baby to languish in a Barnardos home for the homeless, in London. Then I was – let's say – acquired. Long story; family rift, a father who left the fold and all that, but it's not for now, K. And no, I don't belong to the Squeedlys. They were my . . . rescuers, once . . . but they won't be rescuing me now. With you. So I'm stuck here, aren't I? In this room, hiding, with four kids who can't get out of here. So, Company T, welcome to your very first mission. Any suggestions?'

'We get you out of here secretly,' Scruff says, 'then we Caddys surrender and take the flak.'

'My orders are to hold this field. *With* my men,' Bone grins, 'so no can do.' They salute each other.

'But is he safe?' I look across at the waiting man. 'What will he do to us, Bone? To you?'

'If he finds me here with you right now, hmm, not good. Maybe we should just sit this one out, Company T.'

Silent Mountain stays frozen by the door, silently mountainous, searching the room with his eyes; content to play the waiting game. Pin squirms, it's impossible for him to be still. 'You can be my brand new brother!' he whispers happily to Bone, oblivious to the need to keep quiet. 'Stay here forever, with us. I get so sick of Scruff. All he does is eat and talk slingshots and army tanks.'

Bert and I are astounded – Pin never talks mean like this. Exactly who is this mysterious Bone that has everyone so entranced? He just nods in sympathy at Pin, winking at Scruff. 'I'm not going anywhere, P. That beam above your biscuit – sorry, spiffingly comfy army mattress – is my new bed forthwith!'

'What's your real name?' Pin asks, ignoring my urgent shush.

Bone screws up his face. 'Lachlan, P,' he whispers. 'Lachie. It means from the land of the lakes. But I'd much prefer something that means from the land of the volcanoes or the roaring thunderclouds, wouldn't you, Company T?'

'Oh yes.' Bert jumps in.

'But instead, somehow I got stuck with brittle, old, lonely Bone,' he shrugs.

'But you're the best!' Pin exclaims loudly and throws his arms around his new best friend in sympathy, which – eeeeek! – wobbles them both off balance and they tumble to the ground in a loud, squirmy, crashing heap. Silent Mountain looks across. Gotcha! Strides straight over to our wooden barrier. Stares up at it, expressionless.

At all of us, now poking our heads over the edge.

'Mission aborted, Company T,' Bone says wearily. Despite ourselves, we giggle.

Silent Mountain does not. He's looking at Bone and Bone only, and his expressionless face melts before him into the saddest, most stricken look; the look of a father, our father, when Scruff's thrown the cricket ball into the stew or Pin's drawn finger paintings across the floor with the last of the flour. It's as if Bone has no idea what he's just done by being here, with us. Our friend changes in an instant as he realises the anguish it's caused Mr Squeedly.

'Well then, K, S, B and P,' he says quietly, 'I'd better be off. Toodle pip.'

Our mighty commander jumps down, everything about him different – subdued. Meekly he walks out of the room beside the tall man, without looking back. Silent Mountain puts an arm tenderly, protectively, around the boy's shoulder just before they reach the door and he does not drop it. The door, which is our only way out. Which is once again firmly bolted shut from the outside, leaving us stuck. And alone, all over again.

Right. That's that. Back to square one. Pin starts to cry. 'But he was my friend.'

'There'll be others,' I soothe, not believing it. 'Come on, let's get back to bed.' Which we do, with barely a word, too tired and shocked with all that's gone on in this room. We curl away from each other on our thin army mattresses, lost in thought, thinking of Dad and Mum and Bone and home, falling into sleep, Pin cuddling his teddy, Banjo, tight like it's his last friend left.

'But is there *anyone* else to play with, Kicky?' he asks suddenly into the dark.

'P, old boy, now there's the rub. You see, Lady Adora has a daughter –'

We all gasp. Look up. Bone Boy, of course! Back with us, on his beam holding his ball and completely his old self, grinning his cheeky grin from ear to ear. It's a sight to behold. Bert's squeal again.

'You can't keep me down for long, Company T! You're just too much jolly good fun to stay away from, despite orders from Central Command. Insubordination? I'm the master of it. Just don't let on to Mr Squeedly that I found my way back.'

'Really? No,' Bert giggles. 'But he seems to like you.'

'Oh, he does, B, he does. He's just very protective. Doesn't want me near you lot because you might rub off on me. He's petrified of losing me. Bad influences, Company T.' He wags his finger gleefully at the four of us.

'But what's this about a daughter?' I jump in.

'Ah yes. To be avoided at all costs. Even though she's not here very often because she's always away at boarding school. But urgh, ghastly. Strict instructions: no one's to go near her. The stories I've heard from the Squeedlys, I tell you. They won't let me anywhere close because she'd turn me in, just like that. Avoid, avoid one Hebe Horatina Ellicott, my friends. You've been warned.'

'Hebe *what?*' We laugh.

'Yes, that is actually the horrid girl's name. It sounds like a deadly and contagious disease, I know, but it's a flower. And you won't be laughing when you see her.' He proceeds to tell us stories about her that are legendary: she hits little children on their legs with a riding crop just to see the nasty red welts; she'll take the one teddy you brought from home and declare that it's hers now, then stab it with scissors just so she can watch your face; she'll rip the coat that you've carefully accessorised off your back because she'd like it right now, thank you very much. And she certainly doesn't like pets, which is why the Squeedlys have never been able to have one. Horrified silence; we can't bear to think. '*That* is the daughter of this house, Company T. She'll do me in, crash my entire world down, be the death of me.

So never, ever mention me to her – or her mother. Got it?'

'But why are *we* here?' I ask him in frustration, stalking to the window and peering out, wondering if there's any way along the roof. Do I dare risk that idea again?

And Bone relates the most horrifying news: Basti's Kensington Reptilarium will be securing the future of this house. His vastly valuable estate will one day end up in the lap of Her Ladyship because she's absolutely broke and determined that this great ruin will remain absolutely, Ellicottly, Ellicott. In other words: the Illuminarium will never be sold off on her watch. Lady Adora's going crazy with failure, and she'll go to great lengths to do whatever she can to keep the estate in her family.

'And until about a week ago, Basti had no family he kept in touch with. No one, really . . .'

'Except Darius,' Scruff adds.

'Roger, S. Got it in one. The closest thing to family he had. It was all in his will. But Darius, meanwhile had fallen madly in love with Lady Adora – at the chocolate counter of Fortnum and Mason, no less. Oh, his love may be reciprocated, one day, if Basti's money is ever delivered to her. Then she'll marry Darius, or something like that, she's promised.

That's why he's always trying to win her over – with empty promises of the vast money he'll eventually be inheriting. From your uncle. That will save this place.'

Apparently Lady Adora and Darius were expecting Basti to go quite soon. They thought he was fading. Getting weaker, giving up the ghost, and they had it all worked out. Their windfall was on its way. Because once upon a time Basti's brother was lost to him and the four kids were off, somewhere obscure, he didn't care. But now – voila! – here we are. Four enormously sticky flies in the ointment.

'I get it now,' I whisper in horror. 'Why we're here. Darius's face when he first saw us.'

'Oh, I can just imagine,' Bone nods. 'Because he knew that your arrival would give Basti a new lease of life – something splendid to live for all of a sudden. Which meant that your rejuvenated uncle was suddenly, most inconveniently, in Lady Adora's way,' Bone concludes, his voice dropping low. 'As are you.'

'We need to save Basti.' Scruff rushes up beside me. 'And us. Need slingshots, bows, arrows, those jeeps in the stables. A major assault here, Company T.'

'Can any of you actually drive?' Bone enquires.

'All we need is a brick for the pedals. I've done it before,' I jump in.

Bone looks at me admiringly – 'You Aussie girls are quite something, aren't you?' – then his voice drops, he warns that Lady Adora is quite mad, and she's becoming madder by the minute. Horribly unpredictable, cruel. She's talked in the past about Darius perhaps slipping open a few cages of the Reptilarium one day, while he's visiting, just to nudge things along. And she's getting impatient. Wanting things happening, before Basti starts thinking about his will and the inconvenient new people who should be in it. Kidnapping us was a crazy spur of the moment thing, on Darius's part, but now the two of them have to decide what to do next. 'He'll do anything for love, whatever she says. He's smitten, desperate to please.'

I slam my hand to my mouth, feel sick. We have to alert Basti. Get out of here. Fast. No time to waste. The roof. Out of the oval windows. It has to be done. Without another thought I climb out onto the horribly slippery slate tiles. 'Whooaaa!'

'What are you doing?' Bone barks.

'Getting us out of here.' I wobble . . . slip . . . regain my footing and peer over the edge – shriek and step back, near the window. It's a long way down . . .

but this roof is a way out. Focus here, girl, focus. Basti's in danger. *Imminent* danger. We have to get out of here. Warn him, protect him. Scruff jumps out beside me, just like that, on my wavelength; Bert exclaims in horror; Pin wails, remembering the last terrifying roof experience in his life. 'How did we get tangled up in *this*?' I declare to the freezing night air.

Bone commands me to get inside this instant, this is madness – 'Insubordination in the ranks will not be tolerated here! Running away right now is no way to save it!' Eh? Who says? He goes on to explain that Darius and Lady Adora have it all worked out, that many of Basti's species are endangered and extremely colourful and the Reptilarium is to become the most fabulously exotic fashion house. Basti's never considered the commercial possibilities – but *she* certainly has.

'Perdita!' Berti gasps in horror, thinking of Basti's beloved pet cobra as a handbag.

'Oh yes, B. And now you've come along. They'll be thinking fast, trying to work out what to do – So you, Company T, must think faster. But not from a dangerously slippery, frosty roof. That's five storeys high.'

I look wildly around. Slippery slate tiles, barbed wire left over from the army in big rolls along the gables – a massive drop to instant death. So the Armed Forces didn't want rooftop shenanigans either.

'Nope, it's not going to work,' Bone shrugs at me in triumph. 'Inside, K. Now.'

'Hang on, Lord Bone of Boneland. *You* seem to find your way in – and out – of this place. So you've got to help us out of here.'

'Oh no, we can't have you breaking away from me just yet. Can't have you gone as soon as I've found you. Plus you don't have the skills. Plus you might give me away. Plus I'm the one who knows how the people in this house work.'

I flash my eyes at him – I've met my match here.

'Now don't get all huffy on me, K.' He smiles his widest smile. 'You're my second in command. My 2IC, remember? I need you.'

'Please. Help. Us.' I back closer to the edge of the building, the enormous drop; Pin yelps, blocking his ears, squeezing his eyes shut. 'Bone, I am going alone here if you don't come on board with this. We need your expertise.' I step back another step. Feeling my way. Another. Slip. They all gasp. Right myself, my foot wedged in an old copper gutter. My heart is pumping so hard it feels like it's going to burst out of my chest. But Bone will not win this.

'Stop! You are mad. Think about it, K,' he cries. 'I certainly have. If you escape, it'll take quite some time to make your way to London. Which gives Lady Adora the chance to alert Darius, to put their plan into action super-fast. Darius will make a little visit to Basti, who's always home. Unlock the cages. Let all the deadly snakes slither loose. The reptiles won't escape immediately – Darius will have time to depart. Basti, of course, will not. A tragic accident. So don't give them the excuse to set the ball rolling quite yet. Please. They need to make things happen before he changes his will – but he's too distracted now; they think they've got a bit of time up their sleeves. So hold fire, Miss Scary Roof Girl. Escaping is not the right thing to do right now. You need to fight her from the inside. We have to think here. All of us. Together. Company T.'

'But our dad?' Bert says. 'He would come into it, too . . .'

Bone sighs. 'Yes, yes, another spanner in the works that's appeared out of the blue. Lady Adora is now hoping that your father – who's been jolly well weakened, from what I hear – will die of a broken heart when he learns of your disappearance . . . and possible demise.' He stares at me icily.

Noooooooooo. That's why we're here? Can it get any worse? But he's right: even if we did try to reach Dad or Basti, London is hours by road; Bath even worse. The lonely North Sea is ahead of us and there's a great forest behind us and there's not even an island close, or a boat. Scruff cries that we could tie Hebe up, hold her hostage. I roll my eyes. Climb in through the window, in defeat. Nope, we'll never be escaping from this roof; too much barbed wire and too steep. Bone knows it.

'Okay, stand by, Company T, I have a plan,' I announce as soon as I'm safely back inside. Don't. But no one needs to know that yet. Especially Commander Bone, who really shouldn't be settling into the idea that he's the only leader in this place.

'I knew Kicky would save us!' Pin claps his hands in excitement and relief. 'She's always got a plan, Bone.' Scruff climbs back inside.

'Oh she does, does she?' Bone looks at me in a challenge. Shakes his head like he doesn't believe it, like nothing will save us now. We'll see about that, my smile says right back at him – I'll devise a plan yet, just you wait. He flashes his beautiful smile, raises the V for Victory at me. We'll do this.

'Hey, that's my sign!' Scruff cries. 'Mine and Dad's.'

Nup. It's all of ours now. 'We need to turn in, chaps,' I bark orders, indicating the waiting beds. 'Get a good kip. For tomorrow. Then it's action stations, bright and early.'

Because Bone's not the only army commander here. And I need time to think. Bert, Scruff and Pin make their way to the army mattresses, as do I.

'Well, I think I'll just have to throw one up to you, captain,' our new friend exclaims. 'That means salute.' He raises a crisp hand. 'We'll make a good team yet, Company T. And P, I'm on that beam right above you, don't forget.' With that, Bone jumps up, lies flat on his back on the thick beam, crosses his arms and with a loud snore pretends to sleep.

Pin, of course, is enchanted.

We all are.

But I'm still trembling, from my time on the roof, from the revelations about Darius and Basti's will, from all of it. Tossing and turning, thinking, thinking . . .

19

THE FOOTBALL TRAP

A plan is formulating.

Bone is not going to let us out of here yet. We can't get through the bolted door. The Squeedlys are no help. We have to get to Lady Adora and Darius. Befriend them, talk to them, find out their plans and convince them to let us go – or make a run for it if none of the above works. And we have to find a way to contact Basti as quick as we can. Warn him. Which means getting out of this room. We have to find the Illuminarium's vulnerable point. We have a rough idea of everyone in this house . . .

I wake late. Bone is curled up in an oval window, staring out.

'A plan, K, by any chance?'

'Yep,' I nod firmly.

He grins wide, salutes, jumps down from the window and rushes over. 'No time to waste, then!' We rouse the others.

'Well?' Bert says expectantly, straight up.

'We have to lure Hebe up here, Company T. She'll be on school holidays at the moment, so she must be in the house,' I explain. 'She's the only chink in the armour that I can think of.'

'A pretty terrifying chink, if you ask me.' Bone is shaking his head in disbelief.

'She's worth a try. Dad would want us to. Just to see . . .' Because Dad always says to give things a go, and if you fail, well, so be it. At least you'll have no regrets. 'She's a direct path to Lady Adora's heart, plus she's a kid and we know how kids work.' Unlike grown-ups who are endlessly perplexing and contrary and I can never work them out. 'This might just work. Well, fifty per cent . . . might.'

'Ten,' Bone says. 'No, five.'

But three Caddys nod obediently. Get it. Because Hebe could be a way out of this mess no matter how frightful she sounds. And I can't think of anything else. But no way am I telling Bone Boy that. He needs no ammunition to cement the supremacy here. He just raises a single eyebrow at the plan and swings onto a beam. 'Good luck with that, Company T. I won't be here. I do not want a case of the Hebes in my life – far too delicate a constitution. The Squeedlys have warned that she'll be my downfall.' He lies along the beam on his back, closes his eyes and pretends to snore again, loudly.

'Come *on*,' Scruff urges his new mate.

'I'll be vanishing in a puff of smoke, old chap. I'm good at that, remember? And don't any of you go mentioning me.' He starts snoring again.

Okay, one down, three left. 'So, we need some good thinking here, troops. What would make Hebe come to us? How can we lure her into this room? Get her to unbolt that bolt?'

Bert taps her head. 'Hey, remember when we first got to the Reptilarium, when we'd stare out the window, desperate for escape? Looked at all those kids in the square preparing for their Christmas. Walking up the hill with their dads, playing with sleds. *Playing*. That's the key word. Having fun. With friends. I wanted to be a part of it so much.'

The ache of the alone – yes, me too. I shake my sister's hand. Well done, old girl.

'Playing, fun, friends . . . football. *FOOTBALL*!' Scruff snatches up Dooky, which Bone has most conveniently forgotten. 'A match. A noisy one. The room's big enough.'

'But what if the Squeedlys turn up to investigate, rather than your Hebe,' Bone declares from his beam. 'Just saying.'

'To them, it's just kids letting off steam,' I explain. 'At a regular hour this time, so there's no harm in it. But to a child . . . it's a whole other world.'

'True, true,' Bone says wearily. 'You've got it all worked out, don't you, K?'

'Oh, come on, Bone Boy.' Bert grins.

'I'm really not sure I can get used to someone else calling all the shots in this house.' He looks at me suspiciously.

'This is to help us, mate. Just be here, please, at the start. To get the ball rolling, add to the noise.'

'But I need my beauty sleep.'

'Bone Boy, Bone Boy.' We all giggle. Accompanied by a war clap that gets louder and louder.

'Lord Bone of the Illuminarium to you, thank you very much,' but he starts to smile.

'Lord Bone on high! Illuminarium Man!' We cry and clap in rhythm.

He props a hand on a cheek, basks. Drops down. 'All right, ladies and gentlemen, all right —' the beautiful smile — 'your Bone Boy is back. Just at the start.

Right where you want him. And then I'll be slipping away and you won't even notice.'

I kick the ball at his chest to celebrate. 'Woohoo!'

'Not like that you . . . you . . . desert girl thingy. All wrong. No killer instinct. Let me teach you.'

'If you insist.' I grin back, one side up, one side down. My crooked grin that Mum had exactly and used on Dad far too much, when he was driving her bananas but she'd be secretly laughing at it.

'Goals,' Bone snaps now. 'Two. At either end. Pronto. You can't have a match without them.'

We look around. Goals? Hmmm.

'The hospital beds, Kicky.' Pin points.

Yes! Perfect! Upended. We throw off mattresses and unclip brakes and wheel two metal frames to the far ends of the room. Actually, no, er, whizz them. They slip and spin and run from our grasp and we jump on top of them and glide across the vast expanse of the room. Like pucks on ice! Bert and I take down the net. Now we've got a racetrack! Two can pile on each frame, clinging to the front, then we speed from one end of the room to the other in tandem. Beyond fun!

Then three are piling on, four. Me pushing the most, of course. Wheeeeeeeee! Best combination? Bone and Bert; Bone holding on with one arm stretched high like a charioteer and Bert squealing, yes squealing, her absolute delight of being next to him with massive eye-rolling from the rest of us.

It sounds like thunder along the very floor of heaven with screams of joy arcing like arrows over the top of it. 'I've never had so much fun in my life!' Scruff shouts, his face red and puffed. Pin's suddenly flat on his back on the ground, too exhausted for another round. I join him.

'Up,' Bone claps. 'It's time for battle. We need the goals in place. Beds upended, roger?'

We prop up a metal bed frame at either end. Two goals. Perfect. 'Okay, as much noise as you can,' I command, but no one needs any direction. We're off! Dooky is most obliging. I'm in goal at one end, Scruff in the other, and we play like the country depends on it.

Suddenly, one by one, we realise a girl has slipped inside the door.

Is watching us, her back against the wall.

Is saying nothing.

'The disease,' Scruff whispers, and I shush him quiet, stifling a laugh. Pretend we haven't noticed. Quickly scan the room; Bone has magically disappeared, of course, the canny will-o-the-wisp ahead of the lot of us and not wanting to be infected by any of this. How does he vanish so triumphantly? He's a master of spying and subterfuge; must have been taught by the best and I guess there would have been some amazing men stationed here during the war, spies, part of that Escape and Evasion Unit he talks about.

So. A new girl. In pink satin, like a party dress but there's no party, and it's too small. As if it belonged to a world long ago that she's no longer a part of but she's clinging onto it, playing dress-ups. She's fat. Not comfortable with it. It's in the way she's standing there awkward, one ankle cocked behind her leg. Like she wants to disappear into the wall, actually, but also wants to watch and the result is an avalanche of awkwardness. Hands behind her back. Hands scrunching down her dress. Hands scratching her arms, pulling back her hair. Hands nowhere because she doesn't know where to put them.

She's about ten years old. Curled hair. Glasses. She reminds me of a child in a book, some new girl at school who's left her old one because no one was friends with her there – but she already knows that no one will be friends at this one either. It's in the way she's standing there. Not expecting us to notice, to talk. Can barely look us in the eye when we catch sight of her. As if she suddenly can't remember why she's here at all. But hugely does. But can't admit it.

One by one we stop playing, come up panting, and stare.

20

THE STRIKER IN OUR MIDST

Silence.

'I'm just watching.'

Suddenly. Resentfully. Her voice a scrunch of a scowl.

'I've heard about you lot. I was curious.'

Then she's staring at the ground, her toe at a piece of imaginary fluff, her long hair falling across her face. 'I wanted to see, but . . .' to the floor, and everything about her says she's not expecting us to say anything like a welcome. Like she's been told once too much that she's a contagious disease and believes it. I remember something Mum said to me long ago: that mean people are unhappy people, and never forget it. That when someone says or does something horrible it's because they're crying on the inside and you're not, and they want to drag you right down to be as unhappy as them. And as I look at Hebe standing before us all clotted and wrong I can see where Bone's stories would have come from. But what if you're nice to them? What then?

'I'm Kick.'

'Bert.'

'Pin!'

'Scruff. So get yourself over here!'

'Pardon? What?' She frowns, steps back.

'Come and play,' Scruff insists.

'Really?' Shock.

'Can you play footy?' Bert's eyeing Hebe's scuffed ballet slippers. Too big, too pink, too satiny – and too fabulous.

'Um . . .'

'I'll teach you. No worries.' Scruff bowls right over and takes her by the hand.

'Don't touch!' she snaps. As if Scruff is made of slime. Or she's never been touched in her life. Wrong move: it only makes my brother more determined. 'You're just my type for a partner in crime. You English girls – jolly spiffing. And, um, terrifying. Is that it? Oh, what the heck, just come on. We'll call you H from now on, and you're in Company S.

S for Scruff. Got it?' He pulls her into the middle of the pitch and Bert and I giggle; we know where he's taken his lessons from in the charisma department – Bone – and he's got a long way to go yet. 'With you on board, H, we're going to win this tournament.' He grins a Bone-like, megawatt grin. Well, at least he's got that bit down pat.

'All right,' Hebe says shyly, dragging her hair behind her ears and blushing furiously. A flicker of a smile, as if her face isn't used to it.

Well, let's just say she's hopeless. Lumpy and awkward and a bit stinky to boot. Her limbs don't work together smoothly, it's all a bit wonky. Can't kick, volley, tackle, can't anything and we're not much better, but still. We all try to teach her. Let her score a goal, she misses, then another, she just gets it, and she's barely even realising all the help we're giving her. 'Oh my golly goodness I can do this!' she says in wonder at one point. The smile on her face cracks wider, then wider, until it's completely glowing her up and we all stop: she's become someone else.

Her hair is coming loose, her dress gets ripped. She doesn't care. We're laughing with her astonishment. We're all getting louder and louder, clapping and cheering and leaping on each other, faces red and sweaty and puffed. And every time a goal is scored we crash down the bed frames and whizz them in a thunderous roar of victory across the room – the scorer gets Bone's charioteer's spot and we make sure it's Hebe, a lot.

'Scruff, push me!' She's laughing and laughing so hard we think she'll crack a rib from it. At her twelfth goal, Scruff lifts her up by the knees and spins her around. 'Put me down!' But he doesn't, oh no, she's slipping from him and he drops her, laughing, and she's laughing too as they tumble to the ground. It's an almighty crash of shouting and whooping and giggling.

Hang on. What's that?

A thudding. Furiously. Up the stairs.

'Hebe? Heeeeebeeeeeeee?' The unmistakable voice. 'If you're in there . . .'

Lady Adora. We all stop. Clomp clomp, stomp her roaring feet. Hebe cringes behind Scruff.

And there she is, in the doorway. Standing there resplendent in her full-length tartan taffeta. Clutching the door frame, mopping the sweat from her upper lip. Not used to being dragged up here and not happy with it.

'You're in there.'

Daughter glances at mother – a moment of frozen, cowering tension – then daughter ignores her, magnificently, and just keeps on playing, dragging Scruff up. It feels like a big moment for Hebe, like it's the first time she's ever disobeyed Lady Adora. I watch her closely. This plan has to work.

'Pass!' Hebe yells at Bert, who duly kicks the ball across to her.

'What are you doing?' screeches her mother and we momentarily stop, then, taking the cue from Hebe, play on: 'H, H, pass!'

'H? What?' exclaims Lady Adora.

'Let her win,' I whisper to the rest. Because her mother has to see it. Scruff and Hebe are one team, Bert's with Pin and I'm the ref. Hebe weaves between the lot of us and we fall like skittles in her wake.

'Goal, Hebe, goooooooooal!' The yell is sudden from behind me, from the door. 'Come on. Elbows, girl, use them.' Is it really her? No. *Yes*. Lady Adora, getting far too involved for her own good. Hebe scoots past Berti, Scruff gets up for another attempt at the ball.

'Atta girl, you can do it. The bed, the bed!' her mother shouts. 'Come on, you big lump. Be a *winner* for once.' Hebe stops, in despair, like she's heard this a thousand times before and is absolutely clogged by it.

'Show her what you're made of, H,' I urge her quiet, up close, 'show her what you can do.'

Hebe's in the centre of the court, the goal a ridiculously long way away. She hesitates, loses confidence, slumps.

'Just do it,' I urge. 'Don't think about it. Just kick.'

Hebe gathers herself, takes aim. The ball flies straight past Scruff, straight past Pin.

'*Goooooal!*' her mother screams, then looks around sheepishly. 'Oh. Quite forgot myself there. Yah.'

Hebe's pink satin dress is now startlingly ripped, its matching ribbon halfway down her curls, most of her hair loose. Scruff lifts her in the air and spins her around, Bert too then all of us and then we tumble flat on our backs, in a ragged row, exhausted. Hebe sits up with her hands resting on knees, legs apart, most unladylike. Most Australian, actually, and I grin and raise a thumb at her and sit like it too, in solidarity.

Hebe grins back. 'I did it.' Wondrous.

Lady Adora comes to her senses, staring down at the ragtag jumble of us. 'Downstairs. Immediately, young lady. Away from these . . . these . . . colonials. They're a bad influence.' Her face is screwed up in revulsion. 'You have viola practice immediately. Twenty minutes ago, in fact. Then pianoforte.'

'Can I stay? Five minutes.'

'Absolutely not.'

'Please, Mama.'

'Forbidden. Their ways –' Lady Adora looks at the four of us in distaste '– might rub off. Look at how you're sitting for a start. You've never sat like that in your life.'

Hebe snaps her legs shut. 'Pretty please?'

'Downstairs *now,* or there'll be no lunch. Or supper.' It's roared, we all jump. It's just like Aunty Ethel used to shout, and Mum. It's just like any mother at her wits' end, in fact. I snap my own legs shut.

Hebe looks at me, shrugs shoulders and reluctantly stands up. 'Bye,' she mouths. 'Thanks.'

'Can we come for dinner?' I ask Lady Adora, right out bold, because we have nothing to lose here and it's the next stage of the plan – befriend, or make a run for it – but most of all get out of this room and work out how to contact Basti fast. We just need to get beyond that door, however we can. My fingers are crossed behind my back.

'Oh yes, Mummy, dinner, yes!' Hebe clasps her hands as if I've said the most magical thing in the world.

'What?' Lady Adora hisses. 'The . . . the . . . impertinence.'

'Yes, yes, what fun! Please, Mummy. Tonight! You've not told me why they're here in the first place. Why are they here? For how long? Why can't I play with them?'

'Questions, questions.' Lady Adora holds her hands at her head like she's suddenly got the most enormous headache. 'All in good time. They are friends of friends and they won't be here long and there will be no playing, no dinners, and no uncouth manners rubbing off. No mixing. They are *not* people like us.'

'But they're my new friends. They're kind to me, Mummy. They've been helping me. They make me feel good about myself.'

Lady Adora looks at her daughter, struck, as if she's learnt something extraordinary about her for the very first time. 'But there's no time for attachment,' she says, bewildered. 'They won't be in your life for long.'

I lick my lips, breathe shallow, fast.

'Pleeeeeeeeeeeeeaaaaaase.'

Adora looks at us. Looks at her daughter. Back at us. Like she's trapped.

'I promise promise promise I'll do my viola practice, for *three* hours today. Then pianoforte. Then watercolours. Then callisthenics. Solid work.

Eight hours straight. No daydreaming, no shilly-shallying, every day until school starts. And I'll be as good as Georgiana Coutts-Pagmore by the end of it. I'll beat her, I'll get the music prize this term, I promise. I won't let you down, Mummy. If you just give me this dinner with them. Just one. How long are they here for? Why are they here?'

Lady Adora holds out a hand to her daughter in a huge stop sign, as if she has no idea herself, no answers herself.

I smile at Hebe, lips rolled in tight, raise my secret crossed-fingers sign to her. Lady Adora backs out as if it's all too overwhelming, too much to think about. 'No, no,' she mutters.

I glance at Bert. What's the one thing she'd love more than anything here? That would get her going with interior decorating and designing and enchantment and magic; the biggest sisterly gift I could give her? 'We could have a ball!' I exclaim. It's now or never and I'm going in big; nothing to lose. After all, Lady Adora is a woman who loves her dressing-up just as much as my sister, and she looks like she's swanning around in readiness for a ball every day of her life. 'You know, in that big ballroom. You could invite Mr Davenport. I bet he'd love to have a dance, he just seems like . . . the type. Bert here could decorate it. Real romantic. Candles, the lot. She's a wiz at all that. We could all dress up. You must have *something* you could wear, Lady Adora . . .'

'A ball?' She sighs, lost in thought and shaking her head, wilting.

'Yes! Yes!' Hebe claps her hands, jumping with excitement.

'We could have lanterns,' Bert seizes her moment. 'All over the room! I saw them on a library shelf. We'd just need a few hours to make it magical. Spectacular. There's an old gramophone in the library. And records. I bet there's the Charleston among them, the Pride of Erin. We could dance. The house could come alive again, just like it used to.'

'Pllleeeeeeeeeeaaaaaaaaaaaaaaaaase!' Hebe's eyes are scrunched tight like she's going to explode.

Without further ado Scruff bowls up to her and spins her around then plunges her down just like Dad used to do with Mum, on a Saturday night, when the wireless played the waltzes. He almost drops Hebe but she doesn't notice, just giggles and whoops with excitement at the imminent thrill of it.

'A ball, Mummy. I've never been to one.' Her face is glowing.

'Yes yes yes!' we all exclaim, eyes shining. Because it's our one big chance. The Escape and Evasion Unit is swinging into action here, Bone Boy, oh yes.

Lady Adora sighs, throws up her hands. 'Anything for some peace.'

And to see her daughter's smile again, I bet. The one where her whole face is lit up. Which, right at this moment, is aimed at the four of us. Someone else, entirely, oh yes.

21

SCRUBBING AND SCOURING AND SLEUTHING

Silent Mountain. Half an hour later. Collecting us without a word.

He just appears at the door, in silence. Stands there. We know instinctively to follow. He gives us nothing before turning his back then doesn't turn again until we arrive at the ballroom. Then is gone without a word, melted into the very walls of the house – just like Bone.

But we can't hold in our glee. Out. The plan worked! We dash into the middle of the room and spin in the vastly empty space we've promised to magic up by tonight. Stop. Look around. Oh. Big task. What were we thinking? What was *I* thinking? How can we possibly win Adora and

Darius around? Should we abandon this ball plan and make a dash for it? No, everyone's far too excited by the prospect of what's ahead. And if I can get Adora talking then maybe we're a step closer to Mum; if I can just get her tipsy, happy, loosen her up, it could all work spectacularly and Basti will be saved and I'll be the Commanding Officer of Company T – not Bone – and on my way to a Victoria Cross.

But the room's filthy. Falling apart. Needs cleaning. Hugely. Bird droppings are all over the floor and the frost has intruded through smashed windows that would have been flung wide onto a perfectly manicured lawn once. Rotted silk curtains lie like abandoned silver rivers along the parquet. Plus it's freezing. Covered in ice. Great ropes of ivy cascade from the windows in frozen waterfalls of frost. An enormous chandelier has crashed onto the floor like a beached ship. Others have spilled from their protective cotton bags like dead octopuses from fishing sacks.

Bert catches my look of hopelessness. 'We're from the bush, girl, we can do this.' She smiles. 'Come on. You, out of anyone, cannot give up. Mops. Buckets. We don't need much else.'

'Er, hired help?'

At that moment Lady Adora clickety-clacks into the room in a great cloud of feather boa and perfume, glass in hand, as if she's half dressed for the ball already; followed by Hebe clutching a viola and barely looking at us; followed by Mrs Squeedly, whose entire body is a squirm of disapproval at the new shenanigans in this place; as if she's not enjoying one bit all the meddling with her housekeeping regime. Well, she's got a wild ride ahead of her.

'You're not going to run off on me, are you, little mousies?' Her Ladyship flings out her hand holding the glass and liquid shoots across the room like a golden whip. She bats away the mess. 'Squeedly,' she points dismissively, 'mess, mess.'

'Well, if we run away, Lady Adora, we'll never find out what happened to our mum, will we?' I respond sweetly. (Not adding that we know she'll be alerting Darius quick-smart if we make a dash for it and then he'll have time to execute the releasing of the snakes before we can get to Basti, because even if we could get to a phone, Basti never answers his because he's afraid of it.) 'So no, we're not thinking of bolting on you. And besides, we'd never let Hebe down.' I smile at the girl. She raises her viola back. 'She's our friend.'

I like her. Despite what Bone says.

'Splendid! You're learning, little tiger mousie, aren't you? Now where's the one who's going to transform the place. Dressed in black. Step forward, bat girl.'

Bert leaps in front of Lady Adora. 'Present and ready for action, Your Ladyship. Mrs Squeedly, if I may be so bold? We need mops. Buckets. Cloths.'

'They're quite a way away,' Mrs Squeedly responds. 'In the under parlour, by the kitchen. You'd need bicycles to get them.'

'The clock room!' Hebe exclaims. 'There's a whole stack left behind by the army.' She throws her viola across to her mother, who doesn't quite know what to do with it but too late, no time for bewilderment, we're off; running behind Hebe to a room of a hundred clocks, all silent and broken except for one valiant, feeble tick that's determined not to stop.

I point to the sound. 'That's me,' I whisper to Scruff.

He laughs, adding, 'You've always got Bert to wind you up.' Delicious!

We all grab a bike, Pin balancing on my handlebars, then the five of us weave through empty corridors and echoing rooms, squealing our delight; Bert's feet barely touching the pedals but she manages it on tippy toes, just. We return to the ballroom, balancing tin buckets over handlebars, holding wire brushes and cleaning cloths. Lady Adora and Mrs Squeedly have left, off in the kitchen no doubt, working out the dinner menu. We scrub the room down, laughing and squealing and throwing sponges of warm water at each other then sliding through the soapy slops and swinging on great gathered ropes of the ivy like Tarzan, perfecting our jungle cries and beating our chests.

Hebe too. In fact, er, Hebe the most. 'We're turning my house into a huge adventure park!' she cries gleefully.

'As we should,' Scruff grins.

'Do you steal teddies?' Pin suddenly asks.

'What?' Hebe stops. Looks at me.

'Ignore him,' I jump in, not wanting him launching into a conversation about Bone; we need to keep those two worlds separate. Plus we don't need anything scuppering this ballroom mission right now, there's too much at stake.

'Any other places around here ripe for a Caddy conversion?' Scruff asks fast, getting it.

Hebe chatters on about an abandoned village, adjoining the estate. How the army took it over in 1942, for target practice, and forced all the villagers out. They were never allowed back and it's been completely empty ever since. 'It's all mine now.' Her face glows with the secret.

'You've *got* to take us,' Scruff exclaims.

'If you're nice to me,' Hebe grins.

Scruff flashes his V for Victory sign and she shoots one back.

I tell the lovebirds it'll be our very next mission, but first this room needs a scrub-up. The space is brittle and bare with forgotten-ness. The cold of the dark is already slipping in and we'll need to wrap up warm tonight, plus light the place up.

Bert is straight onto it. She ties the windows' ivy back with army sheets torn into strips (Mrs Squeedly handed Bert a 'trusty' pair of scissors. Trusts her. It's a good sign). Bert demands candles throughout the room, her hands like a camera's viewfinder as she surveys the space. 'Dear Mrs Squeedly, we need some candles here. Can you possibly help?'

'Possibly,' she sighs upon return, as close to warmth as she'll get. She leads us to a locked room nearby. The space is crammed with dozens of gilt candelabras like mannequins abandoned in a shop.

'No!' Bert exclaims. 'This could not be better.'

We set them up by the windows, along the walls. Dot some kerosene lamps on the floor; we find a whole storeroom of them. Drag a mahogany table as long as a cricket pitch into the centre of the space. It takes six of us, with towels under its fourteen legs and Pin lying luxuriously on his back, arms behind his head, on top of it. Like Cleopatra on her barge and, good grief, everyone wants to be him in this place.

Lady Adora flurries back, checks out the preparations. 'Darius won't believe it.' She raises her glass in admiration. 'Daddy, too. He'll be here in ghostly form. Full evening dress.'

Mad, mad, yes.

'Will Mr Davenport be coming?' I ask.

'I requested and he accepted. It's been a long time since this house has seen a ball and we're all curious. Besides, it's the depth of winter – we need some sparkle in this house.'

Bert wails, tragically, that we have absolutely nothing to wear. Says if only she had a needle and thread she'd have me in a ballgown yet, imagine, what a sight. I recoil in horror. Hebe tells us excitedly that there's a fur room downstairs, near the cellars, and it's full of mink coats and hats and we'll so need them tonight. Bert squeals, quite recovered. 'We could have a Russian theme! In our frost room!'

'Oh all right,' Lady Adora sighs, as if she's entirely surrendered to the idea of bringing her beloved house alive again and glowing her daughter up. 'Fur hats! Balalaikas! Dancing bears!' She sings loudly, 'Bring it forth. Sparkle, sparkle!'

Hebe looks at me and scrunches up her face in apology; her mother's always erratic and crazy and all over the place, she's resigned to it, and we must be too. 'It's fine,' I mouth to her.

Because the trap is progressing very nicely here. The worming into Adora's world – to unlock the secrets of Mum and turn Basti's nightmare around, to stop Darius inheriting our uncle's estate and handing it to Her Ladyship – is proceeding to plan. Mum said to me once that if someone is being mean to you, just try connecting, with niceness, because it can shock them into change; it's always worth a try. I stand here now, looking at Hebe putting her arm gently around her mother and giggling in excitement as she points out the sweep of the candelabras, and I smile at the thought of my own mum, of my arm around her, too. Of all her life lessons flooding back.

My eyes prick with, what? Tears, excitement, anticipation.

Her world is close. I can feel it. Soon, soon. This will work. Our entire family will be reunited: Mum, Dad, even Bucket.

I can do this. I'm on the way.

22

BEARBAITING

As the light drops – crazily early in this dimly lit country – Silent Mountain leads us back to the tennis court, then leaves.

Hebe has gone, immersed in her viola and pianoforte practice, as good as her word to her mother. Bert spins us around in a pile of furs, attaching bits and pieces to various parts of our bodies and standing back to adjust. Bone has magically reappeared, to our delight, and is busily directing the dubious operation – urging us (with a great amount of cackling) to become more furry by the second. 'More, Company T! More! More!'

'Don't you go making me look like a grizzly bear, mate,' Scruff says nervously, glancing at Pin, who's beyond help in several mink wraps held in place by diamante clasps.

Now's the moment for the next step in the plan. Deep breath.

'Pinny Pin,' I say in my most wheedling voice. 'I need Dad's scarf. That's tied around Banjo's neck.' He looks at me in horror. 'I'm so sorry. It's really important.'

He shakes his head furiously. 'No, it's my most precious thing. I have to mind it for him.'

This is going to be more difficult than I thought. 'I need to get Bucket back. I need to know what happened. It's eating me up, little man. It's part of the plan.' Because our dingo girl is the next thing I'll make right here.

'Whoooa. Who's this Bucky?' Bone interjects. 'Am I to allow him –'

'Her!' four Caddys interject.

'Am I to allow *her* into our very select band of brothers? This is an exclusive club, you know. No riffraff.'

'Hebe mustn't see her!' Pin cries.

'It's okay,' I soothe, 'I'd never put Bucket in danger. You know that. I just want her here, with us.'

'Excuse me, *who* are we talking about?' Bone snaps.

'She's our dog,' I explain. 'It's a plan I've got, for tonight. To get her back to us. And this is our one big chance, Bone, while we're not locked up. We can't blow it because I don't know when it'll happen again. And Company T, we have to get Lady Adora and Darius tipsy. Keep filling their glasses. But not so they notice. Got it?' Three Caddys nod.

Pin hands the scarf over reluctantly. 'Anything for Bucky, Kicky.'

'Well, I do love a sortie,' Bone sniffs. 'As long as it doesn't involve abandoning poor ol' Bone Boy, eh? I have a phobia about that. But if you're nice to me I can tell you where the wine is stored. In fact, I can even keep the bottles in good supply myself, from all the lovely secret hatches of this house. Just consider me your most obliging ghost.' He bows.

'You just relax tonight, mate. You might need it for what's ahead.'

Bone steps back, surveys us all in various states of furry grizzliness. 'I say, have I met my match here? You lot are quite the doers, aren't you, Company T?' He warns us again about the madly unpredictable Lady Adora, and how she won't like a dog coming into her house one bit. What we're doing is enormously risky; we're playing with fire.

'We have to risk it,' I say. 'Bucket's our link back to Basti. She could get a message to him if we play our cards right.'

'And you too, mate!' Scruff adds.

'Oh, I'm quite beyond saving.' Bone comes up close and taps my forehead. 'But what on earth's in that head of yours, K? I'd love to know. For the future. To put my mind at rest.'

'A master plan, Lord Bone. To win not only this coming battle but the entire war. Do you approve?'

He steps back and surveys, his eyes dancing. 'Quite possibly. It's the best fun I've had in ages. Dooky, cover your ears. K, you make a delectable grizzly bear.'

Yeah, right. He's made me look ridiculous here, hasn't he? As has Bert, no surprises there. She of course looks exquisite, in a long fur cape and matching wrap, swathed in black tulle that even covers her face. I, on the other hand, look like a lump. A brown furry one. Or mole, or rat. Great.

Bone glances at my grumpy face then swings up to the beam where Dooky lives. He passes down a book to me. I gasp. It's a beautiful, leather-bound volume of *Wuthering Heights*. 'I have a secret stash, K.' He smiles mysteriously. 'Mrs Squeedly has spent hours teaching me to read with books like this. She

202

saves them, because Her Ladyship isn't a reader at all. Disturbing, isn't it? Library shelves are for gas masks in this place.'

I punch him in thanks. In absolute, utter chuff.

'Now, don't getting mushy on me,' he says, rubbing his arm like it hurt.

Are you kidding? 'Not on your life,' my face scrunches up.

Bert just stares, furious. 'I read too.'

23

THE FROZEN BANQUET

The night is stopped. Not a breath of breeze, not a cloud, just a large silvery coin of a moon flooding our world with light.

Four Caddys, one Ellicott and one Darius Davenport dash onto the wide ornamental lawn in front of 'The Swallows' among a battalion of limbless statues shining a glary white. Darius knows we won't be going far – there's a band of terrifying darkness beyond us. He languishes back on a stone bench, as if he's imagining being lord and master of this grand estate already (well, we'll see about that, mate). He gazes at us with a look that's not quite straight on, his body twisted and uncomfortable in its dinner jacket, and we know who would have forced him into that. 'Come on!' Scruff yells at one point, then Pin, but Darius shrinks back with a 'Mmm, no, goodness no. I don't do running about. Never have,' determined not to join in our fun despite our best attempts; too wary of us.

Wondrous fire torches are held aloft by all us kids; they were found stacked in a broom cupboard by Mr Squeedly, who even – with much gravity – cut one down to fit Pin's exact height. Magic! Delirious magic! We've even found an old box of animal masks, ripe for a masked ball, of course. Out with the Russian theme! In with the zoo!

And so a fox, a tiger, a zebra, a lion and a hedgehog squeal through the stillness of the frost-laden night, our footsteps leaving patterns on the ice, like lines on a hand. We run and spin and skip, do cartwheels and handstands, exhilarated just to be out in the lovely crisp air. It's a wonderland of ice. The moonlit trees are frozen coral. The endless grounds an ocean of crunchy white, and beyond them lies the dark heaving breath of the real ocean, asleep.

'Ssssssssh,' whispers Hebe the Hedgehog. 'Just breathe it in.' We stop. Absolute stillness.

'You look so beautiful right now,' I whisper to her, and she does, in a purple velvet dress with her hair out and her mask now flung back.

'Really?' she responds in disbelief. But the remark is transforming her, I can tell; making her change, and me in the process; chuffing us both up.

'Believe it,' I say soft, 'you're amazing,' and Hebe suddenly seems taller, straighter. What a gift to make someone feel like that! We stand there, in stillness and solidarity, side by side, and can feel the magic under the full moon, as if everything in this end-of-the-world place is waiting, breaths held . . .

For what?

Lady Adora finally strides from the ballroom in a silver dress that matches the moonlight. The cloth is streaked with age-stained creases and the hem is shredded from too much dancing long ago but she doesn't care, doesn't seem to notice. A wire crown of a moon and stars rests upon her long, white hair. She turns back to the house and stares up at it with her arms languid, empty wine goblet in hand. As if she's in love. Painful love. As if she can't bear it. I stand beside her, whisper 'it's breathtaking,' gazing with her at the vast, ice-encrusted ruin of the Illuminarium.

'Oh yes,' she says. 'And breathtakingly temperamental. Always falling sick. Catastrophically. Like a prize thoroughbred, only worse. The vet bills are enormous.' She snickers at it. 'You're too, too much, aren't you, girl?' Looks at me, shaking her head. 'We care too much, don't we, too much.'

Hebe takes Banjo for Pin while he fumbles with his torch. Asks the teddy's name. Pin snatches it back with a snapped 'Mine!' Hebe lifts up her mask and peers at the little lion in our midst and tells her mother that everyone needs to eat immediately because the guests are starving and starting to act in peculiar ways.

'I second you on that,' Scruff announces, stabbing his torch into the ground and falling on his back and clutching his stomach in fits of giggly agony. I do too, then Bert, then Pin. Oh, you can tell it's been a while since we've been let loose outside. The result: a laughy, squealy jumble of hitting and shrieking and tickling.

Darius rolls his eyes at the mess of it. 'Children, mmm, I'll never understand them.'

Lady Adora steps back, hands out in horror, can't bear the sight. Looks at us suddenly like she's never seen us before; has no idea why we're here. 'Who are you? Supper, did you say, Hebe? Supper. Yes, must. Squeedly will see to it. What have I done?' She waves her wine glass vaguely at the house.

'Yaaaaaaaay!' We all run to it.

So here we are, a raggy, scraggly old ragtag bunch at a cricket-pitch-long table. Furs are piled on like cavemen – except Bert – along with bits and pieces of whatever military uniforms we could find: rows of medals (Pin), a diagonal rope of spent bullet cartridges (Scruff), a velvet choker (Bert), and a pair of Land Army lady's jodhpurs with a bandage as a belt (me). We're all wearing pieces of crystal that Bert has salvaged from the chandeliers and strung with fishing line – as necklaces, earrings, badges, belts – and our masks are thrown off.

Lady Adora has placed four ancient China dolls at one end of the table, on their own gilt chairs, to enjoy the spectacle no doubt. Hebe stares at them in embarrassment, shaking her head and biting her lip.

'Her proper family,' Bert whispers.

'Sssshhhh,' I giggle.

Silent Mountain stands like a footman at the door, expressionless. We sit among yellowing napkins with the initials of some long lost duke, cracked dinner plates with the gold family crest fading off and an enormous soup tureen filled with frozen willow branches and fake roses covered in frost. Candelabra light flutters and trembles all about us and there's a roaring fire from the central fireplace (thanks to a few salvaged chair legs). Great ropes of icy ivy are tied back from the windows to display the lawn with its lace tracery of madly excited footsteps.

'Perfect for swinging on, sis.' Scruff nudges me, indicating the very unique curtains. 'Me first. When that namby pamby dancing bit is over.'

'As long as I've got the chandelier, mate.' I nod to a great central light that's fallen almost to the ground on its thick rope, but not quite. 'And don't forget our mission this evening. The whole point of us being here.'

Scruff winks. 'One Ladyship Love-ora, one fit of wobbliness. Ditto Darius.'

'Those barbarous army thugs,' Lady Adora mutters furiously to her dolls as she holds up two chipped wine goblets to the light. She's in a world of her own, gulping the sight of all her old crockery, feverishly running her hands over it and holding it to her cheek as if she hasn't seen the table properly set for years. Darius gently lifts a plate from her hand, tuts sadly and pours her some wine from a dusty bottle. I secretly refill his glass. Scruff is hovering, itching to fill Her Ladyship's, I can tell. Bert raises a sneaky V for Victory sign to Bone somewhere in the shadows, goodness knows where, and I rub my hands: we're all settling in nicely with this mission. It's going splendidly, Company T.

Mrs Squeedly serves the dinner but Scruff, of all people, doesn't get past the first course before he spits the green liquid into a napkin of the eighth duke. 'Urgh, what *is* this?' He's told off curtly that it's nettle soup, a wartime favourite, and the nation has been living on it for the past six years, as will he. That it will be followed by Everything-in Stew, which is self-explanatory, and Rock Buns, which are guaranteed to live up to their name, and for dessert he'll be enjoying Eggless Bread and Prune Pudding. Mrs Squeedly looks at various un-thrilled faces. Un-thrilled herself.

'Why thank you,' I say politely, staring pointedly at all three of my naughty monkey lot and mouthing 'Bucket' furiously, to shut them up. They're pulling the most unenthusiastic faces here but once it's served, yep, we eat everything – starving, of course. Especially Scruff, who holds his nose through the lot of it.

Then out of the blue Bert asks why on earth Mr Squeedly never talks.

'Ah, dear Squeedly,' Lady Adora jumps in, gulping from her wine goblet. 'He lost a child, didn't he? Somewhere. An accident. I've forgotten now.' Mrs Squeedly has gone utterly pale, her jug of water frozen in midair. 'Never had another,'

Her Ladyship babbles on. 'Never spoke again.' An awkward silence. Mrs Squeedly doesn't look at her, doesn't look at anyone. 'Bottled up with grief, he was. Yes. Well, he does talk, I know, to those he loves . . . but not . . . me. For some reason. Just won't. Jolly bad luck, eh? Was it a boy or a girl? A boy. No. Girl? Goodness, can't remember now.' Lady Adora laughs a nervous laugh. 'I see the two of them every morning going down to the grave near the cliffs, in the old village. I like staring out at that time, at the sunrise. Early, early, yes. Wake at four am, bolt upright. Can't fall back to sleep after that, no matter what. Such a big, whispering house. Every night it whispers, did you know that? Taunts. Mocks. Bad girl, bad girl. That's what it says. How could you allow it?' She shakes her head, grimaces, collects herself. 'And now he has children, four of them, crawling all over his life. Like beetles, ants. Tormenting him, reminding him . . . why did I *do* that?'

'That's awful,' Bert cries, her hands at her cheeks. 'Poor Mr Squeedly!'

'Isn't that right?' Lady Adora throws over her shoulder at him. 'An accident?'

Silent Mountain just stands like granite in the doorway, his face a mask of grief battened down, no doubt, and my heart twists to see him afresh.

No wonder he can't talk to us, can barely look at us. More children. Reminders. Of what he lost. I want to run and hold him.

'Quite so, m'lady,' Mrs Squeedly snaps to life with her lips curled in tight like she's bursting to say something but won't, can't. I catch a flicker of despair on her husband's face before it's resurrected to its normal stony state. But little Pin can't help himself. He's off. Running across the room and crashing into the huge man's knees and squeezing tight, just as he does to Daddy, to Basti, to anyone who needs it and my heart catches at his wide open heart.

Silent Mountain is, as always, silently mountainous. He does not bend. Does not stir. If he did, would it break him? A stew of a silence, rich with everything not said or done. Bert looks like she's going to cry; like she, too, can't bear it.

'Did someone say there was music here?' Hebe declares loudly.

'Yes!' Scruff grabs her and runs to the gramophone set up in a far corner. A scratchy old record is soon playing the Charleston and that's it, we're off. Need the mad flappy relief of Mum's favourite dance. We're soon shrieking and bouncing, can't help ourselves. Holding two hands and spinning, growing more and more bold. I swing on the chandelier that's already askew; Scruff grabs the ivy over the windows and is closely followed by Bert. Pin. Hebe.

Darius rigorously avoids it all. 'Not the dancing type, mmm,' he murmurs to us. 'Or the dashing-about type, for that matter. Or the children type. Or –'

'What *are* you then?' Pin asks him in frustration.

'Er,' the man shakes his head, stuck, like he's not the talking type either now, and all the while Lady Adora is jiggling her foot uncontrollably as her dancing partner is resolutely twisted and turned away on the sidelines then, what the heck, the music gets to him too and something cracks inside and he suddenly grabs the love of his life and flings her back dramatically. 'I say, young man, I say,' she whoops.

He's off, a new man entirely in the spin of music and candles and Adora and Pin's laughter, and without him realising it I refill his glass as he dances and gulps. As does Bert. Scruff. I ask Darius to dance with me, hold his reluctant hands, wheedle 'Come on, *Lord* Davenport,' and oh he likes that title, it's what he's dreamt of, using Basti's money to get him there, of course. I spin him until he's laughing, drunk on the idea. Spin faster, faster. Need him hot, need his coat off. Eventually he removes it. Flings it over his chair.

Bingo. My big chance.

I watch, wait. Slip Dad's scarf into an obscure inside pocket when no one's looking. For Bucket. If she's still around, at the cemetery, waiting for a sign. Which I'm sure she will be. I've got it all worked out. She'll sniff out this scarf, know Darius is connected to her master and sneak into the van to get to us, somehow, using her amazing tracking nose that's been trained in the desert to find Pin whenever he wanders off, which averages about once a week. Oh yes, we need our dog here, our beautiful, clever, endlessly smiling girl. Need her extraordinary tracking skills. To find her way back to London. She's our link to the outside world; to Basti and to Dad.

So there it is, Company T: Stage One of Ballroom Mission, complete.

Stand by for Stage Two!

24

THE BROKEN NIGHT

We all collapse, exhausted, after the dancing frenzy. Hebe and Scruff are side by side, flat on their backs; Pin is curled in my arms as we lean against the wall; Bert is trying to re-attach her outfit, which is coming loose. The evening is stretching into darkness, candles sputter out, one by one. Darius is holding a monogrammed plate high, examining the crest, and Lady Adora is suddenly huddled in a corner, red lips smeared, stroking a wall and crying.

'My darling, I *will* make you happy again. I'm so sorry it's come to this. Forgive me, old girl. Your Addy let you down . . .'

Darius and Hebe look at her like they've seen this a thousand times before and it's no use doing anything anymore, it's hopeless. But Bert strides over. 'I can help you,' she says, trying to put her arm around Lady Adora's shoulders.

She's brushed away. 'What? Who are –?' Her Ladyship looks in horror at Bert's grubby, freckly hands from the bush that dare to touch her.

'I'm your interior decorator, Your Ladyship, remember?' Bert announces with far too much confidence for a child. It won't be liked. 'Well, training to be. As well as dress designer. Here, look.' Berti takes off her necklace made of chandelier crystals and places it over Lady Adora's neck. 'Have it. Please. It's my best.'

Lady Adora scrabbles the object off. Flings it aside. 'Urgh! Who are you? I do not need any of your help, thank you very much. Who ordered you here? Was it you, Darius?'

'Er, mmm . . .' he can't quite answer, stepping back. 'There was some confusion . . . it happened so fast. Panic, remember. What to do.'

'What? Yes. Me? Really? No, no. Most confused. This is all a mistake. Are these mine?' She looks at the crystals strewn on the floor then at us, in revulsion, as if she's only just noticed our strange getup. Which has all come from her house, of course. 'Remind me, where are you from?' Utterly icy.

'The Kensington Reptilarium, Your Ladyboat!' Pin announces proudly.

'That place!' she roars. The mere sound of it has sliced a nerve. 'I'm *sick* of hearing about it. Or anyone associated with it. I need it removed. Now, yes. From my life. Need this episode wrapped up. Darius. Where are you? Darius?' Lady Adora staggers to her feet, rights herself and accidentally smashes her wine glass on the floor.

Darius just stands there, his eyes firmly shut and his face to the heavens in an attempt to somehow block out all the madness. Hebe groans with her hands over her ears; she's mortified. 'Mummy, stop, stop.'

We Caddys step back, embarrassed, gobsmacked. The night has suddenly become very old. Stretched. Weary. Like something has snapped in Lady Adora's head and all the demons have rushed out. We inch back towards the door. Time to go.

Her eyes light up at the retreating sight of us. 'Not so fast,' she hisses. Staggers forward.

'Where's our mama?' Pin cries wildly, not guessing this might not be a good time to ask. 'I want my mama. What have you done with her? Did you eat her?'

Lady Adora stares at him in bewilderment, spits, 'Your mother?' Then pushes past us all, knocking Pin to the ground. He's shocked but unhurt.

I pick him up, furious. 'He's just a child,' I shout.

Lady Adora stops. Like she's suddenly woken up from a dream inside the snow globe of a beautiful winter ball and hard, cold reality has come crashing back.

'Addy,' Darius warns, trying to grab her arm, 'calm down.' She spins on him, on Pin.

'Flora Caddy.' She nods at the memory. 'You're her children, yes, of course.'

'Now now,' Darius warns, low.

'No.' She dismisses him with a flick of her hand. Looks around the vast room, the wallpaper peeling away, the war-damaged roof, as if she's seeing everything for the first time. 'All this talk of your Kensington Reptilarium. Ha. Well, do you know what this is, my little mousies? It's the Icicle Illuminarium and it's far more spectacular. Isn't it, Dari? Our secret world that . . . illuminates. Oh, it contains many, many secrets. About your mother, about her world. But you'll never find them out, will you? Oh no.' She snatches a goblet from Darius's hand, as if she needs to clutch all her possessions now, have no one else touching them. Drinks deeply. 'We used to have so many balls here, didn't we? This very room . . .' She starts to cry. 'It held all my happiness once. The summer ball. Bunty Shearer with his shotgun, Boo Kessel-Jones dressed as a polar bear. The Harvest festival ball. The thanksgiving services in the chapel. Remember, Dari? The chapel! Desecrated! They used the altar as an operating table, those army brutes. The Mayday ball. Flora Caddy in her sky-blue dress with her shouty-red lips. Flora Caddy. Got what she deserved, didn't she?' Lady Adora wags a finger in my face. 'You'll have to hurry if you want to get to her now, tiger girl. Save her? *What*?' She rounds on little Pin, who's now crying heartily, his lion mask trampled on the floor. 'Oh, she's beyond saving, boy.'

'Where *is* she?' I cry, the mission crumbling before my eyes.

Lady Adora spins around, oblivious. 'That midwinter ball when we all had to dress in white. The Hunt ball where Daddy was convinced I'd be married off.' She laughs bitterly. 'Married off . . .' Looks at us, muttering, then gazes at the ruined sweep of the room. 'What happened? Where's the band? Champagne, fireworks?' Suddenly focuses on

Bert, who's shrinking back. 'Thinking of taking over, aren't you, bat girl? Well, you cannot have our Icicle Illuminarium. No, no, you can't. Greedy, greedy. As for your mother, pah, forever haunting me, isn't she? Oh, I see your schemes, your grand plans, I read your mind.' She holds Bert's chin, hurting and tight. 'Want to redecorate?'

'No,' Bert sobs, squirming. 'I don't know what you're talking about.'

'Oh yes, you do. Rip apart. Swallow up. Conceal, change, grab. Like you own the place.' She spits at Bert, right in her face. 'Well, you can't have it. All the furs, the crystals from my chandeliers, you can't have any of them.' She rips the fur cape from Bert's back. 'This is mine.' Holds up a chipped dinner plate, then a goblet. 'All mine.' Smashes them both in triumph.

Bert shrinks back. 'This is not what we're here for.'

But Her Ladyship isn't listening. 'No one forces me from this house. You've come to check it out, haven't you? To drive me out. Oh, they all do. Everyone wants it.'

'We didn't ask to be here,' I butt in but it's no use.

'Swinging on my chandeliers, sizing up what you'd like. For Flora Caddy with her red lips to swan around in.' Like an animal, she hisses, 'Well, she's not getting it.'

'*Where is she?*' I scream.

'Where you'll be going very soon, girl.' She's mad, utterly mad. 'Squeedly, lock them up. Out of my sight.' We back out. Need to run. She's in the way, Silent Mountain's at the door. 'How did this happen? How did I allow it? Lapse. All lapse. Oh yes. I cannot see them anymore, can't bear their sight. If I see them again, I'm getting the hunting rifles out. Bang! Bang! Ladyboat indeed.' She's right in Pin's terrified face now. 'Urgh. Everything they remind me of. The new world, the *brave* new world. All that energy. Living to a hundred years, oh yes.' She looks at Darius in a challenge, hands on hips.

'Madam?' Mrs Squeedly says, faint.

'Impediments, impediments. We're running out of time. Darius!'

'Your Ladyship,' Darius whispers urgently, trying to shut her down.

'Off to London. Tonight. Everything's taking too long,' she whines petulantly. 'I'm getting impatient, Dari. We could do with some action here. You need to visit your friend some time. We need . . . clarification.'

'Mummy,' Pin sobs loud; it's all become too much.

Lady Adora looks at him in wonder. 'Your mother?' She smiles. 'Let me tell you about mothers abandoning children. No, can't.' It's like she's having two conversations at once in her head and is being driven mad by it. 'Oh yes, abandonment. I had to. So long ago. For the house, for the best. No one wanted him. Why can't we forget? Move on.' She shakes her head, holds it tight. Pin continues howling, the rest of us are speechless with shock. What is she talking about? 'Some mothers aren't very good at being mothers, you know. Because of what they do. External pressures. Oh, tell me about it.'

I look at her – this woman who calls her daughter 'Lump' to her face. One thing my mum was, always, was my champion. 'I'm your rock, Kick,' she'd say, 'never forget it, no one will champion you more than I do. You can always come to me, with anything – and I'll be there for you.' I try to shake Lady Adora's poison out of my head as Bert cries that we have to get home, that there's no point in us being here because she's mad, raving, she makes no sense.

'Uh uh uh!' Lady Adora sings. 'The tennis court, little mousies. Where you'll be locked up good and tight.'

We make a dash for the lawn via the French doors.

'STOOOOOOOOP!' she screams.

She's holding Pin.

Pinny! He's squirming, can't break loose from her grasp. She's hurting him, doesn't seem to notice. 'If you don't go up to the tennis court right now, your little lion cub gets shut in the cellar. For a very long time. A very, *very* long time.'

A gasp from Hebe. From all of us. Everyone looks at me. What to do? I look at Hebe. Hands in anguish over her ears again, mouthing 'Mummy, Mummy,' over and over. It's no use. Look at Pin's stricken face. He's crying, in pain.

'All right,' I whisper. 'All right. We'll go upstairs. Just give our brother back.'

Lady Adora pushes him roughly to us and I hold him and hold him, breathe him in deep, our precious boy, like I'll never give him up. Then we're marched off in defeat.

Bone was right: Lady Adora's getting more irrational by the moment; she's a tinderbox of unpredictability and who knows what she'll do next. Bert's right too: we need to get out of this. Fast. We're in too deep. And Darius is heading off to London tonight. With our only hope now – Dad's scarf in his pocket, for Bucket. And he's under instructions to seek out his friend, to get some clarification.

223

We can only presume that means finding Basti . . . and working out a way of executing their plans.

Noooooooooooo.

Frantically I count the days on my fingers, since Boxing Day, since we left the Reptilarium, since we came here. We were heading into a weekend, yes. Thursday, Friday, Saturday, is it Saturday? Yes! So, Sunday is tomorrow. Thank goodness! The one day of the week that Charlie Boo has off so Basti barricades himself in the Reptilarium and doesn't answer the door, to absolutely anyone, and Darius might not know this. So he'd have to wait until Monday at the earliest to visit him, and not too early because our uncle likes sleeping in, he only knows one ten o'clock in a day and it's not the early one. So, we have a day – one single day – to sort everything out.

Our last sight:

Hebe, staring after us, in silence. Her face broken with knowing. Aghast.

25

OUR NEW RECRUIT

'**Booooooo-ooooooooone?**'

We call out, as soon as we're back in the room and the door's safely shut. Where *is* that blasted boy? Because the mission has just failed spectacularly and we need to regroup here, try something else. Fast. With his help.

A hugely empty, hugely silent space.

He's not anywhere. Typical. And impossible. We've searched every inch of this room and just cannot work out how he constantly escapes and slips back. I stamp my foot in one big strop of exasperation. Need him, immediately. To get away from here. Have to have his knowledge of this building to escape. We'll go through cellars and tunnels and wall gaps if we must.

'The Bone Boy is ba-ack!'

A chirpy cry, suddenly, from the far end of the room. And there he is, walking merrily along a roof beam, dipping and skipping with the ever-faithful Dooky tucked under his arm and that enormous sunbeam of a smile on his face, not a care in the world. 'You rang, Company T?'

He leaps down, balancing the ball on his foot then bouncing it high on his heel, shin, calf, toes. I snatch Dooky up. 'No need for grumpiness,' he tuts. But there's no time for games here, mate. I tell him we need to break out because Lady Adora's absolutely mad, as he knows, and it's not safe for us anymore. Grabbing the ball back, he spins it on his finger and declares that he refuses to be left here on his lonesome.

'Come with us!' Bert cries. 'We'll take you to London. Find your family. Get you home.'

'Have no family. Am home.' He winks at her. Bert's whole body fills up with a smile. That's her staying with him, then.

'We're getting out of here now,' I snap. 'With your help. Even if curiosity for anything beyond this house isn't your specialty, mate.'

Uncharacteristic silence from the Bone Boy.

'You don't want to come with us, do you?' Pin's bottom lip trembles. 'You don't like us enough.'

'On the contrary, P. But oh, I have my grand plans, right here in this Illuminarium. For annexation.' He takes the little boy's hand. 'Can you keep a secret? An absolutely spiffing one? The bottom level will be turned into a zoo. All the leopards and lions will come back, and you can help me import the kangaroos. The middle level will be a hotel. Only for extra special guests, mind.' He winks at us. 'The top will be a skating rink. And a football pitch. No grown-ups allowed. The Squeedlys will be at the centre of the vast operation, running the show with brutal efficiency and purple uniforms and dinky little hats. I've got it all worked out.'

I roll my eyes in exasperation. This is Bone's world, his entire existence – it's all he's ever known, it seems.

'Besides, I need to be here, to drive Lady Adora mad. It's my sole purpose in life,' he declares with the cheekiest of grins. Urgh, I wish he'd just be serious for once.

'Plus I'm waiting.'

'For *what*?' Scruff says.

'For life to turn,' he smiles mysteriously.

'Okay.' I've had enough of his games. 'We get it. You don't need us. But we need you. So please just help us to get home from here.' I'm pleading like I've never pleaded in my life.

'You know, K, I wasn't meant to come near you when you arrived but I couldn't resist. Why? Because I needed friends. Company. Needed to know what it's like. I've led a very sheltered life, you know.'

'But we have to leave now.' I come right up close.

'I don't want you to.' He looks me straight in the eyes, absolutely serious, no games anymore. 'I . . . can't.' He's so confident . . . but not.

'Why?' We all yell.

'Because you're friends. At last.'

Gosh. The boy with the smile that could enchant an entire room suddenly seems very small, and lost, and alone. And I can tell that he's being honest here. His true self. And that it's really hard for him. He doesn't want us gone; doesn't want to be alone; without friends, all over again. I smile in understanding.

'If we really are your mates, you'd help us to get out of here,' Scruff hrumphs. 'You didn't see what that mad lady did down there. Pin almost ended up in a cellar. For good.' Our little brother yelps and scrunches into me. Bone shrugs it off.

'All right,' I announce, 'I'm going ahead myself from now on. Company T, you stay put. I'm going alone. I've caused enough problems already.'

'Hang on, hang on, you can't.' Bert stands square in front of me. 'We Caddy kids do not split up. Dad wouldn't want it. It's four of us together – or nothing. I don't want it some new way – and neither do the rest of us, Kick.' I look at her in astonishment: this is the sister who never lets an opportunity pass to tell us how wrong I am. 'And besides, we need Basti on board here. Somehow. And Dad. You can't do this by yourself.' I look at her perplexed. 'Don't leave us,' she cries as if I'm the dolt brain who's just not getting it. 'We don't want you to.'

'Okay, okay.' I smile at her in a new, firmer truce. She needs me, and I need her. I get it. But before we can continue on with our mission, we have to decide our next step. I tell them we can't possibly bring Dad into it, he's too weak, and Basti's fighting days are over, especially with all that happened just before Christmas and the hunt for his Reptilarium. Bert snaps that Basti's all we've got.

I sigh. He is. So. We're stuck for now. Here, in this room, once again. With a Bone who isn't budging and doesn't seem to care about some old guy in London. Time to turn in, for all of us. It's been a long, exhausting day – and night. We need our rest – for whatever's ahead.

❦

The next day we work on our ghostly friend all over again – but he doesn't soften. I strop away, gazing endlessly out the window, biting nails myself now, joining in with Scruff. Can't stop pacing, fretting, worrying; about Darius in London and whether he'll actually visit Basti or not, about Basti's fragile mental state as he wonders where we are, about the scarf finding its way to Bucket. Will Darius come back here before he even gets to Basti? He's obsessed with Lady Adora, it's obvious, can't keep away from her, so he might. I bang the walls, the glass, the door – how to get out! Feel so useless.

The day lengthens, the frost is turning to an endless, soft drizzle and it feels like the house is melting; the land is fuzzy, the sea lost. Hebe doesn't come near us. Has she been banned? Are we too raw, grubby, loud? Too colonial? I bet she's locked in a room just like us. Poor thing, despite what Bone says. Poor us.

'Hebe?' Scruff yells at regular intervals. 'Heebs, we need a match. Where are your striker skills when I need them?' But just an echoing house answers back.

Finally, finally, the sound of a car. I race to the window. The familiar van! Of course! Darius mustn't have known about Uncle Basti's strict Sunday seclusions, his absolute refusal to open the door to anyone. That's why he's back, so swiftly, for his Lady Love-ora – he can't stay away from her. I bet Darius is just about to report that his friend Basti, most oddly, seemed to be out on this Sunday, but not to worry, he'll be returning to the Reptilarium soon to take care of things.

Which is why we have to work on our plan, fast. I gather Company T close. Except for the C.O., who hangs back, doing his pretend-snoring thing on his perch.

'Watch,' I exclaim, my heart swelling as my arms enfold them.

'What are you looking at over there?' Bone enquires.

'Darius's van. The back of it.'

Breaths held. The car halts. Darius gets out. Goes to the back of the van – Bert gasps in suspense – he takes out a bag. Carries it to the front of the house. Then a dog – a dog! – slips out the back of the car.

'Bucket!' we all yell.

'Sssssssshhhh,' I giggle. 'I knew she'd find the scent, Pinny, and it's all thanks to Dad's scarf.' I give him the biggest hug of thanks.

'I am the best!' Pin flashes a V for Victory sign, which gets muddled into three fingers at once. Our Bucky girl has been following Darius's coat without him realising it, knowing that wherever he goes, we must be close. And she's probably been starving, trapped in the catacombs, unable to get out.

We fling open a window and whistle low on the wind, the way we learnt to in the bush, from Dad. Our old hunting signal. Instantly her ears prick up. She gazes up, straight at us. We wave frantically. But Darius! Coming back to the van! Quick, girl, move away! Bert gives a warning whistle, directing her, but she's onto it. She slips under the car. Waits.

Darius retrieves another carpet bag, oblivious, and returns to the house.

When he's gone our girl slinks in behind him. We rush to the door, it won't be long. After a few minutes we can hear her whining and pawing on the other side of the wood. 'Atta girl, sssssshhhh, oh you beautiful thing, you!' Then we hear something else. The heavy footfalls of Silent Mountain bringing up food. Stopping at one point; as if the steps are too steep for him, too much of an effort; but he's determined to do it.

Bucket goes quiet. Growls low. 'Sssshh, girl,' I whisper. 'Don't attack. Sit.'

'Bone?' Bert cries out. 'We need you here. To explain about our dog. Quick.'

'Oh, do I have to?' He yawns from his lazy perch.

'Yes. Now,' Bert snaps like Mum used to at Dad.

A great crash of a tray tumbling to the floor. Mr Squeedly's shock, no doubt, at the sight of a dingo by our door.

'It's okay,' Bone yells, looking at me, then scrambling over with a salute to Bert. 'She's with us. I mean, them. It's their dog. She's found them. Followed, sniffed them out or something. Is that right? They just want a cuddle or whatever it is that dog people do. Can she come in?' He looks at Bert, she nods. We all press our ears to the door. No sound.

The door slowly opens. Bucket slips in as it's opened, whimpering and yelping her happiness to see us. 'Sssh, girl, no barking,' I laugh. We all roll on the floor with her in one licky, squeezy, waggy-taily bundle of amazement. She made it. Our brave, clever Bucky girl. Silent Mountain looks at Bone, asking, why are you here, what's going on? Bone just shrugs a cheeky grin of 'what?' The man's eyes raise to the heavens, like the boy is beyond help.

Our dingo girl gets all the food we've got. Wolfs everything down in great gulps then Bone slips out with Mr Squeedly to get something else for her. We don't know when it was the last time she ate, but we can feel her rib bones too much. She doesn't care – she's licking us so crazily like she'll lick our faces off.

Right. I get down to business. Time's running out. Scribble a note on a torn-out ad from an old tennis magazine.

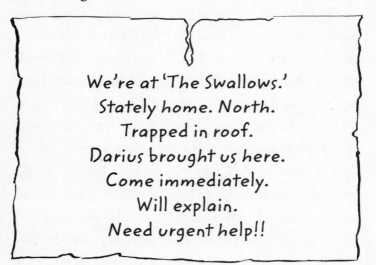

We're at 'The Swallows.'
Stately home. North.
Trapped in roof.
Darius brought us here.
Come immediately.
Will explain.
Need urgent help!!

'We need our names,' Scruff says. 'I don't think he's ever seen our handwriting. What's a codename he'll recognise, Company T? So that he knows no one's forged the note and it's really us.'

'Excuse me.' Bert grabs the pen. 'We have one unique call sign here.' She signs the note:

Childus Desertus
Australis

Of course. His nickname, collectively, for the crazy desert addition to the family. 'Brilliant!'

Pin adds a kiss and a cuddle. 'Will Basti bring the police?' he asks.

'No. They'll only draw attention to the Reptilarium, so he's stuck.' I frown. 'He has no one to turn to, actually. Except Charlie Boo.'

We look at each other doubtfully. Will our uncle and Charlie Boo be enough? Basti's a bit hopeless, has been all his life; since the Great War when it all went wrong for him, and that was a long, long time ago. It feels like we're calling on a ninety-nine-year-old crippled grandmother to climb Mount Everest here. All by herself, without alerting anyone. But it's our only chance.

'We just need to have faith, troops.' I tuck the note under Bucket's collar then ask Pin for our uncle's sleeping cap still around Banjo's neck. Solemnly, without any trauma this time, he hands it over. 'Anything for Basti.' I let Bucket sniff it then with both hands hold her beautiful wet nose close to mine. Stare into her eyes. Say that she has to go to Basti, find him. Have her sniff the cap again. She has to head back to London, with Darius, in his van. I take her to the window, point to the vehicle, tell her over and over again, 'Basti.' Because Darius might be heading to our uncle, or Basti might go back to the cemetery to have another stab at working things out, or Bucket might be clever enough to use her amazing tracking skills to find her way back to him. I have no idea if it will work, but it's worth a shot. Because Mum said to me once that the only failure in life is in doing nothing. To just keep trying and trying because you never know what one day might, miraculously, work.

I give our dingo girl a kiss. She licks me in obedience, her keen, warm eyes brimming with intelligence. 'Atta girl,' I hold her tight.

Later, when Mr Squeedly collects the empty plates, a well-fed Bucket slips out. Within minutes we see her by the van, waiting for the moment when it's opened to slip inside. Bone sighs that she could never be *that* impressive. I bet him an entire lesson of football tricks with Dooky that she'll do it. We shake on it.

Actually, I'm not sure myself that she'll make it back to Basti, but I don't tell anyone that. This is our best bet. Our only bet. It *has* to work. Scruff whispers that our dog's never done anything as massive as this. She'll be fine, just you wait, I soothe.

Crossing fingers behind my back.

26

DOLLHOUSES

**The next day. A tentative knock on the door.
Like no knock we know.**

Extremely un-Bone-like. But he's not here, so
can't interpret. 'Hello?' Scruff yells out. No answer.
Slowly the bolt slides back. Breaths held. What now?
Who?

Hebe. Standing awkward before us. As if she's
been caught out; no one must know. She's looking
fearfully behind her. Can't read her face, which is
encased in an enormous blush.

'I—I found something.'

'What?' 'Hebe!' 'It's so good to see you!' 'Come in.'

'No time. But you might want to see this. Quickly.
You mustn't be seen.'

238

Pin tugs me back, remembering Bone's words of warning about her no doubt. 'It might be a trap, Kicky.'

I shake my head. She's offering us a way out of this room. *A way out.* 'We can't leave any stone unturned, little man. I'm with you. Trust me.' I nod to Hebe.

She smiles, shyly; tells Pin he'll like it, she promises. She leads us a back way down a tiny corridor and narrow service steps, nervous, jumpy. Mr Squeedly is waiting outside, in a car. What? Silent Mountain says nothing. Of course. Very silent and very mountainous. Doesn't look at us, doesn't have any expression on his face, just stares dead ahead. Hebe tells us to get inside, fast; to crouch low on the floor next to the seats at the back. 'Keep your heads down. I'm not meant to have anything to do with you. Mum will kill me if she sees us. You're a bad influence,' she grins. I ask Mr Squeedly: what's happening, where are you taking us?

No answer. Hebe jumps into the front seat. 'I got him to help us. He's my servant, so he does what I say, of course, but . . . he's more than that – he gets me. He's very kind. He's known me since I was a baby. He doesn't talk to many people but he talks to me, even though he's painfully shy. I'm lucky.' She smiles at him. 'He's always been nice to me.

Even when Mum isn't.' A pause. We all know what she means. 'But this is hugely dangerous, so do everything I say, all right? Don't run off. Don't do anything you shouldn't. You haven't got long away from the room. Only an hour or so, but it'll be enough. *If* you do exactly what I say.'

'Where are we going?' Scruff asks.

She smiles. 'Enver. That abandoned village I told you about.' We gasp. 'There's something there you have to see. It was taken over by the War Office a month before Christmas in 1943. They used it to train the US soldiers preparing for the D-Day landings. The place was evacuated, and the village just vanished off the maps. The villagers were praised for their great sacrifice, and promised that their houses would be returned after the war. But it's not looking likely, is it, Mr Squeedly?' He nods. 'Some of them were really upset, but they were seen as these amazing heroes for supporting the war effort. It's still out of bounds to everyone.' She grins, quite someone else. 'Except us.'

'Will Mr Squeedly get us in trouble?' Pin asks.

'Mr Squeedly has a key to the gate, Pin. A big wire fence surrounds Enver, but his dear little son is buried in the church graveyard. He knew someone in the War Office who gave him a secret key. He used to live in the village. Most of the help did.' She pauses, touches the man's shoulder. 'The key is so that Mr and Mrs Squeedly can visit their son whenever they like.' Bert thanks him softly; Silent Mountain nods, his face granite. I want to reach over and touch him in thanks but don't dare.

'I come with the two of them now and then,' Hebe says. 'When Mum's been mean to me and I need to get out of the house. I love being in the fresh air, away from everything.' She shivers. 'The Squeedlys understand that. They don't dare get close to you because my mother has expressly forbidden it, but I think it's more than that – they had a huge loss, and don't want to extend themselves to anyone who might disappear from their lives in an instant.'

'Why would we be disappearing?' Scruff asks.

'I don't know,' she shrugs. 'But Mum told me you might.'

All the more reason to get out of this situation sooner rather than later, I think. Scruff's on my wavelength; he whispers to me that we could escape while we're in the village, find a way out, it's a good chance. Hebe says she can hear us, and tells us not to even think of it because we'll really want to see what she's about to show us.

'But can we trust you?' I look at Pin, who's trembling and not trusting anything at this point.

'You can't,' she laughs, 'but you'll just have to.'

The car stops by a tall gate in a wire fence:

DANGER.
NO PUBLIC ACCESS.
UNEXPLODED SHELLS.

Bert asks what shells are. Bombs, Hebe replies. Pin trembles even more violently. I smile bravely because at this moment we have no choice but to trust everything here – there's nothing else.

We drive past the abandoned church, all alone in the middle of a mishmash of tank tracks. The gravestones lean violently back in unison as if in shock at the endless blasts they've been subjected to – but it's probably the wind that's done it. It's howling straight off the ocean right now, straight through us. And no hands have been here of course, for years, to set the gravestones straight. The battered ruins of houses stand forlorn in the main street. Sandbags are piled high in some windows, barbed wire wraps others. Grass grows up through the road and laps at the doors. A rusty bicycle leans against a lamp post.

'Enver Court' is a manor house at the edge of the main street, with sheets of corrugated iron across its windows. Bert gasps at the possibilities in it – the house would have been beautiful once.

We get out of the car. Mr Squeedly stays in the driver's seat, stares ahead, lost in his thoughts. We walk the ghost village beside Hebe, who strides confidently through it like she's done this many times before, alone; in her very own playground. It's eerily empty, unearthly quiet. Even the birds have fled, as well as the ghosts; everything blasted out. We wipe dust from the windows of the village shop that has bullet holes pockmarking its walls. Step inside. Rusty tins of food are still on the shelves. A till has a few lonely pennies in it.

'Any lollies?' Scruff asks.

'Sorry. Gobbled them up long ago.' Hebe rubs her tummy. 'They were good.'

'Torture!' Then Scruff's eyes light up at a concrete bunker box with slits on its sides lying across the road. 'About turn, P!' Behind it is a rusty tank, the ground rising up and swallowing its wheels like the earth is a mud ocean in this place. The boys disappear into their bliss. A nearby sign reads:

DANGER.
UNEXPLODED MILITARY DEBRIS.
DO NOT LEAVE THE CARRIAGEWAY
UNDER ANY CIRCUMSTANCES.

But the boys ignore it, as does Hebe. She runs across to them. So do Bert and I. 'Should we be scared?' I ask nervously. Nope, she responds with a shake of her head – she trusts the Squeedlys completely.

Scruff yells across his approval: it's the best playground ever! We girls stand back and watch the boys being boys. I ask Hebe if she's excited about getting The Swallows one day and she tells me that she might end up with this playground, too, if she's lucky. She shivers that she wouldn't be wanting her family's big, ghosty house under any circumstances.

'That mouldy old thing? Urgh. It's only brought my family misery. Oh no, I want a cosy little flat in London with a gaslight heater and a wireless in the kitchen and a ginger cat on the window sill. In Soho. With a cake shop right by Covent Garden tube station. I want to spend all day baking. I've got it planned. I use the shop here as practice.'

'Hebe Ellicott, you are something else,' I murmur. Because you could have knocked us down with a feather.

'And anyway, I'm just a girl, so I'll never inherit. It'll go to some musty old cousin or something. Mum's fighting it but she has no hope. She's deluded. It's how it works here and has since the year dot.'

'That's appalling!' Bert says. 'Just because we're girls we've got just as much right as anyone.'

'Try telling the system that. We only get a girl queen when they've exhausted everyone else who could possibly do it.'

'It'd never happen in my world,' I say. 'Dad wouldn't allow it and neither would I. Or Mum.'

'Lucky you,' Hebe says, looking at her watch. Then she tells us we have to get a move on, because we're running out of time. We need to get to the classroom, fast. What is she so insistent about checking out in there?

But Hebe won't tell us. Just grins in a way that entirely changes her face: like she's triumphed with something in her life, at last. I step in line beside her, close, as she heads towards the school.

Bone, I am liking this girl more and more. Sorry, mate.

27

THE CLASSROOM'S
SECRET

'The *school*? No way,' Scruff yells. 'I'm allergic to it.'

'Me too!' Pin starts coughing violently.

'Not convinced,' Hebe says, grabbing Pin's hand and marching him kicking and screaming straight into the one-room school building. I follow, heart singing. A school means books!

On our way we pass by an abandoned set of child's crayons. Several slates on the floor. A broken abacus. Hebe stands at the end of the room, at the old school marm's desk with its seat attached. Hands clutching the back of it like a war general about to impart details for the final battle. By instinct, we all sit. She raises an eyebrow. A new Hebe entirely.

Ready? Oh yes.

She opens the lid of the teacher's desk with great officiousness. Lifts something out. Holds it to her chest. Steps in front of us, her face flushed with the deliciousness of her secret.

It's an old, worn leather satchel. She hands it across. To me.

'I found this a while ago. It's been here for ages. But I only twigged the other night, during our ball. You might want to have a look inside.'

My heart lurches.

I know it, of course. All us Caddys do. And now the tears prick. My mouth is dry as I turn it over, run my fingers across it, breathe in the leather deep.

Mum's. *Mum's.*

Here.

It lived on the wooden hook behind her bedroom door, along with her straw hat with its netting for flies that I haven't been able to put on since, because it smells of her hair, still; Bert neither. Mum used to take this battered old satchel with her on trips to Alice Springs, the Big Smoke; on sketching expeditions into the desert; on cattle musters and bush picnics. Aunt Alice smirked at Flora's strange ways – the bag was so unladylike and practical and blunt – but Mum loved it for exactly that. 'It fits my life in it, Kicky,' she told me once. 'A notebook, a purse, a lipstick, a book. All that's needed. Oh, and love. Of course.'

'Mum,' Scruff whispers.

I croak, 'Yes.' We haven't seen the satchel for years. Since she left. With trembling hands I lift open the flap, the others gather close. Nothing inside but a dried-up lipstick, *her* lipstick, a fiery red; and a book. *The Mill on the Floss.*

'What's a floss?' Bert asks.

'A river, I think,' Hebe says.

I flip open the volume. To the familiar bookplate in all her books, a woodcut of an oak and a swirly sky and a wooden house with a little round window. The name: *Flora Caddy*. Bold in her lovely, distinctive copperplate. As it always was, in all her books, which she treasured. And taught us to. 'HINC EST' is in a scroll on the bottom of the house. Her family motto: 'Curiosity is All.'

And now I weep.

As we crowd around the teacher's desk and flip through the thin, fragile pages we come across a curl of the finest, softest reddy-gold baby hair, then another, and another, and another; all carefully wrapped in a sliver of tissue paper with our names on each in that bold copperplate. *Ralph. Albertina.*

Phineas. Thomasina. But I can barely read as the tears come fast now, blurring the careful ink.

We stare at each other. Prickles up our backs.

'She knew she was going somewhere that night we last saw her,' Bert whispers. 'She must have packed this bag on purpose. It was her security blanket. I remember her telling me once that when she had it with her – and her lipstick on – everything was right with the world. She could face anything.'

'She'd never abandon it.' Scruff punches the air with his fist.

'Not with us in it!' Pin exclaims.

I know, I know. Shutting my eyes on all of it. Because for years I've felt I was somehow responsible for her leaving and I've never told anyone this. That my horribly, tantrumy, attacking words – *'Go away, I want any mother but you, I want someone else'* – had forced her to abandon us, in despair, to just run off. That it was all my fault. But no. Not according to this. Someone else took her here, to this place. And then away from it. By force. She had to leave this satchel behind. Or she didn't get a chance to take it.

And I am released. Can't talk, I'm so filled up.

Bert holds Hebe by the shoulders. 'Your mum said we were close – the other night – when she was talking about our mum. What did she mean by that? Was our mother here once?'

'She must have been. Perhaps. I've no idea, I'm sorry. We need to get back now. We're running out of time. I'll get in so much trouble . . .'

'She knows, she's lying!' Pin cries.

'I don't think so,' I say soft.

Hebe smiles her thanks.

'The satchel could have been here for weeks. Years. When did you find it?' Scruff asks.

'I'd seen it ages ago and just left it here. I can't remember when exactly. Then when Mother mentioned Flora Caddy the other night I thought, hang on, where do I know that name from? Then it dawned. The old bag in the desk. With the book in it.'

I clutch it to my chest, can't let it go. Is it a sign? From Mum. A signal that we're on the right track? She knows I'm a bookworm and wouldn't pass up the opportunity to explore an old school room. She knows I'd eventually be looking in the teacher's desk because I'm such a bossy boots, teachery-kind-of-person myself. Did she guess we might one day find our way to this place?

I pass the book to Bert and hold the abandoned lipstick to my nose – not a trace of scent left; it stopped being used long ago. Mum hated appearing anywhere without it. She was taken by force, must have been.

'She didn't leave here voluntarily, troops,' Bert says, echoing my thoughts. 'Hebe, are there any other clues about Mum?'

'No, just the bag. Take it, Kick. Come on. We haven't got much time.'

Mum would never deliberately abandon her belongings. Or she'd come back to them once she knew they were gone. Goosebumps. Unless she couldn't come back, unless she's still trapped. Out there somewhere. Waiting for Dad.

For us.

'We could make a run for it,' Scruff says, looking around. 'Right now. Get to the bottom of this, away from here. Back at the Reptilarium.'

'But Basti —' Pin leaps in.

'If you escape on my watch I'll be in so much trouble.' Hebe pleads, 'Please, for my sake, just go back to your room. For now. Don't do this to me.' I stare at her. 'I thought you were my friends,' she says quiet.

Standoff.

Her face tells us she's expecting us to let her down, just like all the others do. Scruff's right, we could easily make a run for it; find a way to a train station, to London. The hunch in Hebe's shoulders has already absorbed the betrayal. The devastation, all over again. She doesn't deserve it. Not after the gift of this satchel. She took a huge risk in getting us here and in handing it across. 'Mum will kill me,' she whispers despairingly.

Oh, we don't doubt it.

I smile. 'Come on, Hebe Hedgehog. Let's get back. We won't let you down.'

'Thank you, Kick, thank you.' She's almost crying with relief.

'No, thank *you*,' I say, placing the book back in the satchel and clutching the precious find to my chest. We're never giving this up now.

The car on the way home is heavy with silence, thick and rich. Trying to work it out. All four of us. So, Mum was here. Then not. And she left behind something she'd always take with her. And now – what a coincidence – we found it. Setting us more firmly on the path to finding her. Yet it could have been left years ago. And there's nothing else, no other clue. Except whatever Lady Adora knows. The key is tied up somehow in her Icicle Illuminarium and its past army existence and Mum must have been immersed in it, once, yes.

Everything is connected – but how? Bone said he learnt his master spying from people who were stationed here once, his Escape and Evasion Unit. Did they use the village as practice?

I stare at the mysterious great estate ahead of us, on the horizon, and wonder about all the secrets it still holds: we need some illuminating here ourselves.

I hold my head. It doesn't make sense, any of it. We all peer back at rusted tanks and buildings boarded up, at the eerie emptiness of the abandoned village. Then as the enormous house comes closer we Caddys, one by one, slip below the seats.

For Hebe's sake, as much as anything else.

'Do you feel it?' Bert says, crammed next to me and squeezing my hand.

'Yes,' I whisper, 'yes.'

She smiles. 'Me too.'

Mum, close.

28

THE ARRIVAL

Back in the tennis room. Pacing. Thumping the walls.

Mum's out there somewhere. While we're here. Waiting for a car, a Basti, a Bucket, something, anything, to haul us out. Waiting because we couldn't let Hebe down, because we promised her. Hebe Hebe Hebe – whose side is she on? We're here because of her. The wall is punched again. Is someone playing tricks on us? We take it in turns to scour the horizon with a pair of referee's binoculars. A day of sharp, happy blue is fast disappearing and we need to be out in it, getting things done, as the clock ticks endlessly on. Mum's waiting . . .

A car.

We crowd at the window, peering out. Willing our world to change, come on!

Darius's van, screeching to a stop in front of the house. He bounds out and dashes up the steps.

But nothing else. One by one we slink dejectedly away from the window, except for little Pin, who refuses to give up hope, the binoculars strung around his neck. 'Bucky has the sleeping cap, Kicky. Bucky won't let us down!'

'I know, little man, I know.'

About twenty minutes later, his sudden cry: 'Company T, look!' The rest of us rush back to the window, hearts pounding. Grab the binoculars. Because there behind Darius . . . completely unnoticed . . .

A lone figure walking up the driveway.

Wearing a jaunty green flying cap. A yellow jacket like a sunflower burst open to the light. Red trousers. A blue scarf. Round silver glasses and velvet slippers with initials embroidered on them in thread as golden as egg yolk. And a slow walk that says he's rather stunned to be in such a Basti-licious place.

YEEEEEEEEEEEEESSSSSSSSSSS!

We all cheer. Because we have before us, ladies and gentlemen, one Sebastian Caddy – in all his glory! Like he's landed from another world entirely and wearing his ceremonial best to celebrate. With sleeves scrunched up. For whatever may be ahead. We just know that his weapon of choice is a baby chameleon called Frederique in his left breast pocket because that is where she always lives ('Close to my heart.'). And his walk now looks charged with purpose, as if he's reminded himself of the real reason for being here: to sort his nieces and nephews out, to set the world right.

And Bucket, the Most Amazing Dog in the World, actually found her way to Basti, from Darius, with her secret note intact. How, goodness knows, but what a *champ*. I knew she wouldn't let us down. She never has.

But hang on, no – think, girl, think – we have to get to Basti immediately.

Warn him. Fast. Because he's walking boldly up the driveway with not a care in the world and will soon be in view of the house. Which will be dire. Because he has no idea of the danger he's in. Neither would we, when his rescue mission is discovered by the lady of the house. I suddenly realise our folly in writing the note to him; didn't think it through properly, should have made it clearer. Yes, we needed rescuing, but not by him directly, here, at the Illuminarium. Because now Lady Adora and

Darius have got us all where they want us: our frail, vulnerable uncle is walking straight into a trap. My fault. I got him here. I feel sick.

'Bucket's with him,' Bert reports through the binoculars. 'Just coming into view. Probably been distracted by the rabbits.'

Great. *Two* of them to rescue now.

Scruff now: 'Stand by. No sign of Charlie Boo.' Basti hasn't alerted him, most likely, thinks he can do this all by himself. Well, he can't. He needs us. I grab the binoculars. Basti's dressed ready for a rescue, on his terms, and it's an odd, madly wrong sight. He was once the golden boy of Campden Hill Square, of course, the tree climber extraordinaire who volunteered for the war at fifteen – but has been broken ever since. It'd take a lot to get him over the Reptilarium's threshold now. This expedition is big in his books, but he doesn't know exactly how big it's going to get. And he must have hidden his car – our only means of escape – somewhere near the entrance. Which means that freedom is an awfully long way away. For all of us.

Bert worries that's being a bit reckless, just walking in like that. Oh yes, girl, you're reading my thoughts. Our darling uncle is wonderfully precious and eccentric and adorable – and vulnerable. He won't have thought to change his will yet. Darius will know this. It's their big chance. To have him disappear, in a place at the end of the world, far removed from anyone else.

'Company T, about turn. We have to head him off before Lady Adora and Darius see him.' I look at my watch. 'We've got, I reckon, about twenty–twenty-five minutes before he comes into view.'

We all turn to Bone, asleep on his beam, snoring loudly; it's impossibly hard to wake him without alerting the house – or more likely, he's determined not to be woken up. Without a second's thought Bert swings up and straddles his chest. Tickles him awake while clinging on with her legs. 'Lazybones! Up! We need to get out of here. Right now,' she bosses.

'Our uncle's just arrived,' I add. 'He's walking up the drive as we speak. He's at that distant oak clump.' Scruff: 'We can see him through the binoculars and we need to head him off before he's seen by anyone else.'

'Uncle. Out? What?' Bone's taking his time, as he does, stretching slowly, rubbing his eyes.

'You've got to help us.' We're all crying.

'No, Company T, no, it's too hard. I might be discovered, I've told you that. *And* you. And you are not going to unravel – just like that – everything

I've got invested in this place. Which is a vast amount, actually. I love this house more than anything else, in case you haven't noticed. Except you, K.' He grins, Bert hrumphs. 'And you, B. And P. And S. But none of you will be the cause of my expulsion from it.'

'All right, all right. Just tell us how you get out of here then,' I reason.

A silence. 'Oh, right. Farewell. I see. No, you can't abandon me just like that, in an instant. It's too brutal.' He strokes Bert's hair. 'It was so much fun while it lasted, wasn't it? We could have been a great team.' (I tell you, she glows.) 'But no, you want to leave me here all on my ownsome. I'll get scared, K. I need you.' (Her glow stops.) 'I've grown used to it.' And in that moment, I've got his secret: Bone's one of those people who craves company, someone, anyone – and he'll never let us go if he has the chance.

Scruff tells him that we'll come back to him, we promise, we just need to swing this current mission into action. Right now.

I shake his hand and give him my word that we'll return. But will we? We must. Can't have the Bone Boy disappearing completely from our lives. He wonders aloud if he can trust us; holds his chin, thinks; shakes his head and after agonising seconds murmurs, nope, he's not that sure he can.

What? After all we've been through? Pin yells noooooo in indignation, the rest of us groan. I just want to shove Bone at this point. His games are driving us bananas and it feels like the sole purpose is to keep the spotlight firmly on one Lord Bone, C.O. of Company T, and no one else.

'General Bone,' I snap, 'this is Scale A – meaning huge. Repeat, huge. Someone we dearly love is about to walk into a deadly trap. Only you can save him. And us.' He looks bewildered, throws up his hands; the clock's ticking, he's not moving fast enough here. I look around. What does Bone love more than anything?

Dooky.

I jump up to the crossbeams the football is jammed in, grab it and hold it high.

'Pass!' Bert yells. On my wavelength. I lob it to her and take out Dad's hunting knife. 'I don't want to do this,' I say with the sharp point at the ball's flesh, ready to plunge. Pin and Scruff hold him back. We're all in this. Basti is too important. Sorry, mate. I whisper to him low, 'We need you to get us out of here. To tell us the secret of this room.' I ask him if he's really our friend. 'Or not,' Bert adds. Even *she* has had enough.

Bone looks wildly around, 'No, no, not my Dooky.' Looks directly at Bert. 'Even you, B? How *could* you?'

Yep, even me, she nods grim. Bone screams with his hands over his ears: so, abandoned by everyone here.

We've got him. It's the only thing that will work. Don't want to do this but must. I prick Dooky with the tip of the knife, push its leather in, almost break it through. Bone yelps in pain like his own skin is being attacked. 'All right, all right!' He squeals, quite someone else.

We drop his arms.

'Because I love you,' he says in defeat, snatching the ball back. 'And Dooky.' Thinks, staring at the ball, taking deep breaths. Looks up, smiles sadly. 'I am the ghost of The Swallows, Company T, but yes, I may have a bit of ghostly help.' Pauses. 'And what I am about to show you . . . means with absolute surety that I will lose you.' Tears glitter in his eyes. I stare at him, tears too, yet this is so important for us. 'But if I must, I must.' He walks to the end of the tennis court. Glances back, rubs his hands, winks. 'Can Company T keep a secret?' His voice wobbles.

'Oh yes, yes, Commander Bone. Stand by.' I snatch up the binoculars, put the loop around my neck alongside Dad's hunting knife. Pin stuffs Banjo into his shorts, Scruff does the same with his sling-shot, Bert puts Mum's satchel diagonally across her chest. Right. The Escape and Evasion Unit is present and ready for action. Bone grabs an old ivory towel hook by the bathroom door. Twists it. 'Voila!' And bows a sad, courtly bow.

A soft whirring noise . . .

29
THROUGH THE
MAGIC GARDEN

A sliding panel!

It opens, just enough to squeeze through. 'Isn't it spiffing! Mr Squeedly knows this house even better than Her Ladyship,' Bone explains with chuff. 'And Mr Squeedly is my . . . friend. My very dear friend. My father, in a way. Ever since I was little. He tells me many, many secrets of this house.'

'Well, I wish he'd talk to us like he talks to others in this place,' I grumble.

'He's very shy. He's lost people before . . . those he was close to . . . he's just shut down, over the years. But he's a good egg, believe me. It's just that none of us know how long you'll be here. He wouldn't risk making a connection with people he might grow to like . . . and then . . . never see again. That's how he works.'

'Oh.' I stare at him. Not quite wanting to follow through with that. And all the more reason to get out of here, fast. 'Well, Company T, my watch says time to go.' I peer through the magic door. It opens into a store room.

'Come on.' Bone ushers us through, then rolls his eyes. 'Hang on, you'll never find your way out by yourselves, will you? Commander Bone to the rescue –' a dramatic sigh '– once again.' Many hands clap him on the back in joy. After all, a Bone rescue is the best rescue of the lot! The room is full of tennis racquets and a jumble of nets and, bizarrely, little suits of children's armour. Bert squeals at the sight and tells us she needs to come back to them. I jump in with no you don't.

'You do realise, Company T, that if I lead you to Basti you'll all be together,' Bone says. 'A delicious little bundle of Caddy . . . impediments. Which is just how Her Ladyship would like you. Just thought I'd pass that on.'

'Wha . . . at?' Pin shrinks back.

'For disposal. A job lot. Her grand plan a step closer to realisation.'

I know this well, but Pin is now wailing, turning to me; I drop down, squeeze his shoulders, can't have him bailing out on us at this point. 'Basti's out there, Pinny. Exposed. We have to save him. And stick together, little man. We're not coming back to this room. I promise, *promise*, I'll protect you. Trust me.'

Bone kneels down to Pin, right beside me. 'Hey listen, the C.O. of Company T has had a change of plan. He will now be going all the way here with his troops. Roger? He'll lead you into battle, don't you worry. Because I think you need some local knowledge, old chap. I don't get out into the grounds much because it's so risky – I might be seen by Lady Adora, or Darius, or Hebe – but when they're not in the house Mr Squeedly sometimes lets me out. I've learnt the lie of the land in little sorties over the years, and P – Captain P – needs a navigator, right? All the way to Basti's car.' Bone gets the most ferocious Pinny-squeeze of happiness in return.

I smile my thanks. 'Does this possibly mean no more gritchiness at me, Commander Bone? No more fury? A rare truce?'

'Yes.' A smile that brims me up, and we shake hands on it, me as firm as I can get it.

'Ow!' Bone exclaims.

'You've got to watch those desert girls,' I wink.

'Don't I know it,' he grimaces.

Scruff jumps in that we have to find Hebe fast, to say goodbye, we can't just leave her hanging here. I sigh – we'll find a way to her, somehow, just add it to the list.

'But why?' Bone protests. 'She's so awful. The Squeedlys have been telling me horror stories for years. Who cares about her?'

'We do!' We all chorus.

'Maybe they told you porkies because they just didn't want you going anywhere near her,' Bert snaps. 'Up here for thinking, mate.' She taps his brain. 'If she played with you, then she might have accidentally spilled the beans about her ghostly mate to Lady Adora, especially when she was younger.'

'This place is not called the Icicle Illuminarium for nothing,' I grin to him. 'Don't always believe everything that people tell you, Commander Bone. Trust your heart. And find out for yourself. She's a good egg.'

He looks at us oddly, like he's actually learning something here. 'Well, there it is, Company T. The Illuminarium . . . illuminates.' Then we race down the stairs used by the servants, through service corridors and storerooms, Bone leading the way. Burst through a vast conservatorium full of brown, brittle plants and dirty glass and weak winter light. Bone keeps glancing back – this is a huge risk for him, after all; his world will vanish if he's caught.

'Stand by, Company T.' We gather close, by the back door. 'There's a secret way, across country,' he whispers. 'I found it last summer, when Her Ladyship was in Italy, with Darius. I had the run of the garden for two blissful weeks.' Then he races in a zigzag through the grounds, taking cover by fences and stable walls. 'We'll head your uncle off just as he's passing the glasshouse. Then he can disappear into the garden. You all can. Sob! Just vanish. Be safe. It's through the undergrowth, but it'll get to him quickest. Are you ready for some thorns?' We nod, we're ready for anything. 'Then come on!'

We tear behind him. Crawl, Indian file, on hands and knees at one point under toppled moss-heavy oak. Huge tree trunks have twisted to get at the light and the path darkens; the world closing over us in a jumble of vine and ivy. Now we're on our chests, now standing under a spreading tree that feels like the great skirt of a Victorian giant. Down again, crawling, and it feels like we're entering an underworld of damp and vines and dirt.

We're getting scratched, torn, wet and puffed but we do not stop. Not even Pin, who never complains, never moans.

'How long have we got?' Scruff asks at one point.

'About five minutes.'

'Blast,' says Bone. 'This is more overgrown than I thought.'

'We're running out of time,' I cry. 'Faster, Company T!'

Bone leads us deep into a tangle of a forgotten garden, towards a tiny path ending at a gate that hasn't been opened for centuries. We're stuck. 'Boooooone!' Bert wails, furious. Scruff leaps straight in, tearing at the undergrowth, scrabbling at the gate. We join him, pushing and rocking, trying to break the lashings of brambles on the other side. *This is not going to defeat us.* Basti's close, so close, yet we can't yell out, can't have him shouting back and alerting the house. Finally, finally, the gate falls on its hinges. An enormous stone wall is ahead, plumped out as if it's been bloated by the sun and crowned with weeds that have found footholds on its rim.

'Through here!' Bone cries. A tiny opening, in the wall. Inside, a circular produce garden. Its beds still faintly there among a mess of weeds as tall as us.

On the far side, toppled, the peak of a greenhouse. Its wooden roof frame straining from nature's clutching like a person reaching from quicksand or an earthquake sunk church.

'There's a door in the fence! Through that greenhouse!' Bert yells. We thunder over shattered glass, crawl under a broken roof beam and crouch through the door that's almost completely covered in blackberry thorns. The bush grabs at our flesh – ow! – but no one stops. Basti, ahead. Finally.

'Don't break cover,' I warn. 'We can be seen from the house now.'

We flit behind the great trunks of the oaks, right alongside our oblivious uncle. I quickly scan the house with the binoculars. Catch Lady Adora in a turret, with Darius, gesturing and pointing. They've seen him. They're onto him. Noooooooooo. My heart sinks. This will be harder now. Bucket crashes into us with her joy. Thank goodness the house can't see her – or us.

'Uncle Basti,' I whisper when I'm close to him.

'Eh? What?' He jumps a mile, nervous, glancing around.

'It's Kick. Don't look at us! Just keep walking. Slowly. We're right beside you. Pretend nothing has happened – we aren't here.'

Lady Adora has left the turret. Can't see her anymore. Coming out to greet Basti, no doubt. Preparing for whatever's next.

'Could this be my little fanged Tassie tiger?' Basti sounds so relieved. 'Oh you're safe, you're found.'

I blush. 'Yes, it could well be me. But try not to talk. This is urgent. You're being watched. From the house. You can't do anything to alert them that something's up.'

'Right you are.' He stops, his hand covering his mouth as if he's cold. Good one, Basti. 'My plan was to get close enough to the house to sneak inside,' he explains through his fingers. 'Find you all. Release you. Charlie Boo is waiting by the gatehouse as we speak, the car hidden in bushes. I was hoping to set you free without any confrontation – I do hate attack of any kind, as you well know. When we are safely back in London you are to explain all this madness to me.'

'Stop talking, Basti!' I cry in despair. 'We need to think here. They're on to you.'

'But I'm so delighted to find you!' He walks on, his hand still over his mouth. 'I did miss you quite . . . forcefully . . . Miss Kick. Then I got the note from dear Bucket's collar and was so dreadfully worried. She just turned up on my doorstep, can you believe it?' Bucket gives a little yelp of appreciation, she knows we're talking about her. 'And the other little tiger cubs? All present and accounted for?'

'Yes, yes. I tried to get rid of them but it didn't work,' I say hurriedly.

'Splendid!'

'Basti. Concentrate. This is important.'

'But how thrilling that you lot are actually capable of being hidden and quiet for once. I've been trying to get that happening for days. What's the secret?'

'The secret is imminent death if you *don't listen*. You're in danger. They want to get rid of you. We're all in danger. We have to leave immediately. Get back to London. See your lawyer, Horatio, if we can possibly drag him away from that Henrietta Witchum Maggs.'

'Such a fragrant creature,' Basti says.

'We have to –' deep breath '– change your will.'

'My will? What? I haven't looked at it for years . . .'

'Make it out to anyone but Darius. The Snake Society of India, the Red Cross, whatever. Because Darius wants –'

'Darius?' Basti stops, stock-still. Goes deathly pale. Looks at the house, trying to work everything out here, his friend, the note he received from Bucket, us. 'But – but he's my best friend.'

'No, Basti, no.'

'Oh.' And in that soft 'oh' it's as if everything is suddenly dawning on him. His face is drained, bereft. 'My only friend . . . what did you say . . . my will?' He wipes his mouth like he's going to be sick. His fingers are suddenly trembling. Bucket gives him a lick. 'We need . . . we must . . . I – I don't know what to do,' he stumbles, holding his hand against a tree trunk as if to support the great body blow of what he's just learnt.

'K,' Bone jumps in. 'If Basti just turns around and runs away and disappears – they'll get mightily suspicious up at the house. Jump in the van. Drive after us. Shut the gates ahead. None of you will be able to get out and you'll be stuck in the grounds. With them, chasing after you. Where's your car, Mr Caddy?'

'B-By the gatehouse,' Basti stutters. 'Behind some bushes. But on this side of the estate. Mr Boo is waiting most patiently inside it, under instruction. I told him *I'd* be sorting this one out. It would be my moment of triumph. I gave him strict orders to stay put. Oh dear.'

'Well then, you'll never escape The Swallows and its grounds. Lady Adora knows every inch of it, as does Darius. You'll be starved out. Frozen. Trapped in here forever. All five of you. So just stop for a moment. We need to think this through.'

I stamp my foot. 'Do you actually have a plan, Bone Boy? We don't have long.'

'Actually, K, I do.' Bone smiles his smile that's as wide as a watermelon split. 'I've got Company T this far, remember? So don't go fighting your C.O. Surrender. To me.' I poke out my tongue. 'In other words, just trust me, if you possibly can, for the rest of this.'

I look at him dubiously. He nods. Winks. I smile and yes, urrrrrrrrgh, surrender. Flashing him a V for Victory sign. Pin grabs it down. 'Come on, Kicky,' he urges in terror, looking at Basti, at all of us.

He's right.

'Let's go!' I yell. Bucket barks in agreement.

30

FOLLOW ME

'**You want out, don't you? Well then, you'll just have to follow the most esteemed Lord Bone, commander of all secrets of the Illuminarium, as you well know.**'

He looks at me. A direct challenge. Bucket looks from one of us to the other, not knowing who to choose.

I hate following anyone, most of all a boy. Have to. Nod, setting an example here, especially to Pin. Basti, meanwhile, stops to tie one shoelace then the other. Stalling, waiting, listening.

'Okay, Mr Caddy,' Bone explains, loving being in charge. 'Just keep strolling as you're doing, right up the driveway.'

'I do love a plan,' Basti responds.

'Take it slowly. Look at the trees, the statues, pick some leaves. It buys us time. Then stop in the middle of the circular driveway, right by the entrance. But stay put. Don't go into the house, under any circumstances. Stall, so they have to come out to you. Then wait. And voila, your family will come to rescue you.'

The oak trees come alive with questions. 'How?' 'Where are *you*, Bone?' 'What are we going to do?' 'Don't bail on us!'

'Just do as I say. I'll point you in the right direction. We've got to get to the stables. See that tall roof through the trees –' we all look '– that's where we're headed. There are all these old bits of jeeps and tanks there, and there might be one that actually works.' He grins.

Scruff's eyes are shining. His face says it all: it's our big moment. 'Let's have some fun here, Bone Boy!'

Bone holds up his V for Victory sign. 'Drive you off into the sunset.'

Basti signals to us that he's got it. Rubs his hands down his trousers with the enormity of what's ahead. Slowly he walks on, stopping to examine the great grooves of tree trunks and staring with pretend-interest at the white laden trees that are like strange, still coral. But he's petrified, I can tell. His hands are shaking. He keeps on licking his lips in nervousness. This has to work; he has to get us out, and safe. And he's colluding with a bunch of kids here, including one he's never met in his life.

'Gunners ready?' Four Caddys and one dog nod to Bone. 'Stand by, we're going in.'

Four salutes and we're off, Bucket yappy at our heels. Heading to the stables, our quicksilver navigator always just ahead of us, urging us faster, faster, over fences and through broken gates, flitting past rhododendrons startled through bushes and tree roots like giant, slumbering lizards. Then a path of snow-streaked loam lifts back to reveal a gravel path, waiting for a waking.

'Guess where it leads to?' Bone whispers close.

'I don't know,' I snap, prickling up all of a sudden. That we're entrusting our lives to this enigma of a boy who has to make everything into a grand performance, even this, now; and that our darling Uncle Basti's heading for a very exposed gravel driveway to wait for a rescue that mightn't come. 'Don't be afraid, K.' Bone grabs both my hands, drawing me deeper into the undergrowth. 'Close your eyes. Trust me, just trust.'

I do, for a moment, then snap my eyes open. 'We have an uncle who needs saving here.'

'But of course!' The smile again. 'This way, through this hole in the hedge.' He disappears, we follow. Emerge into a small clearing. 'My magic fairy ring.' Bone sweeps his arm around it.

A flower garden. Almost completely dusted by snow-weighted weed. We spin. What's here? How can this help? Panicky breathing. In the far corner is an old summerhouse with three wide arches veiled by vines. 'K, your chariot awaits,' Bone bows low and indicates. We push through the tangle of weeds – expecting a lover's seat perhaps, the vast emptiness of another of Bone's pranks – but find something absolutely exhilarating and bang on: an old army jeep. Protected by dank coolness and crucially, miraculously, with a key still in its ignition. Bone says he recalls someone mentioning they could drive, but who, who?

'That might have been me,' I smile, running my hands over the rusty bonnet. Will it work? Will it save us? Dad taught me how to drive Matilda on my eleventh birthday – 'We'll make a man of you yet, Kick!' – but I'm not telling Bone that our car ended up in the dam.

'Kick drove our car into the d–' Scruff says excitedly. Bert's hand slams across his mouth.

'What?' Bone says, hauling vines off the jeep's seats.

'Desert. Once,' says Scruff, dejectedly.

'I got it working last summer,' Bone mutters. 'Well, started up. Then I didn't know how to proceed from that point.'

I look at the gears. The enormous steering wheel. Declare that I might be able to help because I'm an Aussie bush girl, after all, and everyone needs to stand back so I can show them what Aussie girls are made of! I jump into the front seat. Don't have a convenient brick to tie on the pedal but my legs are just long enough, I reckon, yep, I can do this. Kick the ignition over. A cough, a splutter. Again and again. Four tries and bingo, she roars into life. The others cheer. Three Caddys and one dog jump in around me. 'Yay, Kicky, yay!' 'Basti to the rescue!' 'Avoid the dams!' I ask Bone how we get to the house. He points vaguely, stepping back and saluting us in farewell.

'What? NO. You're coming too, mate. You've got to navigate,' I cry over the roar of the jeep.

'Do you really need me?' Bone sighs. 'You have Bucket, and besides, I have some crystal to polish.'

'We don't know the clearest path. We'll get stuck.'
I glare. 'Bone, we need you. *I* need you. Right now.'

'You don't need *anyone,* K.'

'Sometimes, actually, I do.'

He raises an eyebrow. Shakes his head with a smile. 'I'll remember that comment.' Climbs in. Pats me on the back then crouches behind the driver's seat, well hidden.

With screeching, grunting gears and then great kangaroo lurches – 'Hold on tight!' – we head joltingly towards the house. To the gravel drive. To Lady Adora, Darius and Hebe walking down the front steps. Adora has changed into a black velvet gown or what's left of it and spindly black heels; dressed for dinner and matching Basti, magnificently, in sartorial splendour. Hebe, in sky-blue satin, is cowed and pale by her side, not wanting a new guest, I can tell, not wanting any of this.

'Drive straight up to your uncle and haul him in,' Bone yells. 'Then leave the rest to your trusty navigator, K.'

I raise a thumb. Got it, Bone Boy. We'll grab Basti and tear away to the gatehouse and the waiting car and get us all safe and sound and then, only then, will we get back to the detective work on Mum. Work out how all the strands in this vast seething octopus of a mystery are connected; because they are, I just know it. We might have to return to the Illuminarium one day, to the army village and its school room and Hebe and Bone, but at least Charlie Boo and Dad will be on board and Basti will be out of Lady Adora's line of sight. Rock-solid safe. The main thing right now. Because we love him very much, and can't bear to see him hurt.

We career onto the gravel. Lurch with a kangaroo hop right by Basti, who's staring at us, at his friend Darius, at Lady Adora, at the whole crazy, cacophonous lot of it and suddenly looking very old and lost.

'Jump in!' we yell to our uncle as I swerve just slow enough for Basti to run and take a flying leap – he makes it! Head first, feet sticking out, then rights himself, flying cap still intact. 'I say! I jolly well say!' he says, breathless.

Adora and Darius are racing down the steps, yelling, 'Stop, stop!' Adora enormously wobbly in her heels.

'You Aussies are always doing it your way, aren't you?' Basti shakes his head in shock and I drive off in a jerky mess of joyous squealing and whooping and licking (Bucket). Straight onto the ornamental lawn. Whoops. 'Where am I going?' I shout to Bone.

'This way!' he roars, pointing to the sea. 'It's a shortcut to the entrance gate. Across country. Atta girl!'

'Stop immediately!' Darius yells, but we most certainly do not and the two of them dash to his van. He can't find his keys, gets out, pats himself down, retrieves them, revs up. 'Hebe!' Lady Adora commands. 'Get in the car immediately. Move, lump!'

'We have to get to my car – it's faster, more reliable – it'll save us,' Basti yells, nudging me aside, taking over the jeep's wheel, automatically snapping on his seatbelt and smoothing the ride out.

'This way!' Bone shouts behind his ear as the rest of us cling on for dear life, the car swerving and swaying around headless statues and topiary gone wild. Darius chases us through the grounds with Lady Adora leaning most unladylike out the window of his passenger seat, urging him on and yelling, 'Stop, obey, you appalling children, at *once*.'

Bone bobs up at one point and crashes back down. 'Lady Adora. She saw me,' he gasps, his face terrified and white. He holds my hand, clutches it.

'You've got to direct us, Bone Boy,' I cry. 'Don't give up on us now, just stay low.'

He smiles at me. 'Stand by, K, I'll draw the flak off you.' He rises, crouching behind Basti's shoulders, knowing full well the consequences of being seen by those following us. 'This way . . . left . . . along this path,' he directs, hoarse. 'Hold tight, Company T! It's a wild ride ahead. Follow the tank tracks.'

Whooooaaaaa, as we slip and slide and skid.

'Where are we going?' Basti yells at one point.

'Into the grass. Quicker. And harder for them to follow us.'

'Oh dear, my eyes aren't the best. Old age.'

'You can do it, Uncle Basti.' Bert squeezes his shoulder and Bucket barks.

'Barely, Miss Albertina.'

'To the left,' Bone directs.

Er, we seem to be heading straight to the sea. What's happening here? 'My car is near the gate-house,' Basti shouts.

'It's the shortcut.' Bone glances behind him, at Darius. 'They're gaining.' We all look: he's right.

Pin screams. 'Don't worry, Pinny,' I yell.

'No, Kick, it's a cliff!'

Aaaaaaaaaaaaahhhhhhhh!

Straight ahead, suddenly, a ravine, as we burst through a bank of trees. A ravine too-close and cut severely into the cliff. We hadn't noticed it until it was almost upon us. The trees go right up to the cliff edge at this place.

'The brakes!' Basti yells, pumping his leg on a pedal. 'They're not working properly.' He keeps pumping but can't slow the car down quick enough. He's swerving but can't do it sharply. 'Evacuate! Evacuate!' he yells to everyone.

'Quick, *out!*' Bone shouts as he leaps and tumbles in the grass, followed by Bert. 'Come on!' Bone yells furiously; Scruff's next and I'm literally throwing Pin out, he's clinging on tight as if I'm the best bet here of the lot but I'm absolutely not and over he goes, flung. Rolling in the grass, bobbing up. Safe. Phew.

'I can't get . . .' Basti's scrabbling at his seatbelt. 'It's stuck. In the clasp. Quick, Kick. MOVE. *GOOOoooooooo!*'

Bucket's whining and barking and refusing to jump, she's nudging at my neck – Dad's hunting knife – of course, where it always is, and I'm scrambling for it and get it out and saw and saw and saw at the belt, cutting my hand in the process and ripping Basti free and he jumps up into the air like a diver scrabbling for a last breath as I dive out just as the jeep turns, turns, then careers over the edge of the cliff.

Noooooooooooooooooooooooo!

Basti leaps up to a branch of a tree growing stubbornly on the cliff edge, grabs it and holds tight.

He's okay.

I laugh. He's all right.

He swings around on his two hands like a monkey, checks we're all accounted for in the long grass and yells cheerily, 'I told you I was once the number one Master Tree Climber of the Universe, troops.'

'Bucky!' Pin cries in anguish.

What?

Oh. Bucket's not here. SHE'S NOT WITH US.

No, please no.

We look wildly around. Nope, she's not in the grass, bobbing up like the rest of us, not anywhere in sight.

I feel sick. The jeep. She's in the fallen jeep. Still.

We rush over to the edge of the cliff. Darius's van has just arrived. The three of them get out and peer over, too.

The jeep has landed upside down. No sign of our beautiful girl on the sand.

No, no, no.

'What are we looking at?' Hebe asks.

None of us Caddys can answer.

Our hearts too full in our mouths.

OUR GIRL

At the bottom of the steep cliff, the smoking wreck of the jeep.

Silence. A long way down, the black prows of rocks jutting out of the water like battleships. The sand almost black, as if a permanent smear of coal has been stained into it. Flat, grey waves.

And Bucket?

No sound.

'Where is she?' Bert whispers.

'She must be under the car.' It's really hard to speak here, to push words out.

'Get her, Kicky.' Pin tugs at me.

I nod. But this is something I quite possibly can't make right, little fella, and how do I tell him that? That I don't want him to see her broken.

Gone. Perhaps.

A lone bird calls from a wide slit in the cliff like it's trapped in a high room but it can't be, of course; it's the saddest, most forlorn cry I've ever heard in my life. But there's no bark, no whining, no whimpering. No sound of the most beautiful, smartest, bravest dingo in the world. Who shouldn't be in this world in the first place.

The steep, slippery cliff will be hard to get down. It's as tall as a double-decker bus. Even the rocks are tinged a moss green.

'I'll do it.' Uncle Basti looks at me soft like he's reading my thoughts. He's down in a flash – the golden boy of Campden Hill Square once, of course – grabbing on to tree branches that are growing almost horizontally out of the rock face. He looks up at us with infinite sadness when he gets to the smoking wreck of the car, takes a deep breath, then peers underneath.

'She's alive! Quick.'

'We're coming!' 'Hang on!'

Uncle Basti dashes back up the cliff and leads us Caddys down one by one – 'Careful, careful' –

showing us footholds and branches to cling to, guiding and lifting where he can. We peer under the upturned jeep. Alive, just, yes. Our darling girl. Hurt. In terrible pain. I can see it in her eyes, which stare out at us, pleading. For what?

She whimpers. I hold my hand across my mouth in horror. *'Keep her close, she'll look after you,'* they were the last words Dad spoke to me about our Bucky girl and look what I've done. What I've lured her into.

Smearing away furious tears I crawl under the smoking wreck. 'Kick!' 'No!' 'Careful!' everyone's shouting behind me but I have to get to her, hold her, feel her warmth. I've got her, I'm here, Kicky's with you, lovely girl. She can still lick, oh yes. She licks my face like she wants to lick it right off, like she always does.

'Hey, hey,' I murmur, laughing, crying. 'It's okay, I'm getting you out of here.' I gather her huge, floppy weight and push and drag her through tears into the open air and Bert and Scruff take her the last bit into it, then we all drop to her, stroke her and kiss. One of her hind legs hangs limp; it's been crushed. Her speaking brown eyes look at us, pleading, then close in agony to mere slits. I hold her tight, we all do; tell her we love her; she's so brave, our girl.

'Kicky? No, Kicky, no,' Pin shakes his head, stepping back, not believing it, not understanding.

I shake my head, crying, 'I don't know, Pinny. I just don't know.'

As my head is turned to my brother's anguish, a soft lick on my neck.

Then another.

I turn to Bucket, and as I stare into her soft eyes she licks me again, on the lips, as if to say, 'Hey, shhh, I can do this. Come on.'

'Actually, Pin, actually –' a whole smile is filling me up here '– we might be okay here. We just need to get her out. Get her fixed.' Cheering all around me. And from Bucket, a bark that turns into a yelp, but it's enough: our girl is with us, she's back. Just. I close my eyes in thanks.

Then glance up to the empty, milky sky. The cliff the jeep careered over. The three people peering over, but not the one who led us into all this. Of course.

The dragon inside me is roaring up. Because this one person needs to be here. To explain, to apologise, to show his face; to show us he's okay if nothing else. But it's one person who's completely, spectacularly gone – and why would we expect anything else? As soon as Commander Bone leapt from the jeep and rolled through the long grass he was out of here, vanished. Lord of this place who led us to this cliff – deliberately or not, mortifed or not. Where is he now?

'Booooooooooone,' I howl furiously, to the sky, the wind, the trees, summoning him forth.

Only the gentle slap of the sea answers me. And Bert's soft keening, as she cradles Bucket's head in her lap.

'Bone!' Scruff stands strong next to me. 'Where are you? Are you all right?'

'Who's Bone?' Adora yells down at us.

'Wait, we're coming,' I say. Basti lifts up the injured Bucket, ever so gently; we all help him.

'So sorry, sorry, your poor dog,' Lady Adora says as we near the top. 'Oh dear. This cliff. Back, back. We should bail out, don't you think? Don't like it here, no. Ghosts. Shouldn't be here. Hasn't changed. And your jeep, the chase, and here we are. Goodness, all of it. Ropey, ropey to be in this place. Haven't been back –' She nods to Basti. 'Sebastian Caddy! What was I thinking? Foolish, what?' She's distracted, jittery, staring at all of us, counting in her head. 'I'm quite beside myself here. Actually. Everything, too much. But Bone. Who is that? What a singular name. Is he that boy? With you, who popped up in the jeep. Bone. Where did he come from? Where is he now? Can someone kindly tell me what's going on.'

We're silent. Can't get words out. Too brimmed up with tears and tired and shock and hurt, the lot of us. None of us can engage with Lady Adora right now, this broken woman whose life is falling down all around her; yet she's the entire reason we're in this predicament. I pity her, oh yes, but want to push her hard at the same time. So I just stand there, fists clenched and furious, as all her questions go unanswered.

'That boy. With the blond hair. *Who* is he?' Lady Adora shouts in frustration. Darius tries to soothe her – 'Adi, Adi' – to draw her away, but she won't budge. Hebe is as still as a statue. Her eyes are squeezed shut, her hands clamped over her ears, as if she can't bear any of it.

'He's just Bone, Your Ladyboat – ship,' Pin says finally, always the peacemaker. 'From your house.'

'What? There's no one else in The Swallows but us.'

'Mr and Mrs Squeedly know him,' Pin prattles on. 'He's Bone. He's our friend.'

'Who? How is this possible. Where did he come from? The *Squeedlys*? How old is he?'

'Eleven,' Bert replies reluctantly.

'Eleven. Eleven. Oh . . .' She's going off into somewhere else here, we're losing her. 'I see. Anything else? What's his real name? I'm sorry but "Bone" is not a name. Pray tell.'

'He's been in your house forever, I think,' Pin explains. 'Like he owns the place.'

'*What?*'

'His real name is Lachlan. Lachie,' Scruff adds. 'He told us that right at the start. He knows your house like the back of his hand.'

'Better than you!' Pin adds.

Lady Adora is very still. A clenched fist is pressed into her cheek. 'Where is this . . . Lachie?' Her voice has dropped, is sapped of life.

We all look around.

He's completely, magically disappeared. As always. Like he never existed, he's a ghost. He wasn't with us at the cliff or with Bucket; wasn't with us from the moment he leapt. 'He's a master at disappearing,' Bert explains. 'He knows every hidey-hole in your house. In fact, he says he's never leaving it because he knows it too well. He says he'll be lord of the manor one day.'

'He says he's just waiting and waiting, Your Ladyship.' Pin's face cracks in wonder. '*Ship* – I got it!'

'Waiting for what?' Hebe asks.

'Back to the house, yes,' Lady Adora says weakly. 'All of us. Darius? Right now. I need to think. Think.' She's speaking in a voice utterly drained, utterly tired, like she's barely listening anymore, to any of us. 'Your dog, I've got bandages. Good, good. Splints. Morphine syrettes – that's painkillers, mousies, hundreds, left over from the war. In the medicine cabinet. Mr Squeedly can fix your dog, he's good with animals. Yes. Quick.'

Basti is speechless with sorrow. We all are. But Lady Adora is right: Bucket is the priority here and she's in a lot of pain. So. We'll get her fixed and then head out of here, fast. We all troop over to Darius's van and pile in the back. Leaving Lord Bone alone to his sea, his sprightly air, his cliffs. Just as he wants it, no doubt.

I stare out of the scratch in the window's paint-work once again. So, Bone Boy. Master vanisher – and storyteller. 'Bone, you are in *so* much trouble,' I yell furiously to the trees as we pull away, but only the sighing of the wind answers back.

'Where are this boy's parents? His family?' Lady Adora yells at us from the front of the car. Can't let it drop.

'He doesn't have any,' Pin answers.

'Of course . . .' she murmurs, 'of course he'd tell you that.'

We drive in silence, no fight in us left. But halfway down the long gravelly avenue to the great house, we see Mr and Mrs Squeedly, worried, panicked, as though in search of something lost. Darius stops the van. The elderly couple, in their faded and much patched service uniforms, brisk forward. Help us all out. Lady Adora motions them to stop. Holds her head like it hurts, like her thinking is threatening to spill out here and she needs this world immediately sorted out.

'Mrs Squeedly. Mr Squeedly. What is this I hear about a boy named Bone? Real name: Lachie. Aged eleven.' She comes right up close, too close, claws a finger at them. 'Bone? Bone? Eleven, mind. In my house. Right under my nose.' She laughs bitterly. 'Apparently he's been living here for years. *Years.*' A pause. Her voice drops to a kernel of coldness. 'With your help.'

Mrs Squeedly goes white. Mr Squeedly's eyes shut and remain shut. As if he's blocking out everything in his life from this point.

32

THE TRUTH OF THE MATTER

'**Tell. Me. Everything.**'

Lady Adora's fists are clenched.

'I ... I ...' Mrs Squeedly can barely speak. She looks around, at all of us, but there's no one to help her. We all want to know here; despite an injured Bucket we have to find this out. Her husband comes up close and lays his hand on her shoulder and it's as if a charge of strength flows through her. She steps forward. Takes a deep breath. Eyes at the ground, like the very earth's helping her to get things straight.

'We found a boy. A wee bairn of a thing. Eleven years ago. A little more. At the base of the cliff here. It was winter. The very dead of it. Bitterly cold.

He was freezing, poor thing. Skin like marble to touch, no warmth. Such a tiny little mite. A shock of white blond hair, even then.'

Her eyes turn to Lady Adora and lock on her. 'We had no child, as you know. We'd lost our Kenneth.' Mr Squeedly squeezes her shoulder. 'I couldn't have another after his birth. I almost died bringing him into this world.' Her eyes prick up with tears. 'You do not know the anguish, m'lady, of the childless. The daily, nightly torment. When they're wanted so much and then God – in his wisdom – takes them from you. And never gives one back. Oh we tried, tried.' She is breaking as she speaks, trying to get the jumble of words out. 'One can go quite mad with it, the pain of it.' She looks Lady Adora square in the face. 'And then your foundling child, well, he was a gift. That is how we saw it. Still do. God's gift. To love. Just that. That's all they need.'

A thick silence.

'We made him ours. Raised him. We knew he was a distant cousin of your Hebe. That you'd travelled to the Barnardos home in London to bring him into the fold of the family, so you told them; a blood rift, long ago, the father long lost to the Ellicott dynasty. He'd walked away in disgust, hadn't he? And how grateful the Barnados people were to have you visit them. You hadn't told anyone here, of course. But we knew. We servants often know.'

Lady Adora's hand is clamped in horror at her mouth. Stepping back, like she can't begin to take in what's coming next.

'He was the only male heir, set to inherit it all – The Swallows, everything. And you lost him, didn't you? Most careless, m'lady. You went for a walk just after arriving here with him. But we knew, oh, we knew. Nothing must stand in the way of your daughter. Her rightful inheritance. Yet you underestimated us. We couldn't have a wee bairn left out in the cold, to be washed away to sea, couldn't have nature – *your* nature – taking its course. When we found him, we were going to go to the police, of course we were, but then we had a thought, Mr Squeedly and I.'

She gives Silent Mountain a furtive glance, can hardly bear it. 'As we looked after that wee bairn, fed him and held him, we got thinking, oh yes, cuddled him like.' She lurches into a sob. 'The days just went on. We called him our little Bone because he was as skinny as one at the start, all skin and bone. But we didn't tell anyone else. And then we thought . . . we thought . . .' She can't go on. Mr Squeedly holds her tighter, his head is bowed. 'We'd wanted a child so much. The need ate me up.'

She's whispering now. 'It was beyond anything, the want. It took over my life. My senses. *Our* senses. That then suddenly we had a child.'

Mrs Squeedly is shrunken, all her fierceness gone as she stands before us. 'I do not want him lost to me. He is mine now. Our son. Our only son. You leave him alone.' Mr Squeedly does nothing but inch closer so that they're shoulder to shoulder, touching her, facing all of us; becoming one.

'We saw everything. My husband was going to fetch you with an umbrella, to tell you a dreadful storm was coming and you had to get home. But there was a flash of lightning and you reeled and the pushchair careered over the edge of the cliff and you just left him and ran, mad like. Yes, you did. Abandoned him on the rocks, at the base of the cliff. To die. Don't shake your head at me.' She points furiously. 'You had one of your "episodes", and presumed you'd gotten away with it. It was easy to hide him on such a large estate, wasn't it? In a storm, tide coming in. You, the mistress of this place, you could tell anyone anything and get away with it. You assured Barnardos and his very poor London family that he'd be taken care of, that you'd be honouring his father who'd passed away in estrangement from the Ellicotts. Then you told them that he was lost to you, to everyone . . . a sickly baby . . . a great tragedy . . . and left it at that.' Lady Adora's shutting her eyes, on everything. 'As Bone grew up he played in this house – the best playground in the world for a young boy. Knew every nook and cranny.' Lady Adora is cowering now. 'As he should.' Mrs Squeedly snaps back into something like her own self.

I look around at the trees, at the house. Feel the stillness, the silence. Know Bone's here somewhere, listening in.

'All the army men said it was haunted,' Mrs Squeedly continues. 'We didn't discourage that, didn't explain. Didn't want anyone around. Couldn't have anyone finding out about him. Our big secret. Whether it be visitors, or Hebe, or you. And the only way Bone could survive here – as our son, with us – was to stay hidden and quiet. It was to keep him safe. To keep him alive.' Her voice drops into hatred. 'He haunted *you* most of all, Your Ladyship. Who tried to get rid of him all those years ago. He knows who's really meant to have this place.' Lady Adora lets out a cry of distress. 'You were just like me, of course. More similar than you could imagine. You could only have one child, oh yes, because she came so late in your life. Your little miracle. Your little miracle of a . . . girl. And she wouldn't inherit if there was a male heir somewhere, however distant. But you wanted her to. Couldn't bear some commoner, with common blood, to get it. But the world's changing, m'lady. Your Illuminarium is illuminating a big, bold new world. The old order is being swept away. People should be earning the right to be in such a place.' Her Ladyship gasps in horror; Mrs Squeedly turns to us, to me. 'Where is Bone now? Is he all right?'

'He's fine. He's where he always is,' I shrug, looking around. 'Anywhere and nowhere. Just how he likes it.'

'We'll have to go to the police, of course,' Mrs Squeedly nods to herself. 'Now that it's out. We've lived with the lie for too long. They'll need to know everything. What you did, Your Ladyship. What we all did.'

Lady Adora's hand floats from her mouth. She turns to her beloved house, gazes. Turns to Basti. Darius. Back to the house.

All is lost, all, it's in her face.

'The police, yes, the cliff, goodness, all those years ago, yes,' she murmurs. 'Thank you, Mrs Squeedly. What I did, of course. Yes.'

She walks away, in a daze, towards the house in the distance, stumbling in her shoes. Hebe runs after her, but her mother brushes her off. 'Go away, leave me alone, I need to be alone.'

'But our Bucket?' Bert's cries are ignored. Lady Adora picks herself up, hauls herself on.

'Mama!' Hebe cries in despair, looking at her departing, lone back.

'Stay with Mrs Squeedly for the moment.' She bats her off. 'And that tiger girl. She's got enough growl for both of you. Girls need it, in this world, oh yes. And stay by Mr Squeedly, who's always been your ally. Oh yes, I saw it. Talking to you, but never to me, like he knew. Of course. Yes. Oh just go, all of you. Do as I say. Find a vet. Away, away from here. Go to the police. I need to . . . prepare . . . yes. Stop looking at me, gooooo!' she screeches. To Basti, Darius, us, the Squeedlys, to Bone out there somewhere, who's crashed into Lady Adora's world so spectacularly and always intended to, some day. Waiting . . . for now we know what. And she is screeching to Hebe most of all, who just stands there, staring at her mother, crying, her mouth a web of wet.

'I love you,' Lady Adora yells to her daughter. 'Know that. No matter what. All the shouting, the carping, the tears. There has always, *always* been love.'

'Where's our mother?' I cry after her, one last time. 'You promised us.'

Lady Adora hesitates. Stops. Turns. 'The answers to all your questions, tiger girl, are right under your nose.'

'What?'

'Go home. Look at yourself, look at her world, and you will see. Your love will save her, no doubt. Oh, and this . . .' She hesitates then takes the necklace of black velvet from around her neck and hands it to me. On the end of it is the tiny silver key she's always fingering. 'This opens all the trunks, at your home. Every single one of them. Flora entrusted me . . . we were friends once. She was here, yes, in this place. During the war. The Illuminarium. Oh yes indeed, it illuminates, this building that has seen so much love. But everything turns. Everything upends, changes. That is the way of the world, little mousies, don't count on anything staying the same, it's the one rule of life. Why didn't I listen to that? A boy named Lachie – ha! My ghost. All these years. Now off, off you go. All of you. *Leave me alone*!'

Then Lady Adora turns and walks from all of us, shooing us away, laughing wildly and flapping her hands, heading to the house. We squint, shield our eyes: she gets smaller and smaller as she heads off into the distance, utterly alone. What's she *doing*? She walks under the great oaks, past the rosebushes, across the ornamental lawn, stumbling in her spindly heels and nodding to the limbless statues. A tiny figure now, she walks through the broken French doors into the ballroom with its candles lit in readiness, in her beautiful dress that's ripe for a banquet; she walks past the great cascade of ivy still tied neatly into curtains thanks to Bert; she walks into the space that held all her happiness once; she walks tall through that grand room and holds her arms high then wobbles on her heels – oh! – and falls, and reaches out a hand, knocking over one candelabra, then another, then another.

We all gasp.

Run forward, but we're so far away and candle flames quickly catch – too quickly, no! – at silk bags cradling broken chandeliers, so fast, too fast. Kerosene lanterns on the floor explode in the heat and fire suddenly rises high into the ceiling like great orange clouds. The flames lick at the silver silk curtains lying in rivers across the floor and run in glee along the length of them then – poof! – the curtains billow up. As Lady Adora struggles to rise, to walk further into her house, to get out, she knocks over more candelabras, and is more overcome by smoke, by heat. No! She's too far away, it's happening too fast.

'Don't look!' Basti shouts to Hebe as Silent Mountain runs to her, to shield her, to stop her racing into the flames herself. Her face is buried firm in his arms, his chest, but she struggles free and dashes towards her mother yet the great man grabs at her and holds her back strong from the heat. We cannot see inside anymore, the room is just a wall of flame from the billowing silk and exploding lanterns and Lady Adora is within it all somewhere but it's no use trying to get to her, it's obvious; we're too far away, helpless.

'Noooooo!' springs forward Darius yelling in anguish, and in his cry is all his love, his life, his future; of course, she's the only person he's got in the world. He's stumbling, sobbing, running to Her Ladyship in great lopey strides, desperate and determined but it's too late for the Lady of the House, for the ballroom, its surrounding rooms, for the entire broken world of the Illuminarium. The great roar of its heat beats him back, its last roar to a new world. Darius falls on his knees before it all, hands loose by his side.

And Hebe, dear Hebe.

Left beside us. Sobbing in anguish, 'Mama, Mama,' as we enfold her in our arms.

33

CHARLIE BOO
TO THE RESCUE

'My dear Caddys, about turn,' Uncle Basti says in shock. 'Make haste, we must alert the authorities. Get help. Save whatever we can of The Swallows. Get Bucket fixed. Can't get near the house, it's just too dangerous.'

We spin to find a car. Long and sleek and panther-black, hurtling up the drive. One Charlie Boo at the wheel, resplendent in his bowler hat and butler's suit. He jumps out. Looks at all of us, our flushed cheeks, skin flecked in ash; our exhausted, bewildered faces. Counts, nods and gazes at the main wing of the great house now collapsing under the spreading flame. 'What on earth is going on?'

'Long story, Mr Boo,' Basti answers wearily, looking at Darius. 'Old chap? Care to begin?' he enquires of his former friend but gets nothing in return, not even a looking in the eyes. Darius is a broken man. 'I'm sorry,' Basti continues, softer. 'But I did think something was odd right back at that visit to Brompton. Nothing felt quite ... right.' Darius, still, is speechless. Ahead of him, I just know it, is a future trapped in the dank and stony world of his cemetery; utterly, utterly alone. Pin goes up beside him and gently slips his little hand in the man's. Darius does not let it go.

'Mr Boo,' Basti declares, 'we need to get out of here, fast. Get fire engines onto this. Save as much of the house as we can. Alert the police. And get some help, immediately, for poor Bucket.'

'But our son,' Mrs Squeedly says desperately. 'The police?'

'I—I'll leave that up to you.' Basti smiles sadly at her, then looks tenderly at the young girl shattered and staggering in the middle of all this. 'Dear, dear Hebe. What do we do? We're here to help you. Your residence is not fit for staying in right now. So perhaps, right at this moment, you should come with us. Just for now. Tidy you up, sort you out, back in London. Get you removed from the, er, immediacy, of all this. Then we can find some relatives, work out what to do next. Yes? We just need to get you warm. Fed.' He looks at us four Caddys. 'Held, cuddled, yes?' I nod, yes.

Hebe's speechless, utterly pale, in shock. Shrugging everyone off, flinching away from the lot of us.

'We're your friends,' I say quiet. 'And we just want to help. Whatever you want.'

'We'll be your new family!' Scruff begs. 'We'll have so many adventures. Chocolate ones. And iguana-as-pets ones. And circus shows. Not a viola in sight. And we'll teach you how to do a double backflip. Well, Bert will. And . . . and . . .'

'Not now, Scruff,' Bert soothes.

Silent Mountain holds Hebe tight, her face to his chest.

'Come with us,' I say gently. 'Just for now. If you want.'

'Until everything is sorted out, perhaps,' Basti adds, putting a fatherly arm around her shoulder.

'But . . . but . . . where?' Hebe manages to get out, looking wildly at all of us.

'We're going home,' I say strong. 'As soon as we can. It's where we belong. We have to go back to Australia.' I clutch the precious silver key now around my neck. 'The Illuminarium has illuminated one huge thing for us: our mother is alive, and we need to find her. We have a key to her now. You can come too, if you like. But we'll be in London first. Come and see the Reptilarium.'

'It's the most amazing building in the entire world!' Scruff says.

'And it's not too far from Soho, I think. Your cake shop . . .' Bert smiles.

'Ha,' Hebe laughs softly, despite herself. 'The dream. You remembered.'

'Of course.'

We're all suddenly quiet, gazing at the fire-swallowed house.

Then high up, from a nearby oak tree, comes an unearthly wail. Louder than the smash and crackle of flames, louder than any of us. Ghostly, other-worldly, like a sound inside a shell inside the deepest ocean. A cry of utter, absolute despair and anguish and loss. A cry of a world crashing down.

'Bone Boy!' I yell.

Abrupt silence from the tree.

'Come with us.'

Only the roar of the flames and the wind answer back.

'Commander Bone? Company T is standing by. We need you.'

'No, he's with us,' Mrs Squeedly interjects. 'He's our son. No matter what. We will not leave this estate, the cottages on it, the abandoned village. We'll live in the stables if we have to. This world is our home, our only home. And we have to sort out the, the . . . matters . . . of the house. If it can be rescued. All that.' She looks quickly at Hebe, bites her lip.

Our friend just shuts her eyes and bats it all away, as if to say, take it, for now, just have it; I can't absorb all this.

I nod to Mrs Squeedly. Shake her hand in farewell. They're where they belong, all three of her odd little family group.

'My husband and I, we love children. But . . . it's so hard to explain . . . we didn't want to get close to you all.' She's talking to us Caddy kids by way of apology. 'Didn't want Bone anywhere near you – but couldn't stop him, of course.' She rolls her eyes. 'Didn't want him luring you away, into another world outside of this. The house. He means everything to us. None of us know anything else. I'm sorry.'

I nod 'I know.' The four of us look back at Charlie Boo. He tips his hat, urging us into the car. We have to find a phone. Get to the authorities, fast. Find help for Bucket, get to Dad. It's time to hand over responsibility here. Dad said I had to look after the family while he's away and I haven't done it very well so far.

A sob catches in my throat: Dad was relying on me and I almost lost a few of us several times here. It's time for the next adventure, oh yes, but with him by our side this time.

We have to unravel the mystery of Mum. Get home, to the desert, and open those trunks; find out just how deeply Flora and Lady Adora were connected and what on earth our mum was doing in that school room and where she went to next. I look at Pin crying, 'Bone, Bone, come out,' to the oak tree, trying to understand all that's just happened. 'Where's Her Ladyboat, Boney?'

Uncle Basti hugs me, guiding me into the car. 'You've done well, kid.'

'Really?'

'Oh yes. You're alive. All four of you. Boo and I are so grateful for that. For your help, as always. Knowing you were with them, guiding them – however bouncy they proved to be – was of great comfort to us. We knew they'd be all right, because they were with you.'

My disbelieving crooked smile, one side up one side down.

'Come with us, just for now,' Charlie Boo says to Hebe. 'Until we sort out what to do.'

She looks at Mrs Squeedly, who nods. 'It's for the best. It'll mean fresh clothes, a proper bed, rest. With friends.' The old lady looks at us strong, in approval. And besides, we all know they've got their own son to take care of.

'But I don't know who I am anymore,' Hebe cries. 'I have no family. No home.'

'You can be whomever you want to be, my dear girl,' Basti says. 'That is my philosophy. I celebrate the courage to be different, as this mad Caddy lot well know.' He looks at us dubiously; they both laugh. 'It's the courage to decide your own fate – however singular that may be. So come on, come with us. Just for now. We want you very much. And like you just the way you are.'

'Why?' A smile bursts through her face.

'Because we think you're rather magnificent – and need to experience more of you.'

We cheer her into the car.

'The Reptilarium's 300-year-old motto is *Custodi Vulnerant*,' Basti adds, 'which means to protect – not crush. It's never been broken yet. You'll be safe with us.'

'New family! New family!' Pin exclaims, clapping his hands with glee. 'Duddle?' he adds.

It's Hebe's big test. She turns and cuddles him good and tight.

'You'll do, striker girl,' Scruff says, punching her playfully. He gets a sniffly punch back. As we shut the car doors the wailing starts up again from the oak tree.

'What's your real name, Lord Bone?' I yell out, winding the window down.

'Lachlan,' he says.

'No, your surname.'

'Lachlan Ellicott, of course.'

I shake my head. 'If only you'd told us that, mate.'

'You might see me again, K.'

'Yes, we may well need you one day in our lives. Your skills might come in handy. Company T isn't done with you yet!'

But only silence answers back.

I smile. *Know* we'll see him again. We wave to the tree. To Mr and Mrs Squeedly. They'll be servants, once again of course, but to their Lord Bone. Who gave them a promise that one day he'd make the Illuminarium as glorious as it had been a long while ago – with them firmly at the centre of it. The Illuminarium has only illuminated what a rotten, dying world it inhabits; that its time has passed. There's a new order on the way – and our different energy will be a part of it, I just know. The Illuminarium has also shown us the importance of working people out for yourself; listening to your heart about them rather than relying on other people's opinions – which can be horribly wrong. Hebe, dear Hebe, is a case in point.

As Charlie Boo finally drives south towards London, after a long, long day, he turns and shakes his head at the jumbly, tumbly, exhausted lot of us. The full Boo eyebrow. The full Boo glare.

'Up to your old tricks again, eh, you Caddy lot?'

He glances at our Hebe, fast asleep in her sky-blue satin on Scruff's shoulder. She's filthy and utterly worn out.

'Pin, you'll do anything for a new friend, won't you?'

'Oh yes, Mr Boo!'

Bert points to a stain of grubbiness and soot across the length of her dress and declares that she's ours now; that we knew all along the Caddy world would eventually get to her.

'You lot are not getting near any of my grand-children,' Charlie Boo murmurs back in mock horror.

'Oh yes, we are!' four Caddys yell out in delight.

EPILOGUE

It's the twelfth night after Christmas and not a Caddy is complaining here – whingeing, shoving, hitting or tongue-poking – nope, there's not even a peep (miraculously) from young Master Phineas.

He's just staring, rapt, at two silver curtains in the Lumen Room, the most magical room in the entire Kensington Reptilarium. A great gathering of new mates is sitting on gilded chairs all around him – Basti and Dinda; Charlie Boo and twelve of his grandchildren (Linus positioning himself a little too close to me, but most astonishingly I do not seem to be moving my chair); Hen, Lina and Hannah, Max and Dave and Ethan, Georgie, Saskia and Harry from Campden Hill Square; Horatio the lawyer and his lady friend, Henrietta Witchum Maggs, with a rather spectacular emerald ring on her finger ('a gift from Charles the Second to my great great great – oh – whatever grandmother') and the guest of honour?

One Hebe Horatina Ellicott – the newest, most tentative member of the family. For now. Who needs a lot of cheering up.

But look! Look!

It's starting.

The curtains are flung wide and out steps Albertina the Younger, most resplendent in the bare hoops of a Victorian skirt over sequined circus tights with a child's fitted military jacket on top and two black feather boas wrapped rather splendidly around her neck.

'Sssssssssh,' she commands, her eyes dancing merrily.

She clicks her fingers high. Out steps her assistant – one Master Ralph, known as Scruff – in a Spartan's helmet, thigh-high pirate boots and a calico convict's shirt.

'Let there be light!' he pronounces solemnly.

Then Berti leans in close. 'If music be the food of love, play on,' she whispers trillingly, to all of us, and Scruff softly beats the drum on a golden rope around his neck. Louder, louder, and one by one every glow worm in the room wakes up and the light spreads like a golden liquid across the walls and roof and we all gasp at the wondrous beauty of it.

And so the show commences. With backflips and triple cartwheels and synchronised green tree snakes and one Perdita the cobra, who insists on being a scarf around Berti's neck at one point. Followed by a skit involving Uncle Rasti the lovable red rat and Minda the Mighty Mouse, black-haired of course, and their grand and complicated love, which ends most appropriately at the altar of a church. (Basti actually blushes, miraculous.) The grand Caddy spectacle finishes up with a song from us four scruffy, squealy kids from the bush; Pin on my shoulders with his hands curled in giggly rapture at his cheeks, staring at everyone before him – all the wonderfully lovely new friends in his life.

> 'When that I was and a little tiny boy,
> With hey, ho, the wind and the rain,
> A foolish thing was but a toy,
> For the rain it raineth every day.
>
> But when I came to man's estate,
> With hey, ho, the wind and the rain,

'Gainst knaves and thieves men shut their gate,
For the rain it raineth every day.

A great while ago the world begun,
With hey, ho, the wind and the rain,
But that's all one, our play is done,

– we grab Hebe at this point and urge her up to the stage, arms around her –

And we'll strive to please you every day.'

The production is applauded rapturously – success! And it's due to be repeated when one Caddy Senior is released from his sanatorium – which is soon, perhaps, any day now. And it will be repeated all over again when our mother walks back into our lives. That's Company T's next mission: to find her, to be a family of six all over again – beginning from home in the Central Australian desert and we can't wait!

The show's grand finale?

Four Aussies from the bush bursting through the curtains bearing trays of the most delicious, most forbidden, most black-markety wartime foods imaginable – bananas and oranges and plates of tiny chocolate airplanes. Then afterwards, in the glow of the winter quiet, Scruff asks Charlie Boo why on earth he mentioned our mother, so carelessly, on that fevery last night with our dad, when our world imploded and the icy adventure into the Illuminarium began.

''Cause if you hadn't, Mr Boo, we never would have gone on that mad secret mission to Darius's,' Scruff adds, 'we would never have ended up at The Swallows. Never would have met Hebe –'

'And thank goodness we did,' Bert jumps in, wrapping a feather boa around her new best friend's neck.

'Well, Master Scruff.' Mr Boo has a think. 'I just wanted to put things right, I guess.' He sighs. 'I wanted your Uncle Basti's life sorted out. Very much. And by extension, yours. You see, I have known your uncle since he was a child. And I am a perfectionist, in case you haven't noticed. I very much like all knots untied and straightened out. And you cannot deny that the mystery of your mother is a very big one. But of course, I almost lost you in the process. Ridiculous, hopeless, aren't I, Master Phineas?'

Pin nods his head vigorously. Charlie Boo raises a most Charlie Boo eyebrow.

Pin thinks again. Rapidly changes his nodding to a shaking. Is that right? says his face.

'You're not hopeless!' Scruff cries and we all join in (which is exactly what Charlie Boo was hoping for, of course). 'You're the best.' 'The most talented butler in the Empire. Sorry, world.' 'Trained in Rangoon, right?' 'Plus we got a new sister out of it. *And* a brother.'

'What?' I snap.

'Lord Bone of the Icicle Illuminarium!' Scruff exclaims and Bert yells her delight; yells that we'll be back for him, Kicky, just you wait. I raise an eyebrow, most Charlie-Boo-like, and the man himself sighs that he's not so sure a ghostly boy who leads jeeps over cliffs is a very good influence on us lot. Scruff's face tells us he doesn't believe that one bit; that it was all one ghastly accident; and he's already scheming to get Bone back into our lives.

'But most importantly, troops, we'll be here for Dad, for when he's let out,' Bert says. 'Imagine what a day that will be. Then we can jump straight in Basti's plane and go and get Mum.'

I smile that crooked smile that's one side up, one side down. Because, yes, Bert's right. Our mother's alive. It's the one miraculous thing the Icicle Illuminarium has taught us. She's out there somewhere, against her will, and she's waiting for us; the clues in a desert baked as red as rust. And I know she'll be proud of me for looking after the family over the past week or so. We're all safe, in one piece. Miraculous! And now that I've been a bit of a mum myself I know how impossibly difficult and exhausting the job is – so I'd never be so hard on my own mum again. No more pushing away, no more shouting; I get her now, more.

'Now where was I?' Charlie Boo holds his finger to his chin. 'There's much to be done here. An entire Reptilarium to be put to sleep, in fact. Grasshoppers to be dispersed, goannas to be kissed. Caddys major, intermediate and minor –' an eyebrow is raised in a challenge '– pick up your snakes.'

We most certainly do.

MISSED OUT ON THE CADDY KIDS'
FIRST ADVENTURE,

THE KENSINGTON REPTILARIUM?

READ ON FOR AN EXCITING EXTRACT!

'**How long do you reckon it'd take to fry an egg
on Matilda's bonnet?**'

Scruff is looking longingly at our car, which is
already boiling hot in the 44-degree heat – and it's
only nine a.m.

'Fifty-two seconds!' Bert rises to the challenge. 'Do
it, Scruffy boy, come on. *Anything* would be better
than Kick's cooking.' She shoots a glance at me,
knowing I'll take the bait. Which I most certainly do.

'Just *you* try being a mum plus a dad around here,
young lady.' I poke out my tongue. Everyone knows
that any experiment at being a grown-up ended
months ago. 'Twenty-nine seconds,' I exclaim, 'and
not a fly's fart more!'

My attempt at breakfast – a frypan with a rug of eggs tastefully congealed on its bottom – is grabbed and said eggs are flung wide into the yard. They spin like a dinner plate. Land – plop! – in the red dust.

Cooking. Pah. I give up. I've had enough of it.

Our dog, Bucket, scoots for the mess of the breakfast and gobbles it up. I bow to her exquisite taste. 'Well, at least *someone* appreciates me around here.'

Then I stand on the table in my leather flying cap, fix Mum's old driving goggles firmly over my eyes, straighten my back and salute.

'Troops, as of this moment I hereby resign from the positions of cook, cleaner, mother, father, storyteller, governess, putterer-to-bed, chief hunter, nose-wiper, Pin-tracker, master spy and war general. You're free. The whole blinkin' lot of you! I'm off.'

'Yaaaaaaay!'

My three siblings – Scruff, eleven, Bert, nine, and Pin, four – hoot with glee and do an instant war dance; Bucket joins in for good measure with a great flurry of leaps and barks. A finger's waggled at her. I expect mutiny in the ranks from the humans who inhabit this adult-forsaken place but not from our dingo we've raised since a pup. Obediently she sits and pants. That's better. I wink my thanks.

'Forty-eight seconds, girls. The bet's on!' Scruff sings, rushing to the larder to gather more eggs. Dad left him his old wristwatch from World War I, complete with its stopwatch, and he's been timing the entire world ever since.

'Twelve eleven! Twelve eleven!' Pin exclaims.

This is the biggest number he knows, and, er, as you can see, I've been a bit slack in the governess department of late. We'll get to numbers one day.

We all scramble out to Matilda, our trusty car, which I can drive (with three blocks of wood tied with ropes to the pedals and a pillow on the seat) at the grand old age of thirteen, thank you very much.

'A minute's silence please.' Bert clasps her chest dramatically when we get there (ever the drama queen). She raises her head to the wide blue heavens. Bucket takes her place behind the wheel. 'Please bring Daddy back to us by Christmas Eve. With the following: a rifle for Scruff, a slingshot for Pin, a black velvet dress from Paris for me and a . . . a little . . . *book* . . . of some sort . . . for the ex-governess.' She wrinkles her nose in distaste in my direction.

My eyes narrow. 'Dinner's all yours, Madame Pompadour. Tonight. Just see what *you* can do with a roo tail, two cups of flour and a chocolate bar.'

'Forty-eight seconds, ladies!' Scruff exclaims, ever the peacemaker, his palms wide between both of us as he scrutinises the tall blue sky.

We all do. Oh, it'll deliver all right. Cook those eggs in the blink of an eye. Because we live smack bang in the middle of the hottest place on earth – the Central Australian desert. And we live here, at the moment, all by our glorious selves.

Dad's gone away on yet another of his expeditions. He's always heading off, ever since I could talk he's been disappearing and then coming back with a great wallop of presents and stories about princes and paupers, India and Ceylon and Paris, samurai swords and civil war muskets, spies and saboteurs, crocs and stingrays and sharks. He's an adventure hunter, that's all we know, liberating peoples and animals across the world, and it's always of the highest importance and the most mysterious intelligence. His latest mission: yep, you guessed it, top secret. But it's to save the world from imminent destruction – even though the war, er, ended several months ago. Apparently. We've spent World War II on our station in the middle of Woop Woop, scouring the horizon for Japs, which always turn into camels as they get close through the haze of heat. But we're ready for 'em!

And Mum? She died when Pin was born; Dad says she ran away to God, because another little Caddy surprise was just too shocking for this world to ever cope with and she needed to instruct God how to do it. Mum's always up there, with us, close, we must never forget it.

The four of us climb onto Matilda's bonnet, which creaks companionably with our weight but never gives, thank goodness, 'cause we're on here a lot. Our darling, faithful old girl of a ute, she's taken us to every waterhole within a hundred-mile radius thanks to Dad. She's sped between sand dunes trailing an old mattress that we've all clung onto for dear life, she's carried swags and firewood and dead roos and goannas piled high for feasts, as well as endless gaggles of kids on hunting expeditions with our blackfella mates.

Dad organised for Aunty Ethel to stay with us during this latest absence – something about me 'becoming a woman and needing some help', which he couldn't talk about, and he would blush whenever I tried to ask, but excuse me, I'm more than all right now, thank you very much. I've got his war pistol and his whip, his car key and a stash of books – what more does a girl need?

Aunty Ethel agreed that her services might no longer be required after she found the entire occupants of Bert's scorpion farm in her sheets. Which came the day after Pin whacked Scruff with a fresh roo tail and sprayed blood across Aunty Ethel's white Sunday-best dress, and Scruff used her glasses to set fire to the straw under the chook house as a liberation experiment.

'Your father was always the black sheep of the family – but he's got nothing on you lot,' she'd said as she slammed the door of her car. 'I'll write and tell him to get back instantly. No one else will have you. Kick, you'll just just have to work out how to become a lady all by yourself. And clean up that potty mouth of yours, because your father certainly won't!'

The last sight of our visitor from hoity toity down south: her Morris Minor coughing and spluttering as it disappeared in a cloud of dust.

Excellent. That's how we like it. We rubbed our hands in glee. Me free to do and say what I want. Kids free of supervision and baths. Plus the most superb development of the lot: Dad on his way back to look after us.

Except he's not here. Yet.

And it's been an awfully long time. Every day we expect him to arrive. The days are ticking on, the tins are running low, as well as the powdered milk and flour with too many weevils in it, and Christmas is in a week, the bush pine will have to be selected and chopped and Dad's always in command of that. Along with bagging the bush turkey, tuning the piano for the singalong, directing the Christmas pantomine (sole audience member: Bucket), and painting across the entire tin roof, in bright red, our yearly message to Santa on his flying kangaroos in case he misses it: 'STOP! BEER + GOOD KIDS HERE.'

'Ah, shouldn't that be written the other way round?' Scruff had asked last year.

'In this heat,' Dad had laughed, 'Father Christmas needs a beer before anything,' and clapped his son on the back.

'I do too!' Scruff had jumped in right quick.

'You're only ten, mate. I'll tell you what. I'll give you one when you've grown some hairs on your chest – and you're all of eleven.' Then they'd both cackled with laughter that wouldn't stop. Little boys, both of them, especially on December 25th. So. Scruff's come of age now and Dad needs to hurry up. Any moment, I just know it, can feel it.

Dad Junior now holds an egg high. 'Troops, are we ready? Steady?'

Pin holds my hand, squeezes with excitement.

Bert examines her nails, which she's just covered with old blackboard paint that's still hanging around, miraculously, even though all the governesses have long fled. 'Excuse me, stop. We're not ready yet because I have a question. A crucial one. What does the winner get?'

Scruff looks at her, thinking. It'll be something to do with warfare, I bet. 'My entire grenade collection.'

'Do any of them work?' Bert's now looking straight at me, planning her attack.

That'd be right. Just because I told her she has to pull her weight and help with a week's worth of dishes now that we have nothing left to eat off.

'Not a single one, sis!' Scruff cackles then cracks the egg with great aplomb between his spread legs. 'Breakfast is on its way, ladies and gentleman – the best feast you have ever tasted in your life!' He counts from his watch, 'One – two – three – four –'

Pin's tugging me, trying to get me off the car. 'Sssh,' I tell him, 'don't interrupt, pup.'

'But Kicky . . .' he whines.

'Twelve – eleven –' Scruff winks at Pin '– thirteen – fourteen –'

But Pin's head is somewhere else. Our little man can be distracted by an ant, a fly, anything but the task at hand, and that usually leads to him wandering off, which always gives us heart attacks. Right on cue he jumps from Matilda. Heads to the front gate. Our gaze follows him.

To an enormous plume of angry red dust, bulleting straight at us from the horizon.

The egg is forgotten as we rush to Pin . . . hearts in our mouths.

What is it?

It's not Dad, it's too fast. It's something else.

THE KENSINGTON REPTILARIUM
is available now. Find out more about
N.J. Gemmell and her books at
www.randomhouse.com.au